DRAGONS of WILD

UPON DRAGON'S BREATH TRILOGY
BOOK ONE

AVA RICHARDSON

BLURB

In a time of darkness, unlikely heroes will rise.

The once-peaceful kingdom of Torvald has been ravaged by evil magic, forcing Riders to forget their dragons and their noble beasts to flee to the wilds. Now, anyone who dares to speak of dragons is deemed insane and put to death. Into this dark and twisted land, Saffron was born sixteen years ago. Blessed with the gift of dragon affinity, she has been forced into a life of exile, secretly dreaming of a normal life and the family she lost.

Scholarly and reclusive, Bower is the son of a noble house on the brink of destruction. His mission is to fulfill a mysterious prophecy and save his kingdom from the rule of the evil King Enric, but all he wants is to be left alone. When he meets Saffron, Bower gains a powerful ally—but her magic is too wild to control.

Their friendship might just have the power to change the course of history, but when the Dark Mage King Enric makes Saffron a tempting offer, their alliance will be shaken to the core.

Thank you for purchasing 'Dragons of Wild'

(Upon Dragon's Breath Trilogy Book One)

If you would like to hear more about what I am up to, or continue to follow the stories set in this world with these characters—then please sign up for my mailing list at

http://www.subscribepage.com/b7o3i0

You can also find me on me on

Facebook: www.facebook.com/AvaRichardsonBooks/

Homepage: www.AvaRichardsonBooks.com

TABLE OF CONTENTS

PROLOGUE
FIRE, BLOOD, AND SWORD

The Salamander Prophecy:

"Old and young will unite to rule the land from above.
Upon the dragon's breath comes the return of the True
King. It will be his to rebuild the glory of Torvald"

(date and author unknown)

Vance Maddox

The city is in uproar. I have never seen the like—even in the old days when the wild dragons would raid from the north. Never has there been so much terror, so much bloodshed and so much anguish. Screams fill the air as people are thrown from their homes. The ringing of bells, the call of the Dragon Horns, and above it all the fire and shriek of the agonized, enraged dragons.

Another beam from the roof splinters and explodes in a shower of sparks on the flagstones at my feet. I dodge to one side. Through the gap in the tiles above I see the red and orange scales of something vast and threatening. The dragon tries once more to get at us inside—to get at me!

"Protect the prince!" I call to the guards, all of them Maddox men and women like myself: tall, light-haired and pale-skinned. They have that rangy look those of the Maddox line never seem to quite outgrow.

"Captain!" The guard chief gives me a quick, stern nod. Gone are the smiles and the fine tunics that marked this small group of bodyguards as ambassadors. We've all thrown aside finery, replacing it with the hardened steel and iron armor of my family.

A hissing roar comes from above. The red-orange dragon once again throws its weight onto the roof. We can all hear the intake of its breath like a giant bellows.

"Flame shields," I call, falling to one knee and holding up the specially-treated oval shield over my head, and not a moment too soon as a firestorm bursts into the hall from the dragon.

One of my guards is not so lucky. He screams and the stink of burning hair and flesh choke the hall. The dragon's fire is fast, incinerating him in seconds, leaving ash floating on the air.

The flames last only a brief second, but already my arm aches from the force of the dragon's breath. Maybe my brother and late father were right—how can any human live near such dangerous beasts, let alone build a city underneath their nests? This is the day that my brother, Prince Hacon Maddox, has decided to overthrow the rulers of Torvald and seize it for himself. May the storms guide me; I have sworn to help him.

"Up! Up and to the prince!" Lowering my shield, I stand and leap forward, knowing we have only a little time before the orange and red dragon will be able to breathe fire down on us again. I catch a glimpse of the charred armor of the soldier who has died, melted now into slag. I don't even know his first name.

No time for misery or cold feet now. We run through the long hall, feet pounding and armor rattling. Above us, dragons pound at the roof and walls and roar. Luckily for us, but not so lucky for Torvald royalty, this palace has been designed to withstand rogue dragon attacks. Its many halls are reinforced stone, shot through with metal bars.

The king and queen's best protection will become their prison.

Turning a corner, we face the next phalanx of Torvald guards, all wearing the imperial red and purple of the Flamma-Torvald household. Scars show how many battles they have fought, and their stance is that of fighting men and women.

But Flamma-Torvald, for all of its might, for all of its fame throughout the Three Kingdoms, has grown soft. The Maddox clan hails from the furthest east some generations ago. We've fought every tribe, every bandit and every upstart warlord between here and the ends of creation. The people of the Middle Kingdom have no idea what we can do—or what strange and terrible things we have already done.

"Death to the traitors!" shouts one of Flamma-Torvald guards, throwing his longsword forward in a jab that would have skewered me were it not for my reflexes. I catch and turn the blow, spinning to step inside the man's guard.

A kick to his solar plexus sends him back. He falls, sprawling onto the floor. My second-in-command dispatches him with a solid thrust of his blade. The battle is fast and hard. I spin and parry. I hack until my sword no longer connects with armor and tissue and bone. Half my guard has been slain by the time we're done, but all the Flamma-Torvald troops have fallen under our blades. My men and women look as though they have been drenched in red by the time that we finish, and I lean on my sword, panting.

"Sir?"

Looking up, I see one of the women of my guard pointing to the brick dust and mortar raining down from above us. She is right. We don't have time for even a breath.

Ahead of us is our goal—what looks to be the ornate, wooden double-doors of the throne room. All this carnage has been planned months in advance by Hacon, my brother by our late father—and by me as well. Hacon and the Iron Guard are to be inside the throne room, seizing the king and queen, while I lead a group of soldiers through the palace halls to deal with any Dragon Riders we might meet.

Hacon has said the people of Torvald have no chance against us. I'd thought that mostly bravado. It is only now, standing outside the doors of the throne room with blood dripping down my blades that I start to believe. How long have I heard him and father rail about the day we would take the city? I never truly believed it possible.

Even now, I can hear Hacon's shouts. 'They are abominations! Dragons are evil, vile creatures—and they have enslaved the entire Middle Kingdom through their control of House Flamma-Torvald!' Our father never tired of repeating those same rants.

Why should I feel uneasy now?

The twin doors of the throne room open. Two of the Iron Guards step out, their full-plate suits looking like the scales of dragons and gleaming in the torch light. Behind them, I see the opulent throne room of House Flamma-Torvald. A ring of the Iron Guard surrounding King Mason and Queen Druella Roule.

The carpets of the throne room seem washed in blood. Bodies of the royal guards lay hacked apart. The stench is almost unbearable. Looking at the blood, my stomach clenches and turns. It wasn't meant to be like this. It wasn't meant that so many should die. What have we done?

From behind his prison of blades, King Mason shouts, "How could you? We welcomed you to the citadel! We gave you a home!" I hear tears in his voice as well as anger.

My brother, his black hair revealed with his helmet off, walks to the window. Outside, dragons swoop through the sky as the city burns. Just a scant few years ago, we came to this citadel with our Iron Guard as a fine gift for the 'glory of the dragon-king.' King Mason had been pleased then, giving us high places at court, installing our Iron Guard at every city gate and guard house. Little did he know this day would come, when our gifts would spring into action under our orders, seizing power and delivering the city to us.

Turning away from the window, Hacon smiles. His face seems sharper than ever, narrow and long. "Call off your dragons." Hacon points his sword at the queen. "Or she will be the first to die."

"Cowards!" King Mason snarls the word. "Try me first, man to man!"

He is brave, I'll give him that. I stride to my brother's side. "Hacon, let them live. We have seized the city, and with a word from this man, the dragons will retreat. There is no need to wallow in blood."

"Silence, brother!" He slashes the air with his sword and turns to Mason again. "Call your beasts off, or your wife and child both die."

"Hacon, this wasn't part of the plan." This is a holy mission—or so I'd thought. I knew it would be ugly, but I also thought this is the right thing. "We are here to liberate the city, not kill innocent babes. Imprison these two or exile them. We have broken their power. It is enough!"

"It is never enough," Hacon hisses. "Exiles have a habit of returning, and babes grow up, brother!" With a motion and a thought, he orders the Iron Guard seize Roule, a queen no more. I knew my brother hid a cruel streak. I knew he sometimes used our family magic without wisdom or thought. But I had hoped he'd grown up over these past few months. That he had learned a little from our late father.

With a mournful call like the herons in autumn, the dragons call out. Glancing out the window, I see them disperse into the thunderclouds above the city, circling ever farther and farther. Sweat breaks out on Mason's forehead. I know he is using his unholy connection to these beasts to send them far away. Every now and then, a dragon swoops to pick up a rider—another unhappy alliance. Those that can flee are doing so, snatching handfuls of humans in their claws. But the Iron Guard raise long spears to show them never to return.

"There. It is done." Mason hangs his head and reaches out to take his wife's hand. "Leave my child and my Roule. Let us flee. You have the citadel. Take our riches, the crown, but let my family live!" He looks up, his eyes red, but his voice is firm.

Hacon's smile widens. "You really are all fools." Hacon nods. The Iron Guards lift their blades and strike down the royal couple. I turn away, sickened by the waste of it. A battle is one thing—to bring down an enemy who will take your life if you do not take his is a glorious thing. But to slaughter a man and a woman as if they were pigs meant for a feast brings no honor and tests no skill.

Hacon's voice calls me back to my duty. "The rest of you—go find the babe and destroy it." The Iron Guard lacks the intelligence to question orders. They are things, soulless and mindless, made of magic and metal. They storm out, clanking, to find the royal chambers.

I turn and slam a fist into my brother's shoulder, making him stagger. "A child? You mean murder. I don't know what you have become, Hacon, but I want no part in slaughter."

Turning, I stride from the throne room. Hacon's plans and maps are in my head and I know some backstairs the servants use. I can reach the babe ahead of the Iron Guard.

The door stands open. Bursting in, I find two Dragon Riders—man and a woman—standing between me and a crib that contains the royal babe. The man draws his sword. The woman bends over the babe.

I close and bar the door behind me. A shadow dims the light from the window. Then a flash of orange and red brightens the light. Storms protect us. Is that the same red and orange beast that attacked before? Has it bonded to the child? My throat dries, but the baby gives a gurgling laugh, and I know that allowing it to be murdered is something I cannot stomach.

Glancing at the riders, I tell them, "If you seek a glorious end, it follows just behind me! But if you seek to keep the baby alive, you must flee now! Forget the child's true name! Never speak of the parents, and you may spare its life! But go–go now!" I must look—and smell—hideous, covered as I am with blood. I can only hope they will listen.

"But the king and queen?" The man's voice shakes slightly. The woman seems to size me up with a look and seizes the baby to wrap it in her cloak. The man lifts his sword and his voice firms. "Where are they? We leave together."

The heavy clank of iron boots is muffled by the door—the Iron Guards are coming. "There is no time! Just get that child somewhere safe and never, never come back, please!"

The woman nods to the other Dragon Rider.

My brother's angry words echo outside. "Break open the door! Kill my brother if he stands in your way!"

The man glances at me, eyes side. "You are Vance Maddox?"

The door at my back shudders. A powerful fist rattles it again, shaking the hinges. It won't take much for them to get through. "Does it matter? Now please. Go. Save what you can. I will hold them as long as possible."

"Come on, this one is right. The flame must live on." The woman gives me one final look and pulls on her friend's sleeve, tugging him to the window. They flee to the waiting dragon. Its lands on the rock tower, clings there as they jump for its back. For an instant, I wonder at this horrible alliance—for an instant it almost seems an amazing thing. But I cannot think that—dragons are beasts and meant to live far from all humans.

Behind me, wood splinters. Just one more blow and they will be through. Metal hinges shriek. Turning, I step back and lift my blade. Outside, the rising mournful calls of the dragons that circled the citadel reverberate, unsure, and I wonder if they understand what is going on, or do they cry just to cry.

The door shatters, and Hacon steps through the splinters. He glances once around the room. "So, my brother—you would seek to undermine my rule?"

"It is done. You have won."

"Done?" My brother swears and shakes his head. "It will never be done until these half-humans, half-dragons never walk the land again. I will work a magic so deep and so powerful no dragon will ever remember having a human rider, and no child will ever think of dragons as anything but nightmares."

I give a shrug. "Fine. Work the magic. But the killing is done this day."

The Iron Guard step into the room. I summon the tendrils of magic within me—the ancient Maddox storm-magic that speaks to us of wolves and thunder, of the wild and forgotten places.

My brother's eyes narrow. He glances at the empty crib and back to me. "You were to be my right-hand man, my trusted adviser, my own blood who is all I can trust. Instead, you stab me in the back. You make your own plans instead of heeding mind. For this, I strip you of your name. I strip you of your family. No one shall befriend you wherever in my whole realm you go. I forbid any to feed you, to clothe you, or to shelter you. You shall be the scourge of all, and a curse I place upon your soul!"

He lifts a hand. The dark wave of his magic washes toward me. He is going to curse me into the grave, but I also have some power. I throw myself forward, the old storm magic clean and pure against his darkness. It may do me some good. But next to me, one of the Iron Guard swings a fist larger than my head. I have no time to duck the blow.

As I fall to pain and blackness, I know I have bought myself—and the Dragon Riders some time. The child survives. The flame still burns. And I can only mutter a prayer that the flame will one day purge Hacon's black heart.

*   *   *

Part 1

Out Of Water

Chapter 1

The Western Isles

I leapt off the cliff. The branches of the trees and small shrubs whipped and snapped at my bare calves, biting into my skin. Stray twigs snatched at my hair. I didn't care. I should have trembled with fear, but I didn't. Holding my arms outstretched in a perfect imitation of the diving, shrieking seabirds that flocked to our shores, I was flying like a dragon.

Blue sky. White sun. Cold air.

Time seemed to slow. The pounding of my heart proved I was still alive even as it drowned out the haunting calls of the birds behind me.

Below me the broad expanse of the Great Western Ocean spread out like a blanket. The distant islands seemed little more than dots in the distance. No ships rode the waves. The sea was flecked with white spray and I could even pick out the smaller shapes of the seabirds, which seemed the size of butterflies beneath me.

How high up was I? Panic tricked though me. This was the highest I'd ever dove from, only I wasn't diving anymore. Looking around had caused my body to shift and turn. I started to spin and tumble. I was falling.

With half a scream, I twisted and righted myself. I let out a whoop as I dove again for the water. Energy surged through me. I was like one of the great dragons. I didn't have time to question why I was doing this as the water and rocks rose at me, faster and faster.

What had old Zenema told me?

The crashing froth of waves lashed into the rocky coastline of my island.

Hands forward. Breathe. Be like the gulls.

Zenema, the matriarch-dragon was always wise. Despite the years that lay on her, she could still dive as elegantly as any seabird. I tried to shape my body as she had instructed, but the wind pulled my legs and my arms out of place. It tugged on the clothes Zenema insisted I wear and whipped my hair across my eyes so I couldn't see where I was aiming. And there were rocks down there!

Foolish child! A female voice rang in my ears and heart. A shape swooped down like an arrow out of the sun.

"Jaydra!" I gasped out the word, but the wind tore it away. Flipping first one way and then another, Jaydra, the blue-green sea dragon, my den-sister, sought to match my dive. She was trying to save me. She was my closest friend and ally on the island. I'd grown up with her, and she even brought me food when I was ill. But could she save me now from my own foolishness.

Blue skies. Gray sea. Black rock.

I was falling faster now and almost out of control. If I hit rock, I was going to die. Closing my eyes against the onrushing sea, I felt for the crystal-clear moment within my heart I knew was there. It was the same feeling I got on the back of Jaydra, or when I ran as fast as I could. The power of the magic that coursed through my veins was always waiting to bubble up. I didn't really know what it was or where it came from—only that, in some extreme situations, it could pour out of me. I had only moments before I would be dashed on the rocks below. I willed my mind into the trance, and my hands moved in complicated patterns of their own accord.

Jaydra snarled and gave a low roar.

My eyes flew open as power poured from my fingertips. A bolt that looked like golden light hit Jaydra squarely on the chest. Power erupted from my fingertips, blowing both of us apart. My fall became a slow arc away from the rocks, and Jaydra flew back, spiraling across the sea like a skimmed stone.

"Jaydra!" I screamed at my sister-dragon seconds before I hit the water.

Cold slammed into me, knocking the air from my lungs. Salt water gushed into my nose and mouth, bitter and chilled. I tumbled head over heels, every muscle straining and every joint aching.

I knew Jaydra had been thrown across the waves, but in my mind, I could see her with her leathery wings wrapped around her protectively as she plunged into the waters, sending up a wall of water in her wake.

White water. Warm water. Pain.

Jaydra-daughter? Saffron-child? Zenema's voice rippled across my mind. The den-mother of the dragons that nested in the clutch must have heard our terrified thoughts. But I had other things to worry about. I rolled in the sea, fighting to swim, my lungs burning. At last I reach up to break the surface with one of my hands. Dizzy and hurting, all I could think about was Jaydra. Was she alive? Had I killed her with my uncontrolled magic?

A shadow eclipsed the sun, and bands of soft iron wrapped around my torso. Claws the size of my thighs lifted me from the sea. Coughing and spluttering, I came out of the waves.

'Saffron Flame-Hair, what have I told you about using your magic without guidance? Zenema kept on admonishing me, her thoughts stern and patient. She carried me over to the nearest beach. Jaydra stood on the white sand already, her tail still draped into the low surf.

Zenema dropped me unceremoniously. Air rushed out of my lungs, and so did salt water. My mouth tasted like salt and sand and I felt as if I had just been through a whirlpool, but nothing was broken. When the ringing in my ears started to fade, and I stopped coughing up water, I looked over to where Zenema was nuzzling her much smaller daughter, Jaydra, checking that she hadn't ripped or torn her wings. Water streamed off Jaydra's bright, blue-green scales, and her golden-green eyes were near-closed with pain. My chest tightened. I pushed up on one fist on the sand and faced Jaydra. "I am so sorry. I should never have tried to dive off the sea cliff, I thought that I could use my magic to—"

You thought to use magic you have never been trained in? Zenema's thoughts came over to me in an even tone. She wasn't angry, but I caught a blast of cold disapproval that made me wince.

Having any dragon annoyed at you was scary, but Zenema was taller than a house, longer than the entire nearby human village, with each leg wider than some of the island's palm trees. She had teeth as long as my forearm and silver eyes like sparkling mother-of-pearl. She was a rare, gigantic white-dragon. At this close distance, the fading sunlight caught every scale on Zenema's face, brushing the white with a fiery red. She shone, always bright and gleaming. But I could glimpse signs of age—ancient scars of busted scales which had broken and fused or formed multiple mini-scales across her snout, jawline and down her neck.

"Zenema." Crawling to my feet, I stood on shaky legs and bow deeply. "You are right. I almost killed us both."

Child. She sighed and her reptilian voice reverberated through my mind. Her thought-voice felt like sunlight in a drowsy afternoon in the clutch caverns. *You know I care for you, bringing you into my clutch as if you were my own. But I feared this—your magic grows too strong. It pulls at Saffron and must be used. You become a danger to your den-brothers and sisters. Magic will control Saffron—and destroy all—if you do not first learn its secrets. Such has happened before.*

I couldn't argue with her. My natural magic—what I thought of as dragon tricks—had been appearing more frequently of late and at odd times. Recently, I'd blown Jaydra off course and into a storm when I'd gotten frightened. And the last time I'd been angry, I'd flattened an entire stand of palm trees.

I wiped a hand down my soggy, baggy trousers.

I was becoming a danger to the only family I have ever known, and now—just like the human parents who had abandoned me—Zenema would want me gone, too.

Saffron-daughter…you must be brave, and I know how brave you are. Zenema curled her tail protectively around me even as she stayed close to Jaydra. I could feel the warmth radiating from her scales. *Was I not the one who found you in the cave so long ago? You would not cry or mewl, but looked me in the eyes and I knew you would be special. When the other dragons hissed, it was I who*

snarled at them to leave you alone. Before you were old
enough, I would find you riding Jaydra's back as she
taught herself to fly. I know the strength in you, Saffron—
and know you must use all of that strength to master the
magic inside your blood.

"But how?" I blurted the words out, feeling childish and
sounding petulant even to myself. "You just said it. I was
abandoned in a cave by parents who obviously couldn't
care for me. They were probably afraid of me. How am I
going to find why I have this stupid magic?" I almost
stamped my foot, I felt so desperate. Almost, because one
does not stamp at any dragon.

The answer is in your blood. Zenema pulled me closer
to her with her tail. *You must find where you come from. It*
is time.

I looked at Jaydra, still snuffing seawater out of her
lungs. What if, one of these days I really hurt one of the
dragons? Zenema was right. I had to go. I had to find out
who I was, for my own sake if not for theirs. I nodded and
wiped the salt water from my face. I wasn't going to call it
tears.

Come. I will take you to the place where it all began.
Maybe you will find the answers that you seek there.

Zenema uncurled herself and leaped into the air as fast and agile as one of the forest cats. She swept me up in her claws. Below us, Jaydra chirruped mournfully, but she did not follow. I knew she was still hurting from her fall. Looking down, I saw the island forest swirled away, the greens and browns growing smaller as the den-mother's powerful wings lifted me into the sky. I didn't want to go back—but I had no choice.

*   *   *

After we'd flown a long distance, Zenema's thoughts filtered into my mind. *Humans, Saffron. You must go to where the humans live. There are many, many more of your kind out there. And not one of them wants anything to do with dragons.* Her sadness over this lingered in my thoughts.

Glancing down at the vast sea below us, I wondered about her words. More like me, and like those in the island villages? Why did they fear dragons like the island villagers?

I had always known there were other humans. Jaydra and I had watched the sailors on the boats that were always coming and going to the islands. To me, they all seemed crude, loud, and noisy. Not true dragon-friends. There had been so much to learn about the forest that I had no interest in smelly, old boats or tiny huts.

But now I started to wonder about them. What did all of those humans do? Who was their headwoman? Was she like Zenema?

And why did Zenema want to take me to where things began—what did that even mean?

The questions left me dizzy and uncertain. They left me wondering if I even belonged with dragons. Which was ridiculous.

I had been with Zenema for longer than I could remember, and had been riding dragons for almost all that time.

Of course, faint memories stirred. A crib...soft blankets...a woman's voice.

No. That was the same, old nightmare—of being a baby, of a house burning. That was no memory. Zenema had cured me of that horrible dream. A dragon had swooped in to save me in the dream, or so Zenema had always told me, and now there was no need to dream of such things ever again. Even so, I shivered and leaned closer to Zenema's neck to let her warmth brush against my chest and face.

And I ignored the fear nibbling at me that there really had been fire and humans and angry people…and a woman's voice that I would never hear again.

Some of my fear must have spilled into Zenema. She suddenly wobbled in her flight and wheeled down to a distant, shingle beach. I clutched tightly at her scales.

Zenema landed on the beach and the rocks clattered under her claws. I slipped from her back. A wind blew cold off the sea and the sound of the waves was a low, hushed sound almost like a dragon's breathing. Her thoughts came to me, soothing and calm. *Here, child. I found you just here, on the teeth of a storm, wrapped up in the scrap of cloth that you still carry.*

My hand went to my belt and the pouch that hung next to my knife. I'd made the pouch myself, after those I'd seen all the island villagers wearing. It contained everything I had ever owned—a sewing kit that had been found with me and a scrap of cloth, threadbare and hardly bigger than my palm. It was now only a fragment of the blanket I'd once been wrapped in. I'd used it over the years to patch clothes for myself, for Zenema insisted humans had skins that were too soft without coverings. I knew if I brought it into the light I could just make out the name picked out in gold.

Amelia.

I thought I could remember the smell of a woman's hair; earthy and slightly fragranced with lavender. I hoped it had been my mother's name and that she had left this with me so I might know her. I wanted to think she had not willingly left me. But the old anger and hurt rose, bitter in my mouth and a hard burn in my chest. My father and mother had left me. *Amelia...my mother's name is Amelia.* And now I was even angrier at Zenema for bringing me back to this spot.

The beach stood empty, with sheer cliffs between us and the rest of the island. Just behind us, stood the cave—a shallow, high-mouthed cavern—where I had been left, over ten years ago. I put my back to the cave and stared out at the green-blue sea and the white foam of the low surf. "You think that until I find out about my human family— who I am and where I'm from—I'll never be able to control my magic? That makes no sense. I don't need to know where my magic comes from. I just need..." I let the words trail off. What did I need?

I knew the answer but I dared not say it aloud. I wanted to hide the thought.

What if I could find my parents—still alive and searching for me?

Glancing down, I kicked at one of the smooth rocks on the beach.

Zenema nudged me with her nose, urging me to turn and look toward the cave. I hesitated, but Zenema kept shoving, so I looked.

It looked like any other sea cliff cave—weathered, old and dark. The droppings of seabirds whitened the top of the cave, but the birds knew better than to fly near a dragon—I couldn't see any of them or hear them now.

The sun dipped lower in the sky and the light fell into the cave, slanting low and golden. Something odd stood out at once inside the cave's walls. Lines in the rocks that had a moment ago seemed random began to take shape. "What is that?" I breathed out the words.

Behind me, Zenema kept silent.

I stepped closer.

The light in the cave brightened even more. Curves and swirls took shape, and one stood out more than the others—an elongated arrow that I knew so well because I had drawn and redrawn it again and again. That shape had been in my dream.

Other shapes began to form in the slanting, golden sunlight.

"Dragons!" I let out another breath. My heart was pounding now.

These weren't the dragons of the home island. Tall dragons and thin dragons, fat dragons and squat dragons had been carved into the cave walls. I knew they wouldn't be the predominant whites and sea-blues of the dragons here on the island. They would be orange, green and even red.

Stepping closer, I walked up to the cave and squinted at the images. They were starting to fade now as the light changed. But I could see something else. I put a hand on the carvings and traced the lines.

Whoever had carved these lines into the cave wall had added human figures, riding dragons just as I rode Jaydra. But the carvings had two people on every dragon.

"Dragon riders." The words came out of me in a startled gasp. I turned fast to face Zenema. "Why did you never show me this before?"

Zenema snorted. *The time is not always now for everything.*

I rolled my eyes and waved at the carvings. "Don't you see? This means that there are others like me. There are others who live with dragons. You said all humans fear dragons, but they don't. So, I really do belong...somewhere.

Saffron belongs with Jaydra. The blue-green Jaydra settled onto the rocky beach. She shook herself and a slight tremor ran along her scales as if she were a bird ruffling her feathers. Head high, she stared at her mother.

Zenema stared back, her gold-green eyes glittering. Her thoughts carried a stern warning. *Jaydra stay away. This is Saffron's duty!*

Jaydra snorted and a small puff of steam warmed the air. *Jaydra and Saffron den-sisters. Where Saffron goes, Jaydra goes.* Jaydra raised a foreleg and thumped it down on the rocks, which scattered, some skipping into the sea.

For a long moment, Zenema looked at Jaydra. At last, her head lowered and she nodded. *It is done then. Already bonded and become one as in the old days.* Zenema turned her head to glance at me and it flashed into my thoughts that she seemed a little pleased as well as sad. *The choice is made. None can stop you.*

My throat tightened. The breath seemed caught in my chest. The world was changing for me—I knew it. I could feel a new destiny tugging at me.

I waved at the carvings inside the cave. It wasn't just dragons and riders that had been carved here. Dragons flew over undulating lines that almost looked like tall waves. But I knew these were mountains.

I pointed at one of the mountains—the tallest one that had been carved to show caves and smaller dragons, and what looked like the biggest village I had ever seen. "You think, Zenema, that I should find my own kind. Well, if I have a kind, if anyone knows about my magic, it will be at that place. I'll go."

Jaydra echoed my words with a cough of flame and smoke into the salt-tanged air.

Zenema nodded again. *The magic inside Saffron is strong—let it lead where it must. Be safe, my daughters. But even more so—be wise and strong.*

Jaydra picked her way across the rocks and stopped at my side.

We both glanced at Zenema as she took to the sky, her strong wings beating the air, leaving me clutching at my hair and Jaydra's eyes glinting with tears. I knew in my heart I was saying farewell to all I had known—my heart thudded slow and hard and I almost wanted to call out to Zenema that I would not go.

But I must.

I had to learn about my magic.

Even more so, I had to find the others who knew what it was to ride a dragon. I put a hand on Jaydra's warm scales.

All the questions I had about my past would have to wait. For now, we had to find a mountain like that carved into the cave walls. But where would we even start with such a search?

*   *   *

CHAPTER 2

HOUSE DARIS

"Bower, you're missing all the excitement. Don't you know someone denounced Master Julian as one of those traitorous rebels?"

I looked over to the other side of the lane. Vic Cassus waved me to come to his side, urging me to hurry. He was about my age, but broader in body and more cheerful in disposition. Vic had the sort of shoulders that should wear armor, frizzy brown hair and a man's beard already sprouting. He would have better fit into long ago times when he might have been a general or a great dragon-warrior and not the scion of a failing house in an ever-diminishing city.

When I reached his side, Vic grabbed my arm and pulled me with him. We'd both been heading to the Torvald courthouse, which sat in the higher tier of the city, behind some of the other, older noble houses. There was so few nobles left that it had become an almost unwritten rule to stay together. We strode up the steps to the courthouse along with others who were streaming in to see what the fuss was all about. Master Julian wasn't the only one to be accused of late, and it seemed to me that more and more names were being added to the list of the king's enemies. This was not good for the city or its citizens, but I had no idea what I could do.

I also worried that perhaps Master Julian was one of the dreaded Salamanders—those who wanted the king overthrown. We would soon find out.

Inside, Vic and I headed for the largest and the most elaborate chamber of the courthouse. The building itself was a series of round, circular chambers. The main one was large with stepped levels that held wooden benches for different blocks to sit together. The room echoed with mumbling, stamping and voices headed to angry arguing. The accusation had stirred up strong feelings. Even though I had every right to be here as Bower of House Daris–one of the original five great noble houses of the citadel of Torvald—most times I felt a fraud for just sitting in session at the courthouse. Too few ever listened to my words, and many thought I was too young to even attend. As always my skin chilled and my stomach knotted. The room stank already of sweat, perfume and fear. I hated this.

But I knew my duty. I could push where I could to get the people food released from the city stores. I had used much of my own fortune to help others, spending it to at least provide housing for those who would otherwise be out in the cold. But the resources of House Daris had dwindled to little enough—our house still managed to offer up soup for those who had none and bread once a week. I feared, however, this would soon stop—the lines of those in need were growing longer, and House Daris had little money left. I would soon be selling my library—if anyone would buy it.

These were grim thoughts for the day, so I pushed them away and tried to listen to the clamor of voices lifted in the stone chamber.

"…land reforms! That's the only way to improve matters and settle these traitors!"

"No—the king has sent for troops from the southern border to come here. That'll soon sort all of this business out."

"Soldiers—what do we need them for? Let them stay at the border. The Iron Guard is all we need. What do we pay our taxes for if not for them to keep order?"

"He's a traitor. I have it on good authority the king is coming this very session to declare it so."

Vic flopped onto a bench and grinned. He actually liked the noise and arguments at the courts. He had always been belligerent, even when we were younger. Now that we were of age to attend hearings and help decide the course of the city, he never missed a session.

I sat next to him and looked down over the sea of heads below. The room seemed washed with bright colors—cloaks and fine tunics, silks and even a few satin breeches. Our seats were always in the top row and the sound echoed hard here. I shook my head. "I'm not sure what good I do. No one wants to hear my opinion, and I would much rather be doing some good in the city, or spend an hour studying."

"Those fairy tales again?" Vic laughed.

"Vic, you know well such words could get *me* accused of treason." Any tales of the old times when there was said to be dragons, sorcerers, magic and knights that rode dragons to battle had been forbidden. In fact, it seemed of late that more and more laws were being passed—curfews to restrict movement after dark, laws against more than two meeting in the street, and more and more people seemed to vanish without explanation. I had become uneasy about living in my own city.

Vic clapped me on the back with one hand. "You worry too much, Bower." Leaning forward, he whispered, "It may be against the law to read that unapproved stuff, but I don't see the harm in it. You're not one of those wild-eyed Salamander prophecy rebels."

I nodded. Everyone had heard of the prophecy rebels— those that sought the downfall of King Enric with some old story of how the Maddox line would end. But it seemed to me that specific details of any prophecy were sadly lacking. And I didn't really believe a prophecy was enough to change our city. We needed…well, I wasn't certain what we needed, other than change. But how could we bring that about? And did others even want such change?

Vic certainly didn't look as if he wished such a thing. Leaning back, he spread his arms over the back of the bench. He looked a young man who owned the world.

I cast a quick look around. No one sat near to us yet, but if anyone ever found out about the library I had hidden inside my house—most of it about the most treasonous topic of all, I would be lucky if I wasn't lynched in my own house.

Trying to take Vic's mind off such things, I leaned back and crossed my arms. I'd worn my best leather jerkin and breeches, and a silken tunic. All of it felt stiff and awkward. I wished I was back in my own house in my old clothes. Voice raised a little to be heard over the others, I asked, "Just what is all this about Master Julian? Is it true?"

"That bloated old fool?" Vic laughed, waving over the hubbub to where the Master sat, surrounded by cronies and completely oblivious. "I doubt he's guilty of anything. But, then again, you never know these days who is a Salamander and who is for the king—except those with the king tend to stay alive." Vic pointed down to where the proceedings were about to start. "Looks as if the fun is about to begin."

The magister, an old man bent with age and bald as well, walked slowly up to the podium that stood in the center of the main floor. He rapped his staff of office on the table three times as was tradition. The crowd mostly ignored him—a fact that I found incredibly frustrating. Did these newer nobles have no respect for the past at all?

"Gentlemen and gentlewomen of Torvald and its principalities, protectorates and outlying regions." The magister's voice, wavering and high-pitched, barely carried to me. "We are gathered here to administer the justice of the court, under the counsel of the elders of the citadel and the wisdom of the king."

"Yawn," Vic muttered. It was the traditional statement the magister always had to give, and yes, it was getting a little boring.

A shout rose from the side of the hall, near the lobby doors. People were roughly shoved back. The clanking of the Iron Guards echoed as they moved in unison into the chamber. Nobles and merchants scrambled away from the path of those unstoppable guards. Their arrival could mean only one thing—the king had arrived at the chamber.

The royal herald's shrill voice split the air as he shouted, "Make way for the king! Make way for King Enric!" The royal herald walked in first, a woman in a rich, red velvet gown decorated with gold embroidered around the hem and the wide cuffs of the sleeves. An old man, dressed in a severe black tunic, breeches and boots, hobbled beside her.

Hobbled? I shook my head. Where was the king? He had certainly never hobbled in his whole life.

Sitting straighter, I craned for a better view. I looked away, searching for the king. When I looked back again, there was no sign of the old man, but the king himself now strode into the chamber, proud and confident as always, also dressed in black from head to toe. I had no idea where the old man had gone, most likely he had blended into the crowd. The magister bowed and backed away, merging himself with the others in the front row.

Everyone stood now, and the Iron Guard marched onto the main floor to stand in a line between those gathered and the king.

King Enric, a man in his prime with black hair smoothed and oiled back as was the fashion, a high forehead and steel-gray eyes, lifted his hands and a hush settled over the chamber. He wasn't a tall man, nor large, but he knew how to command a room. It seemed to me that everyone was holding their breaths—as I was. "Subjects! Nobles of Torvald, I am thankful for your attendance today, and I have come to congratulate you all on your fine work in the service of the throne and of the city."

An enthusiastic drumming of feet and cheers erupted. *What fine work?* I looked around. To me, the chamber seemed half empty. The nobles here looked a rapacious lot, eager to line their own pockets. The merchants who attended had fat bellies and smug expressions. Not one of them would hear a word about repairing the city walls, or putting in new drains or rebuilding old parts of the city that had become slums. I knew for those were the things I had once mentioned in this chamber, only to be laughed down and mocked until I learned to keep my own council. I was as useless as they were at addressing the many problems Torvald faced—but at least I knew it.

The king seemed far too unaware.

"Torvald is growing strong!" King Enric smiled and lifted his hands again. "Just as she has always deserved to. We control more territory than ever before, and the other powers of the world all look to us as their rightful leader. The iron will of Torvald is strong and the Iron Guard is stronger!"

More cheers and shouts answered the king. His smile widened. He nodded and tucked his hands into the wide belt he wore over his black velvet tunic. I was beginning to wonder if anyone here had arrived by walking through the same impoverished streets I had seen this morning.

The king lifted a hand and silence fell again. "But, my loyal courtiers and nobles, not *all* is well within our walls. We might be well-respected outside of them, but inside Torvald is a growing danger that seeks to undo all our prosperity and peace." A few shifted, making the wood benches creek. Someone coughed. The king's gaze swept the room. "It has come to my attention that there is more than one amongst you who is a traitor."

My heart began to pound. It seemed to me the king's stare had stopped on me. Was he about to scream, *Bower of House Daris.* He turned instead and thrust out a hand, pointing toward the double doors of the entrance.

"Master Julian!" The king shouted the name.

Two more of the Iron Guard stepped into the room, dragging Master Julian, one of the newer nobles, into the chamber. The man's fat face sagged with despair and bruises darkened the right side of his face. His fine tunic—satin by the gleam of it—had been torn in places, and his leather breeches looked as if he had been dragged through the city's muddy ditches. The Iron Guards dropped him at the feet of the king.

I knew Master Julian only by reputation—he had built a fortune by trading in fine art and rare antiquities, but rumor was that he overcharged and was not averse to creating goods to sell that were no older than a day in their making. Had he cheated the king? Or even worse...was he a rebel? One who believed the king should be overthrown?

The king glanced down at the man now quivering at his booted feet. "Master Julian, I have it on good authority you have been seen in the vicinity of the old monastery at the top of Mount Hammal." The king's voice dropped to a low whisper that everyone could still hear. "The forbidden land. The accursed place. Is there truth in this—or do you deny it?"

"Oh, by the king's iron! He hasn't, has he?" Vic muttered. I glanced at him. His face looked pale and taut, and his eyes glittered with fear.

Mount Hammal was the long-dead volcano that the citadel of Torvald had been built upon. To be more precise, it was the volcano the citadel was built *out* of. You couldn't dig any depth in this city without hitting the hard, black rock that glittered with crystals. It made any building difficult. Old ruins haunted the summit of Mount Hammal, just under the ridge that separated us from the volcano crater. It was accursed ground, forbidden to any save the king and his Iron Guard. Everyone knew spirits walked in those ruins, and dark shadows gathered in the shattered remnants of what was said to have been an old monastery. It was bad luck to so much as take a stone from those walls.

The king thrust out a finger to point at the man, quivering on his knees before him. "Do you deny it, Master Julian?"

A hushed silence swept through the entire court.

Master Julian bowed his head. His voice came out a soft sob, but everyone could hear his words. "Sire! I would never—it must be a mistake."

"Are you calling your king a liar?" King Enric's face reddened. A wave of dizziness swept over me. For an instant, it seemed as if I was looking at two men—both the proud king at the height of his powers and an old man's face that seemed to shimmer underneath. I blinked and brushed fingertips over my eyes. I had been up late reading—was this just fatigue from being up too late reading now making me see things?

Master Julian cowered even lower and stammered out a scattered denial, but even from where I sat, I could see everyone drawing away from him. He was tainted goods. And I could think of nothing to do to support the poor man. He had done wrong—he had broken the law. I shuddered to even think what his punishment might be.

King Enric's words sliced through the air, cutting as arrows in flight. "Either you think your king is wrong— that you are more knowledgeable than your king. Or you are a liar. Now, which is it?"

"I…it's not that…it's just…" The man looked up and around as if searching for friends. He folded and refolded his fine map scarf in his hands. His heavy face was pulled into lines and his skin had paled to the color of parchment.

"Enough! A man who cannot protest his innocence is obviously not without guilt. You know that forbidden land is held in high regard by the traitors who would see your king fallen. Yet you willingly stepped foot there. It sorrows me to see my love for my people turned against me." King Enric turned away and flicked one hand. "Guards, do your duty."

Master Julian stilled. The Iron Guards stepped forward, their metal armor creaking and whatever internal mechanisms operated whined. They seized the man by the shoulders and started to drag him away.

"Mercy," Master Julian begged, half sobbing the word.

My stomach knotted and the taste of bile rose to my mouth. "Come on," I muttered to Vic. "We must do something."

"What? Are you mad?" Vic grabbed my arm and held me in place. "You will end with the Iron Guards dragging you away as well. Do you want to be dead?"

My heart was pounding, but I couldn't just sit still. I might not think much of Master Julian, but he deserved better than to be hauled away like that. Shaking off Vic's hold, I stood. No sooner had I done so than a shrill scream split the air. The sound was awful—the worst I had ever heard. The chamber fell silent again.

Vic tugged on my arm, pulling me back into my seat. "Sit down. Sit down, you fool, or the Iron Guards will haul you away next.

I kept shaking my head. "What…what did they do to him?"

Vic frowned and he pushed out a breath. "You know the law—it's death to go near Mount Hammal."

Hands bunched into fists, I stared at the doorway Master Julian had been dragged through. "Death for breaking a ridiculous law—a law no one even understands. It's not as if the man sold weapons to our enemies. He was supposed to just have been seen in the wrong place. This is unbelievable." I looked down at my hands, forced my fingers to open and pressed them against my thighs.

I should have done more—but what more could I have done? Vic was right. Anyone who spoke up for Master Julian would have been killed as well. Murdered.

The clanking of the Iron Guard echoed again as they returned. Dark, dripping blood stained their armor.

Whispers started to fill the room. I glanced around, seeing worry in the eyes of man, and fear. This day seemed like a horrible nightmare from which I could not wake. But the king's Iron Guard left us powerless—useless.

"I can't stay here." I stood and glanced down at Vic.

He raised one eyebrow and crossed his arms. "Bower, you need a sterner stomach."

"And when did you become so callous? That wasn't a trial. It wasn't even an execution. It was—"

"Hold your words, Bower." Vic straightened and glanced around, suddenly worried. "You seemed determined to put yourself before the king next, and I have no wish to be anywhere near you if you do. Stick to your books if you must, but do not criticize the king." His face blanked for a moment, and for an instant the room fell silent. Another wave of dizziness swept over me. Swaying, I closed my eyes.

When I opened them gain, Vic was smiling. The normal conversation of the chamber rose up around us, and Vic leaned back in his seat. "I don't even know why you are upset. It's only prison for Master Julian. He'll get his sons to pay a fine to the crown or something."

"What?"

Around us, the arguments and conversations of the court continued. Looking down to the main floor, the Iron Guard was gone—but I hadn't heard them leave. The king was gone as well. It was almost as if nothing had happened.

Something isn't right here.

Uneasy now, I searched the crowd to see if others shared my uneasy sense. My skin pricked and a shiver slid down my back. The crowd was mostly older men. Even the newer nobles, with their garish clothes and outrageous hats, looked to be middle-aged and complacent. That was why so few would ever listen to me—I was too young to know as much as they did, or so they'd told me on a regular basis.

But Master Julian was dead. Wasn't he?

A slight hint of nervousness hovered in the air—and it seemed to me that even my memories of this morning were faded. Or distorted.

Was Vic right? Had the Iron Guard simply dragged Master Julian off to jail? Was that scream simply a protest and not a death cry? Who was I to know? And yet…that voice, that horrible cry, echoed in my mind.

Knees buckling, I sat down with a thump. "I thought I heard them kill him."

"King Enric? The king is a fair and just man." For some reason, the words sounded flat, as if Vic had said them so many times they no longer meant anything. He put a hand on my shoulder. "Maybe it's all that *literature* you read."

I knew what he meant. Those fanciful legends of heroes and dragons and sorcerers had tainted my mind. The king thought those stories evil— something to be used by dangerous, seditious lunatics to corrupt the city.

Putting a hand to my forehead, I touched cold sweat. I stood. "I'm going to go and get something to eat. It's too hot in here."

"You do that," Vic called out.

Half stumbling, I staggered back down to the main doors and out onto the steps. The air seemed dank and foul just outside the room. A splash of red stained the entrance.

My stomach turned and I fled down the street.

I didn't stop until my breath came in ragged gasps and I was far from the chambers and courts. That splash of red stayed in my mind. My mouth dried and my head spun. I didn't quite know how long I'd been walking. The day seemed wrong. Hadn't I gone to the courts in the morning? It was already late in the day, with clouds overhead and a sharp wind. It would be dark soon. Stopping, I leaned against a wall and pressed my hands against the stone wall.

This part of the city was in worse repair than others. Buildings sagged as did the wooden doors. Most windows had bars over them. Trash fluttered down the street, and the gutters stank of filth. A few ragged children ran past, eyeing me as if they might try for my money—they seemed to decide I was not worth the effort.

On the house opposite, dark paint in a reddish brown stained the wall with a roughly drawn W that had a small spark above it.

The fire within.

It was the sign of the Salamanders, the resistance movement, the dangerous lunatics the king was always raving about. This looked the type of neighborhood to harbor resentment and anger. The mark almost looked like the wings of a dragon.

I shivered, pushed off the wall and started for home.

The streets of the noble quarter were quieter than the rest of the city, and I had to climb upwards to my family's house. Below, the dull yellow glow of the lights began to flicker in the windows of the mansions. The curfew bell began to toll—a deep, sad sound. How had it gotten so late?

Shoulders sagging and legs aching, I stepped into my family's mansion. Brown and yellow leaves dusted the courtyard, iron knocker on the door had rusted and most of the windows in the two side wings had been boarded over years ago. House Daris had fallen on hard times, as had most of the city. I could not bring myself to sell the aging mansion nor did I have the funds to keep it in good repair. The roof needed new slates, the chimneys all smoked, and I had four floors of vast rooms, most of which had been emptied by my parents and myself in auctions to keep the household together and to do what we could to help our neighbors. They hadn't succeeded in stopping the growing poor of the city, and neither had I.

I opened the front door—we had given up a porter for the door years ago—being careful not to ring the bell. It was already so late and I saw no need to disturb the two servants who had stayed with me.

Inside, the lantern hung high in the vast entrance hallway had burned down. Gloom clung to the corners of a room as tall as it was wide and long. The house smelled damp and musty and seemed full of night air and the sigh of the wind. My steps echoed on the marble floors, which needed scrubbing, but it was hard to keep up with the cleaning needed. My stomach rumbled, and I realized I hadn't had anything to eat since early this morning.

Deciding to make my way to the kitchens, I slipped into the door that would take me to the scullery and past the servants' quarters. Even if the cook wasn't still up, I was sure to find something bubbling on the stove—she always had a soup or a stew cooking, for it was the best way to stretch whatever meat I could afford for the house.

My boots were soft enough to make hardly a sound on the old, stone steps that led from the main hallway. I was tired enough that when I first heard the whispering, I stopped, thinking of ghost and unquiet souls.

Wavering firelight danced out from the door that led into the kitchen, and then voices slipped into the stone stairway.

Gernigan said, "It was sitting right there. I saw it with my own eyes." My butler and steward, sounded upset, but then Gernigan managed to upset himself over most things. The lack of money in the household, how far House Daris had fallen, the dearth of visitors to the family mansion—all of it he would complain about and give a sniff and an accusing stare. He felt it was all my fault for giving away funds to the poor. His favorite phrase was, 'Things would have been different if your father was alive.'

Cook gave a laugh, her voice rough and low and said, "You must be mistaken."

"I'm not. And I did what any sane person would do," Gernigan replied.

I stiffened. What had he done? What had he seen?

A pan clanked and then Cook said, "You didn't destroy it? You know what Master Bower thinks about us going into his library. If he finds out you took a book, why, you'll be lucky to ever have a job again."

"Dragons," Gernigan hissed.

My throat tightened. With one hand on the stone of the wall, I took a step forward. *Oh, Gernigan, what have you done?*

His voice dropped lower and took on an unpleasant scratch. "Dragons it was. Drawings and descriptions, with writing about their names, their colors and all sorts of terrible, untrue things."

Cook gave a disapproving sniff, and I could almost have bounded in there and kissed her. "The master isn't like that, Gernigan. He's sensible. Who could believe in dragons? It's just ridiculous. And a book don't mean he thinks anything of it."

"Don't it?" Gernigan's voice rose and hardened. "I tell you it will come out that he is one of them Salamanders himself."

Cold swept over me. I wanted to leave, but I had to hear what Gernigan had done—for I knew in my bones he'd done something rash.

"A traitor, that's what he is. This wouldn't have happened if his father were alive. And there was nothing to be done but to inform the king's men. They took my complaint, they did."

Metal clattered onto stone, and I could picture Cook having dropped a spoon. She might have been shocked, but nowhere near as much as I.

I sucked in a breath. My face seemed both chilled and numb. I couldn't believe Gernigan had disobeyed my orders, and he had seen one of my dragon books.

What if he had destroyed it?

My stomach knotted at the idea that he might have actually burned one of my prized possessions. It was worse than his calling the king's wrath down upon me.

My hunger forgotten, I backed up the steps and headed into the entrance hall again. I had to protect the books— and then myself.

The house no longer seemed the same mansion I had once called my own. My trust had been betrayed by someone I had thought reliable. I had been betrayed. Running up the stairs, I headed to the library. Closing the door, I leaned against it. But then I saw the dragon book, still on my desk.

I had left it closed, but it lay open now. Hurrying to it, I touched a hand to the page. At least Gernigan had not burned it. But what now?

I had so little left to me—and so few books. And yet, I probably had the largest collection of literature in the entirety of Torvald. I could not leave it for Gernigan or the Iron Guard. If I hid them all, would the king believe me when I denied any wrongdoing? That had not helped Master Julian.

I thought of the scream I had heard—and yes, I had heard it. Master Julian's last breath had been in that scream. I knew I could not stay.

Hurriedly, I pulled the books from the shelves. I picked out only five to pile into an old, leather scribe's satchel— one on maps, a collection of old stories, two histories and one on dragons. The others could be hidden behind a false bookcase in a hiding room that had been known only to my father, my mother and myself. My father had built it himself, foreseeing troubled times looming. He had been right to worry. Now I would just have to hope the secret was enough to keep the rest of my library safe.

The five books I took with me would be a heavy load to carry but I could not leave these—they were rare volumes and could never be replaced. And the scribe's case would suit my plans. Like any noble born, I could wield a sword, but I could also read and write almost a dozen languages. I would make myself into a scribe. A wandering scribe. I could do no more here other than to save myself now.

Heading to my room, hauling my books with me, I packed a few clothes, what money I had left to me, and a few precious reminders of my parents in a soft-sided bag. I could imagine myself traipsing along the highways and byways, and I almost grinned at the thought.

And then I heard a pounding on the main door.

My heart gave a lurch. Sweat slicked my palms and my upper lip. Heading to a window, I glanced out and saw moonlight glint on metal.

The Iron Guard! They're here for me.

Grabbing a heavy cloak, I glanced around for an escape. A small, high window let out into the Rose Conservatory, which was little more than a summer-room whose windows had long since been cracked and smashed, making it very wintery indeed. I could exit my room into the conservatory and then head onto the roof and go down one of the back stairs. I could flee into the city where I could lose myself in the winding, narrow streets of the slums. I would make for King's Village and take on a new life for myself.

The pounding below sounded again, and I heard Gernigan call out that he was coming. Coming to let my doom into the house. Going to betray me again. With a last glance around me, I opened the window, took up my scribe's case and my bag and headed into the cold night. Behind me, the clank of metal boots filled the house—but it was no longer my house, no longer my home. I was now not just a man with a dying name—I was nothing at all.

And oddly, it felt as if I was free for the first time in my life.

CHAPTER 3

ON THE RUN

The great sage of the Thirteenth Age, Tantalus Mas, wrote that 'every step along the journey toward your destiny is a blessing.' Tanatalus Mas clearly never had to escape a city, hugging the shadows and walking in the thinnest of calfskin boots. I cursed myself for not changing my boots before I'd left, but there had been no time. And I cursed myself for ever having collected books—but what else would I have done with myself?

I had been raised an only son of a noble house. I'd never had brothers to play with or sisters to defend or tease. My parents never encouraged me to fight duels or to brawl with the lower classes, as had some of my friends. But I'd had books, and my love of reading had been smiled upon. It had been my life. Now, it seemed to me that the way King Enric was ruining the land was linked to this ruination of me. I could only hold out a small defiance against him by denying him my life and my books. But my feet still hurt, as did my shoulders from carrying the weight I must take with me. But I could not leave the books to be thrown onto a fire.

In these books were tales of pageants that had lasted days, festivals that had lasted weeks, tales of battles and feats of strength. Someone must hold to the past and keep alive the stories of a long-ago world. I would be that person and I would take my strength from that. But it saddened me that I had to run away like a thief just now.

Heading into the poorer parts of town, down past the lower-middle tier of the city and past the second and third bridges across the ravine-rivers that scored through the mountain, I knew I could hide myself here. But this was a city under curfew. While there might be no other citizens out to see me, the Iron Guards would be on patrol and would be stationed at key spots.

I made my way slowly, stopping to listen for the clank of metal at every corner, keeping to the narrowest, meanest streets. But I knew just where the Iron Guards should be stationed. They would be at each bridge, at the Carpenter's Mark, at the Courtyard of the Lost and at the Square of Remembrance. The Iron Guard were a constant in the city, never moving from where they were placed unless they had a direct order to move or had seen a violation of the king's law. They just stood watch, silent, metal giants. Or they searched for fugitives such as myself.

Still, they made a lot of noise and that would make it easier to avoid them. But that didn't lessen the pounding of my heart or the speed of my breath.

By now every Iron Guard must know that I was on the run. I had read in one book years ago that the Iron Guards were mechanical—and somehow they were all connected. If one Iron Guard knew one thing, they all knew it. It wasn't magic, or at least it wasn't magic in the old sense that I had read about. But it meant that I must treat every Iron Guard as if it wanted me dead.

I had once seen one of the huge, metal Iron Guards explode into action. It had been terrifying. A shout had gone up to stop a thief, and then a small man, dressed in rags, had pushed his way out of a crowded set of stalls. The Iron Guard stationed at the market had swung out a metal fist, catching the thief in the middle of his chest and dropping him.

With two fast steps, the Iron Guards towered over the thief, grabbed him by the leg, picked him up and tossed him down again, as if the man was nothing more than a sliver of wood to toss about. The Iron Guards had dragged the thief away and I never knew what happened to that poor man. That was the way of it—those who broke the king's law paid the penalty.

And I had broken the law.

But I didn't feel guilt for that—unjust laws should not be followed. But I knew I had to watch my step now.

The streets around me narrowed even more. This was an old, abandoned part of the city that had been ravaged by fire many years ago and had never been rebuilt. There were a few such places in the city—tangled streets with half-fallen houses. The building materials had long ago been taken by others. Rats scrabbled in the ruins and I saw a cat slink past, on the hunt for its meal. The place had an odd smell to it—dusty and dry, for no one lived here. And I had a chance to stop and slow my breaths and pat the very few coins I had in my pocket.

It would be wise to hold them back—to use them only if the need for food became dire. For tonight, I would need to wait and get as near to a gate out of the city as I could. I might find a friendly trader who needed help with their records, or a merchant with a wagon bound out of the city. For tonight, I needed shelter.

An hour later I came upon a house with half a roof and walls to break the chill wind. It would do. I put down my bags and used them to make a seat for myself so I would not be on cold stone. My empty stomach flapped at me and a headache had started. I would need water soon, and food, but for now I wrapped my cloak tight and tried to get what sleep I could.

A gray light woke me from a light and uneasy sleep and dreams of blood and an ancient king. I shook myself awake and rubbed my arms. Even with my cloak, this seemed a freezing time of day. Clouds hid the sun, and I was more accustomed to staying up to greet the dawn, not waking to find it a cold and miserable morning. I stood and stretched. Every muscle ached, and I knew I must smell of sweat and dust, but I had to push on. The Iron Guards did not rest. Picking up my bags, I headed for the nearest gate. With dawn, the city was waking and the curfew lifted.

The day brightened and so did my mood.

Voices lifted, shouts and whistles of the merchants and traders as they began their day.

The smell of cooking pulled me down a lane and to a narrow, mean house with a stall outside. A lady was selling a hot pie for a copper. I bought two and sat by the edge of the fountain in the square, watching the world wake. I ate the pie and wondered if I could perhaps send a gold piece to Cook—she had been good to me and I hated to leave her with no salary and now she would have no job. But I knew she could take pots and silverware from the house and sell it. It would have to do.

Gernigan would most likely raid the house, and then others, but that did not matter now. I was the last surviving heir, and without me, the house will be given by the king to someone else.

A solid thump to my back had me rising and turning, dodging in time to avoid a second blow. "'Ere! Get off with you, lazing about like you was a lord." I glanced over at a wash woman, come to do her basket of laundry. She wore a red scarf on her head, a badge of her office, and smelled of onions and ale. She set the basket down on the spot near the fountain where I had been sitting. She looked me up and down, dark brown eyes dismissive and hands propped on wide hips.

The woman who had sold me the hot pie gave a laugh and called out, "Oh, don't be treating the poor fellow badly, Das. He didn't know he was stealing your spot."

The wash woman gave a snort. "Didn't know? I didn't know him. What do you think you are, Knight of the Pigeon Poo and Rat Tail, huh?"

Chin lifting, I stared down at her. "I am…" The words dried and faded away. I could not and should not give her my name. Glancing down at my dusty breeches and boots, I knew I must look more like a vagabond with borrowed finery than any kind of lord. Which was probably a very good thing.

I swept the wash woman a bow. "I am most sorry. I am but a scribe searching for work and I've found none in this city, so I'm looking to travel on." I offered her my best smile.

She didn't smile back. "Taking my place. Looking to offer your services. Well, none around here need a scribe to write out their letters. Ger'on with you." She slapped my arm and turned away, muttering, "Monger's Lane would be too good for the likes of you!"

Monger's Lane! Of course!

Gratitude warmed my chest and I could have hugged this horrid old woman. She might believe the king's decrees that beggars and the poor lack moral character and are one step away from being as dangerous as the Salamanders, but she had pointed out the best escape route from the city.

*　　*　　*

The bridge to the district known as Monger's Lane had been built in the old style, meaning tall and high, and wide enough for two carts. It was also no longer a bridge, for the water underneath had dried up decades ago, and so it was not deemed worth guarding by the king. There were no Iron Guards here.

Laborers strode into the city across the bridge. In my shabby clothes, I seemed to fit right in.

Monger's Lane was even smaller and more cramped than the narrow streets I'd wandered last night. The buildings, mostly of tired wood that sagged, looked outdated by centuries and seemed dry enough that one fire would take out the entire district. The streets curled around and re-knotted with each other. The Iron Guards would have a hard time finding me here, but I was also having a hard time finding my way out and to the gate.

By mid-day, I was hungry again and the first drops of rain wet my face. Putting my books and my bag down, I stopped to rest my arms and catch a breath.

From behind me, a voice said, "Got anywhere to sleep tonight, friend?"

Startled, I turned around, hunching my shoulders and lifting a hand to the dagger at my belt.

"Easy, easy, brother." An older man with wrinkled skin faced me. His hair had not grayed and his blue eyes regarded me with a sharp, glittering stare. I knew he must want something of me, but what? His voice sounded as if he had some education. He carried a knapsack in one hand and an unlit lantern to the other. His clothes looked to be those of a clerk or a palace official—a long, black cassock and a cloak thrown back just now. But a hundred small mends to the fabric and patches showed he held neither of those professions.

"First night on the streets?" he asked with a calm, confident air that seemed to say he knew the answer I would give. He gave a nod for me to follow. I hesitated, but he moved away with purpose and seemed to know where he was headed. I fell into step with him. Why not?

"Second," I said, a little mournfully.

"It gets easier." He turned down a corner and stepped into a narrow alley, then turned again and headed up another street. "Don't worry now, friend. We've all been where you are."

"I—I …my family died of the Black Cough," I blurted out. It was true enough. I had lost my mother to a sickness and all my other relatives, but the healers had had no idea what had struck them down.

"Is that right?" He continued walking, his steps a steady beat on the worn cobbles. "Everyone's got a story. A broken marriage or bad parents or just got on the wrong side of the Iron Guards and the king." He shot me a sharp, sideways look. My heart gave a thump and I almost stopped and ran, but something in his eyes stopped my worry. It wasn't just that I didn't sense an air of violence about it—there was sympathy in his eyes.

He stopped and pointed down an alley. The space was really just a bare spot between a tangle of old houses. Someone had planted an apple tree. Crates stood nearby, along with fresh straw and apples lay strewn on the ground. My stomach rumbled—it had been a long time since the pie. The overhangs of the buildings would keep me dry. I could see I wasn't alone here—a few others had staked out spots for the night.

The man pointed to one, sturdily-built wall. "This here is the blacksmith's. Used to be one of the best in the city, or so they say. That wall gets nice and warm and keeps this whole courtyard toasty. I'll be by in the morning with some bread and water to go around."

I looked at his shabby clothes. "I do have a few coins. And how can you afford it?"

He shrugged and the corner of his mouth curved up. "The bread's only crusts and the straw is only straw. As for payment, you'll know when it's time to return what's owed. And there's not a place I'd advise one such as you to show your face at." He stepped closer and whispered. "When you're under the dragon's wing, no harm can come to you."

Cold slid down my back. He had said the words almost like it was an incantation.

Had he really just said dragon? Was he a Salamander?

Before I could ask, he turned away, gave a wave and strode up the street, leaving me to pick out my space.

It was still light, and I thought to perhaps read, but I dared not pull out any books. Instead I offered up to write letters to any of those who stayed here. None took me up on my offer, so I made my case of books and my bag into a chair and settled myself. I fell asleep with surprising ease, listening to the soft murmurs of my fellow vagabonds. Looking up, I could see the glint of stars through the leaves of the tree. A sense of peace settled over me. It was like a leash had finally been broken. I was no longer Bower of House Daris, struggling to keep alive a name and a mansion that should have faded out long ago. My only responsibility was to stay alive.

I woke early again, but not so stiff and not so cold. I couldn't say I was entirely comfortable—I did miss my bed—but I was rested. The others were still asleep, curled up tight under their blankets. I wondered if they knew where their charity came from.

Sitting up, I found a small roll of crusty bread and a quarter round of strong-smelling cheese wrapped in a cloth and set next to a water skin. I drank the water, wolfed down the bread and opened the cloth for the cheese. Black ink smudged the cloth, but the words stood out.

Wagonmaster Byers Western Gate.

Looking up, I searched for the man I'd met last night. Was this from him? Was it the name of someone who could help get me out of the city? There was only one way to discover the truth.

*   *   *

Wagonmaster Byers turned out to be a young, heavy-set woman, with a large-brimmed floppy hat and a long cigar hanging from her mouth. Upon seeing her, I instantly knew she would help me. The king had passed laws against being drunk and against the foul pollution of cigars and pipes. Wagonmaster Byers didn't seem to care much about such ordinances.

I found her near the Western Gate, leaning against one of her sleepy black mules. Burlap bags of what smelled like hops lay on her wagon, ready to be unloaded and sold. Her name was painted across her wagon as well.

It was still early enough to be chilly and no one took note that I had pulled my cloak hood up to cover my head and hide my face in shadow. Two Iron Guards stood on either side of the city gates, huge and immobile.

At least that means that they haven't spotted me. I intended they never would.

Walking up to the wagonmaster I asked if she was looking for help.

She pulled the cigar from her mouth and looked me over.

"Uh…a man gave me your name." I glanced around and lowered my voice. "He said that when you are under the wing—"

Byers cut me off with a cough and a slash of one hand. With a glance at the Iron Guards, she dropped her cigar and ground it out in the dirt. "Okay. Yup, I see. You any good with horses or mules?" She motioned to her team of four, all big and strong, their coats gleaming and healthy.

"I'm a fair rider." I thought back to the fast horses I'd ridden when my father had still been able to afford a stable.

The wagonmaster pulled a face. "No driving, eh? Can you do sums and figures?" She pushed her floppy hat back and gave me another look up and down. I wasn't sure what she was seeing—a skinny youth? A noble who had never done much work? A man who was now considered a traitor to his king?

But she gave a nod. "I supposed you could help."

A rush of relief spread through me. "That and more. I speak Sushtri, Daelaani, Vril, Ugol and the nearer dialects of the Isles."

Byers chuckled. "You can do my books and help haggle the prices. Now get those scrawny shoulders of yours moving and help me shift this load."

I nodded, casting a sidelong look at the Iron Guards.

The wagonmaster plucked off her wide-brimmed hat and squashed it firmly down onto my head. "Here. It'll be hot work, so take off your cloak and your tunic. You'll soon warm up." She gave me a wink. "Now come stow your gear."

I knew what she meant—the Iron Guards would be looking for Bower of the House Daris, not someone who looked like a farmer's son.

Following her to the back of her wagon, I left my case of books and my pack in the back. I pulled off my cloak and tunic and tucked them next to my books. The wagonmaster frowned at me, reached down and took up a handful of dirt. She scrubbed it into my skin. "No sense you burning that pale hide of yours."

She climbed up onto the wagon and pulled down sacks that she handed to me. Staggering under the weight, I carried them to the scales. Within minutes, I had worked up a sweat and it felt surprisingly nice to be working with my hands and arms. There was no worrying about protocols or if I might offend the wrong noble today. I didn't have a crumbling house to try and maintain. I had no one telling me I was too young to know anything. It was just carry sacks and keep my head down.

By midday, I was hungry again and the wagon was empty. My throat ached for water and my shoulders burned, and I smelled like hops and sweat, and probably like a goat. However, the satisfaction that sat inside me was different from any I had known.

The weighing up and the haggling took longer than I anticipated, but the wagonmaster sent me to an inn with coins to buy us a meal and drink. Just after midday, we climbed into the empty wagon and headed to the gate. Heart beating hard against my ribs, I gripped the side of the wagon. Would the Iron Guards stop us?

The wagonmaster threw a coin purse at me. I caught it as she complained, her voice loud, "Seven gold and three florins? Outrage!" She leaned over and spat out of the wagon side. "Check it, boy. Last time I made at least ten gold."

Head down, I spilled the coins into my lap and counted. The wagonmaster slapped the reins and called out to the mules and we trotted through the open gate. This had to be her way of telling me to keep my head down. The Iron Guards watched our wagon, but made no other move.

Of course, the wagonmaster had been right about the money she had made, as would any trader who depended on coins earned would be.

We passed out of the city and into the outer shanty town. Small huts and a few storehouses stood between the city walls and the wilds of the far west. The king's army patrolled this area, and I was surprised to see so many soldiers camped outside the city gates. I would have thought the king would have his army stationed to protect our borders not here.

Thinking back to how so many within the city had disappeared—and to Master Julian's fate—I started to wonder if perhaps the king was more worried about rebels than anyone knew.

At least we were out of the reach of the Iron Guard, who stayed mostly within the city walls and stood watch at the palace.

The wagon's wheels rumbled over the rutted road, and I was shocked by the poor repair to what should be the king's highway. Potholes dotted the road and deep ditches either side could have swallowed a mule whole.

Gradually, the scenery changed from farm field and rather poor farmhouses to creeks and meadows, and then hills and forest. The wagonmaster called out to her team and told me to put on my tunic again.

"We're safe beyond the city, but have a care. There's been more soldiers on the roads than I've ever seen before. Most of 'em seem to be gathering around the city."

"Why?" I asked.

She shook her head. "Don't know. Don't want to know. It's the king's business what the king does with his soldiers. But I'll tell you clear, I've a feeling it's not something that bodes well for the city."

We passed several other travelers, all of them heading to Torvald, and as Byers noted more than a few mounted troops. Byers waved companionably to every one of them.

The soldiers ignored her, and to the other traders she would shout, "'ware the thieves beyond the walls. Sticks up their behinds in there! Gave me seven bits when they should have paid ten!"

The other traders nodded and sighed.

And I felt suddenly ashamed of my home city.

Torvald had once been deemed the leading light of the entire world, a center for culture and fine goods. Was it now only regarded as a greedy, cruel sort of a place? And why was the king bringing so many soldiers to Torvald?

The road became dirt, not cobblestone, and wandered into curves and woodlands.

The wagonmaster turned to me and reclaimed her hat. She pulled a fresh cigar from inside her tunic, found a sulfur match from beside her seat and struck it against the wood. When the cigar had woven the scent of aromatic tobacco into the air, she said, "Now, young man. I don't care at all what you did and where you came from, or why you have to make your way out of that hellhole back there. And I don't want to know, either. The least you tell me the better. As far as I'm concerned, you're just another runaway, hard on his luck and looking for a new life."

I nodded. "That's true enough."

"Then good. Whatever your story is, fella, let it go. That's my advice. Become someone else. Become the person you always wanted to be when you were younger and let the past go." She turned back to her mules, called out to them and exhaled another pungent cloud of purple smoke.

"When I was younger I wanted to have adventures. On dragons and with wizards and fighting evil sorcerers."

Byers laughed. "Best not be telling that to just any soul."

I nodded and let the rumble of the wagon lull me into a drifting laziness. To me, it seemed that I was already succeeding in the first of those ambitions.

I stayed with Byers for six days all told. She taught me to drive and tend to the mules. We camped at night near lakes or streams and I carried the water. Byers pulled out a flute one night and told stories another. Most nights I fell asleep before it was even dark.

On the sixth day, we came to a fork in the road. She pulled up the team and turned to me. "I go north from here, round to farms I know. My plan is not to be back to

Torvald for some time. I can almost afford to take you on, if you care to stay."

I shook my head. "I'm making for King's Village."

She gave a gusty sigh. "Well, have a care. Even that's not safe ground these days. I've been hearing of arrests of anyone who so much as says a harsh word. You'll want to watch your step."

Climbing down from the wagon, I gave her a smile and pulled down my bags. "Then all the more reason for me to travel on my own. I can't bring trouble to your door— you've been kind to me. But…well, I wanted a real adventure, not to exist thanks only to the charity of others." I dug a coin from my pocket—a gold—and held it out.

She pushed it back at me. "Keep that. You'll have need. And don't be flashing such coin around too freely. There are those who would slit your neck for as little as that. A goodly walk down the road will bring you to an old house. It's a safe haven for travelers, but looks not much more than a ruin in the woods. There'll be food and water there and a roof over your head for the night."

With a nod, I climbed down from the wagon and went to the back to pull out my bag and my books.

The wagonmaster lifted one hand and wagged a finger at me, her eyes dark and her mouth pulled into a deep frown. "You make sure you keep your head down and work hard."

"Don't worry, ma'am, I will. And thank you."

"Forget the past. Embrace the future!" She gave a final wave of her hand. With a puff of purple and blue smoke, she called out to her mules, turned her wagon north and drove off, leaving nothing more than dust behind.

I was sad to see my new friend gone, but I was also excited.

Now...what would one of those heroes from the old books do?

I thought about that as I headed down the road, looking for the ruin Byers had said would be there. I didn't see it, so I parted with the road and headed to the woods, looking for the ruin. The books seemed to get heavier with each step and now I wished I bought food to bring with me from that inn, and not just one meal. I was hungry and tired, and I needed to find water.

Lifting my face, I tried to smell for it—and walked deeper into the woods. Pines and oaks closed around me, oddly frightening. I'd never been far from the city and now I wondered if I might lose my way. But the moon was rising in the east and I could use that as my guide.

The woods weren't quiet, either. Leaves crunched under my boots, night birds called out, and other animals skittered out of my path. I wet my lips and wished for even just a chunk of bread.

In the stories I'd read, the heroes never seemed worried with such things as eating or drinking—or other bodily needs. I was. I wanted to find that house she had mentioned. But the heroes didn't go out alone—there had always been two Dragon Riders or traveling companions, striding through the wilderness in search of lost treasures.

Perhaps I should have stayed with Byers. Or perhaps I would find the house and another traveler would be there. The sun had fully set, the sky darkened to a deep black, and a chill rose in the air. I stopped to put down my books and my bag and pull on my cloak.

As I straightened, something hit me from behind, knocking me face first to the ground.

*　　*　　*

PART 2

IN THE WILDS

CHAPTER 4

SAFFRON ON THE HUNT

He wasn't very well-built, but a spy didn't have to be. The stranger had stopped right next to the thicket where I'd hidden, so I jumped him.

Unluckily for him, he did not know he was dealing with Saffron of the Island Dragons.

I sat on his back, holding him down. I pulled a length of leather from my belt and pulled his wrists behind his back. Once his hands were tied, I turned and tied his booted feet. He was making muffled sounds, rolling on his face in the leaf litter of the woods. The moon was enough light that I could see he was thin, but taller than me, with a dirty cloak. He had bags with him, but I had no interest in that. I wanted to know what he wanted with me.

With him tied, I stood, taking my weight off his back.

He twisted and turned around, tangling himself in his own cloak. "Thief! Murderer!"

I leaned over him and poked him with the end of the stick that I'd used to knock him flat. "What are you doing, sneaking up on me? I think you're the thief."

"What? I'm a...a traveler. Just that. I didn't even know you were here."

I gave a laugh. How could he not know? "You smelled my campfire, there behind the ruined walls of that house."

He glanced over to where I'd waved. "You have a fire going? The house is here? I've been searching for it."

He twisted and his eyes glittered as he stared up at me. "You did this to me. You attacked me. What did you hit me with?

"Nothing that big." I lifted my club. "And of course you're not going to die. I didn't hit you that hard. So, where's the rest of your gang?"

"Gang?"

"You can't be out here on your own, sneaking up on a lonesome traveler like me." I hefted my stick once more.

"I wasn't sneaking." He spat out a leaf. "I was looking for an old building someone told me to search out. She said there'd be food and a place to sleep for the night. And why have you tied me up?"

I took a step back. "That story could be true. You seem too skinny to be a bandit—or at least to be a good one. But maybe you're here to lure me into dropping my guard. I've seen that done before. Just what were you doing out here anyway with no friends?"

"Are *you* traveling with anyone?" He twisted and gave a grunt.

I had tied his ankles and wrists pretty tight. Breathing hard, he seemed to give up on his struggles. His face seemed very pale and he looked worried.

I was worried that he might have seen Jaydra. We had already seen the reaction some had to a dragon—our first encounter on the road had not gone well, and Jaydra had taken more care to hide herself since then.

But I still didn't know what this fellow was doing out here. Bending down, I grabbed the larger of his two bags. This would provide the answers I needed, I was sure.

"Hey…stop that. That's mine and private."

"Ho! So, you *are* a criminal and in here must be your stolen goods. Either that or you have something to hide, at least!"

"Please don't." His voice had dropped to a low tone and I caught a touch of panic in there. But I needed to know. I opened the bag.

It was full of nothing more than books. Lots of old books. A strange, flutter lifted in my stomach.

Growing up, I had only seen two books which stayed within the Hermit's hut. Zenema had said they were great human treasures and wouldn't let anyone touch them. In this bag were more books than I had seen in all of my life. I reached out to stroke the leather and wooden covers. They smelled of vanilla and something aniseed.

"Please don't. They're worth so little."

I glanced at him. "Are you crazy?"

Opening his other bag, I found clothes and some coins, but that wasn't as interesting as his books.

Turning back to the larger bag, I sat down and opened the biggest book. The thin pages creaked under my fingers. I turned to a random page in the middle.

Zenema had had the hermit teach me something of my own language, both to speak it and write and read it. She swapped fish with him for the lessons. But I couldn't read words in his book. The writing seemed strange and blocky, with some of the letters in a pretty, elaborate whirling and twisting designs. I had never seen anything like it.

The thing I could see, even in the bright, silver moonlight was that it had drawings of dragons. Lots of them. I gasped.

I heard a groan, but ignored the stranger as I flipped to another page and then another.

The book had drawings of dragons I had never seen before. I was used to the sea-green island dragons like Jaydra. In the moonlight, I could make out the stocky dragons, slinky ones, immense dragons, and more. The drawings showed the dragons in flight or sweeping across the sky in groups that seemed part of a pattern. It looked so beautiful. I had once tried to get Jaydra and her brothers and sisters to fly like the sea-geese fly, but the dragons had started to squabble over who would lead and then one started fishing and that sent them all hunting for fish.

The island dragons didn't fly like this, so what dragons did? Looking over at my bound captive, I demanded,

"Where did you get this? What land are these pictures of? Where can I find them?"

"The—the dragons?" He wiggled until he could sit up. "You want to talk about dragons? Uh, you're not from around here, are you?"

I thumped the book closed. "How did you guess that?"

"Well, around here…no one talks about dragons. The dragons in the book, they used to fly above us in the Middle Kingdom—in these skies." He spoke slowly, carefully, as if each word was a thorn that might draw blood. "And your accent, of course."

"What's an accent?"

"It's how you say words. It's just not a Torvald accent. It sounds …wilder, I guess."

I narrowed my eyes. "Are you trying to buy some time? Waiting until your friends turned up?"

With a groan, he lay back down on the ground with a thump.

I don't smell anyone else. And so what if others come? Are our claws not long enough? Our teeth not sharp enough? Jaydra's thoughts touched my mind. I could feel her savage joy at the thought of a fight. These last few weeks we had done little except keep out of sight and search for other dragons and magic. I had learned all too soon not to ask about those things—people turned pale and ran from me when I did. And I knew that Jaydra was tired of hiding. She wanted to scrap and play, to hunt and fly and shriek as she swooped across the skies.

Jaydra, I do not have long enough claws or sharp enough teeth. But I agree that this one is probably all on his own. We still have to be careful. This is strange territory.

I sensed Jaydra's agreement, and her disappointment. I glanced down to find the stranger looking at me, his head tipped to one side and his eyes wide.

Could he have heard my conversation with Jaydra? Usually, the island villagers couldn't hear the dragons, although to me their voices had always been clear in my head.

I stood up and pointed at the books. "Tell me about these dragons? Where did they come from? Where did *you* come from?"

He gave a sigh and wiggled and sat up again. "I—I come from a big city—Torvald it's called. The dragons, they don't exist anymore, but they used to. Or so the story goes."

I thought of the drawings on the rock far away on the island. "Is your city in the mountains?"

He shrugged. "There's Mount Hammal. And then there are the mountains to the far north."

"But dragons once lived in your city. Then you can have your books back if you take me to this city and the mountain."

"To Torvald?" He gave a laugh and shook his head. "If you walk into Torvald and start talking about dragons, the Iron Guards will kill you. As in dead. It is against the king's law to even think about dragons!"

"That makes no sense. How can you make a law about thinking? And why would it be against the law to speak of dragons. I mean, perhaps some are annoyed with dragons for eating their pigs and their sheep, but not talking about a dragon is like not talking about the wind or the ocean."

"You're talking like dragons really exist." He shook his head again. His hair was shaggy and fell into his eyes, half covering his face. "You can't go to Torvald. I won't take you."

Squatting down, I put my eyes on the same level as his. "You said you came from there. Don't you want to go back? And after sneaking up on me like that, it's—"

"I wasn't sneaking." He let out a low growl, looked down at the leaves on the ground, then up at the stars and back at me. "I can't take you back to the citadel because I can't go back. And I don't care what you say or do to me. I won't go back."

I stood up again, shocked by the strength of his words. I could hear the pain in his voice, and something else. Fear maybe. It was always hard for me to judge human emotions—things were so much easier with dragons that just let you feel what they felt.

But I could tell something had happened. Maybe he'd lost his family. Maybe, like me, he was an orphan. In any case, he was alone, too.

I couldn't afford to feel sympathy for this stranger, even if he had a book all about dragons. I wasn't sure it would be wise to trust him. Zenema had always taught me to be cautious when dealing with humans because they lied to themselves as well as to others.

"Very well. But I'm going to go there anyway," I told him. "But not until tomorrow. Now are you hungry? You look hungry and your stomach keeps making noises. You might as well eat some food with me and you can tell me more about your book about dragons."

*   *   *

CHAPTER 5
CAPTURED, CORNERED & CONCERNED

I couldn't believe this girl. First, she attacked me out of nowhere. She knocked me around and went through my possessions, then demanded I take her to Torvald. The only place I could never see again.

And now she was offering me food.

Was this what most girls were really like?

The only girls I'd ever known I'd met at the king's court. They were either from the noble families and had no interest in the impoverished House Daris, or came from rich merchant families newly made into nobles who were seeking an alliance with a family held in favor by the king. That had never been House Daris.

This girl seemed...different.

Sharp-features, frizzy hair, a look as fierce as a wild bird. But I couldn't tell if she was mad or just a little simpleminded. Or was she trying to make a fool out of me?

I wanted to lift my tied hands, but they were caught behind my back. At the merest mention of food, my stomach had started growling. "How do I eat if I'm tied like this?"

"I'll free you," she said and held up one finger. "But if you do one thing to try and harm me, it'll be the last thing you do." Pulling out a long-handled dagger with a curiously carved handle, she cut through the bonds she had wrapped around my wrists. I rubbed the chaffed skin.

She cut the fastenings around my wrist and disappeared into the darkness. For a moment, I could only stare into inky-black woods, but then she called out, "Aren't you hungry?"

I stood, pulled together my books back into the case and took up my other bag. I followed the sound of her voice and saw the smooth shape of a wall, and then the flicker of a fire. I stepped around the wall and found the girl had built what looked like a tent made of branches in the middle of what must have once been a large house. A circle of rocks held a small fire, and the aroma of roasting meat curled into the air. Rabbit, I thought.

Squatting down by the fire, she cut strips of meat off whatever animal she had roasting. She tossed me the hot meat and I had to drop my bags to catch it. I sat down and took a bite. It was rabbit and it tasted better than the finest meal I'd ever been served. She cut off meat for herself and sat with her legs folded under her, eating as if she'd never been taught manners.

I kept watching her.

She was a slight girl really, shorter than I was with long, red-gold hair, and by the firelight I could see the tan on her skin. Were it not for her attitude—the one that had her thumping strangers with a club—I might think her pretty. A farmer's daughter perhaps. But she didn't act like any farmer or his daughter. Every move gave off confidence and awareness. She reminded me of a large, not very tame cat—one of the tawny ones that knows it is a great hunter.

Her gaze flickered over to me, every time I moved. Tension kept her body and shoulders taunt.

Finishing my meat, I wiped my hands on my breeches. They were already filthy and I had nothing else to use. I hesitated, wondering if I should tell her my name. I had been using the name of Tarrow, as Byers had said I tarried too much, meaning I was generally too slow for her liking. But it seemed wrong to give this girl a lie—for one thing I worried she might sense the lack of truth. For another, I wanted to know about her—why was she so willing to talk freely about dragons? I could hardly ask questions if I was not willing to trade information. Besides, what harm could it do if she had never been to Torvald?

"I'm Bower." I smiled and offered a hand out to her.

She eyed the hand and slapped more meat into my palm. The light of the fire reflected orange in her eyes. After a moment's hesitation, she said, "Saffron." She touched her hair. "I was given the name because of the color of my hair."

I nodded. A shuffling in the woods had me turning and staring into the blackness where the trees met the ruins of the house. The moon was high, but a breeze kept the trees shifting. For a moment, I saw nothing, and then a dark shape moved out from behind the trees. I caught the impression of a bluish-looking horse, but my mind rebelled at the idea. And then the thing lifted its head and neck into the moonlight.

"Dragon!" I shouted, leaning forward to seize one end of a burning log and leaping to my feet. I don't know what made me grab that log. I was no fighter at all, but the terrible certainty that dragons were real and lived out in the wilds compelled me. I didn't want to hit it—I wanted to see it clearly. I had been drawing for as long as I could remember.

I swung my makeshift torch high.

The burning loge exploded in a shower of sparks and sheets of flame. With a yelp, I let go and jumped back. And then it was as if a giant invisible hand smacked into my chest, knocking me off my feet. I landed painfully on one elbow, muttered a curse, rolled and scrabbled to my feet.

But there was no dragon on the edge of the firelight. Just me, standing there gasping, and Saffron staring at me, her eyes narrowed and her head tipped to one side as if she was now certain I was a madman.

"What—what did you see?" I asked, dragging in air with long, hard breaths. Saffron's face seemed pale in the firelight. She looked from me to the woods and shook her head. "A dragon. I'm certain I saw a dragon!" I spun around, searching for the long snout and sinuous neck. The dragon I had seen was not as tall as those of legend—it was small enough to hide behind a tree and perhaps a little bigger than a good, wagon-pulling mule.

Now I could see nothing more than trees and darkness. I put a hand to my face and brushed off cold sweat. Had my eyes been playing tricks on me? What had I seen?

Saffron crossed her arms over her chest. I noticed then that she was wearing a tunic, breeches and boots made of tanned animal hides. "I thought you said there weren't any more dragons?" Both her eyebrows rose high.

"There are. It was. But this was blue, but not one like the ones in the old books. In fact, I think it was kind of blue-green and...and looked like a horse." I glanced at the torch I'd lifted, now smoldering on the ground. "And why did that explode like that?"

"Could be just sap." Saffron raised her hands, palm up. "And are you listening to yourself? Wouldn't we both have seen a dragon—they're really big in the drawings in your book. Maybe I hit you a little too hard with that club when I knocked you over?" Her stare slid away from mine.

"You think I'm crazy. But...I saw it. Blue and green and I thought it was a horse at first, but it was big, and then it lifted its head and I would swear it looked right at us—it was...curious. And how could I know that if it hadn't been there?" I stopped and stared at Saffron. "Maybe you are right—that doesn't sound very sane." I let out a breath. "I was hit on the head and all this talk of dragons…but the wood, the torch just exploding. It was almost like something hit it—and hit me, too."

Saffron gave a weak laugh. "If a dragon had just breathed fire on us to roast us for a meal, don't you think we would be dead already?" She sat down next to the fire, her back to the woods. "As you say, I'm not from around these parts, but you told me no dragons exist here. No one talks about them or knows about them or is even supposed to think about them. And I don't know about these trees, but I have seen sap pop and a big enough pocket could have flared up. So I just picked the wrong type of wood to use in a fire. Do you know about that sort of thing?"

I shook my head. I didn't know. My experience of building a fire was to ask a servant to do such a task. I didn't even order my own wood—that had been left to others. The short time I'd spent with Byers had taught me little. She had sent me into the woods to pick up dead branches, but had never told me that there was any type of wood that you shouldn't put in the fire. She'd only said it would smoke if the wood was too green.

Slowly, I came back to the fire. Saffron had pulled out a blanket and she wrapped it around herself now. "If you don't feel safe here you're welcome to leave and I'm sorry I attacked you. But I'm getting some sleep now. You can keep a watch for dragons." She lay down near the fire and closed her eyes.

Cheeks burning, I now felt an idiot. I wrapped my cloak around me and used my case with my books for a pillow. But I kept staring into the woods, and thinking about dragons.

*   *   *

Saffron still angry with Jaydra? The thought woke me and I let out a sigh. It was barely first light and I was still angry with Jaydra. How could she have allowed herself to be spotted like that? I'd reacted blindly with my magic, and it was Bower's own luck that I hadn't done more than explode his torch and push him to the ground. At least he'd been distracted enough that Jaydra had time to fade into the shadows. I had almost blinded us all.

Saffron did good. And Bower seems one to trust. Jaydra's thoughts carried a touch of stubborn petulance. She'd thought the same thing to me last night. I still wasn't certain.

As a punishment for having allowed herself to be seen, I had left her on guard. Even a sleeping dragon can smell danger leagues away. Getting up, I stretched and sent my thoughts to Jaydra.

How could you be so careless as you were last night? You know the humans here fear dragons far more than any islander. You know we have not met any human we could trust.

Don't know. Bower just has…a strange way. It felt almost like his mind was close. Just wanted to see Bower." Jaydra's thoughts confirmed my worst fear.

There was something different about Bower, just as there was something odd about everything that had happened last night. So far, Bower seemed to be the one person in this whole land with any knowledge of dragons at all and who might even know the very place I was seeking. It was almost as if our paths were meant to cross.

Mother Zenema used to speak of such things. All life connected. To pull on one scale over here might scratch another scale over there.

I doubted Jaydra knew what that meant.

So? I asked her with my thoughts. *It's no accident we met him. Was he sent to find us? Is he liar after all?*

Not smelling dishonesty. Jaydra gave a throaty growl as she yawned.

Next to the burnt-out fire, Bower snuffled in his sleep, but he didn't wake at the noise.

All things connected by fate. Destiny. You and he have a tie just as you and Jaydra.

It was my turn to give a snort. But whatever we might be facing, Jaydra was more my family than anyone.

But Bower wasn't going back to the city. He didn't want to take me there. I would have to find a way to do this without him. Except if I did that, I would leave him out here, and that wasn't good for him.

Heading into the woods, I gathered fresh fuel for the fire—old branches that had fallen—and I kept thinking of all of the things Jaydra and I had seen during our travels.

From what we'd seen, the roads here were not well cared for or marked. I'd seen better paths on any island. That told me it had been a long time—years even—since anyone had traveled very far.

When we had flown over the cliffs of the shore, we'd seen ruins of huge houses and small cottages, all left and broken apart. There were even entire villages that seemed to have been lost in the middle of the forests—these I could see from the sky, but from the ground they would be impossible to find. Tracks like faint scars crossed the land, and it seemed to me that this land had fallen on hard times. Jaydra and I had learned to be cautious for we'd had to avoid more than one camp of bandits—rough, armed people who drank too much and boasted of the villages they had raided. Farmers didn't wish to talk to me—a stranger—and now Bower didn't want to take me to the one city that might hold some answers for me.

I started back to the camp, settled the wood on the ground and started to build a new fire. I didn't trust my magic enough to use it to light a fire—I'd tried that a couple of times a few nights ago and had set a tree ablaze. Maybe Bower was right to be cautious around me and others. But he had also said he couldn't go back—was he in trouble?

Bower gave a cough and woke suddenly, sitting up and flinching. He glanced around, eyes wide, and I wondered if he was looking for Jaydra.

"Morning." I nodded at the fire I'd started with my flint and my knife blade. "There's water, and rabbit for breakfast."

"Lash tea?" He pushed back his cloak and pushed at his hair. He had thick, dark hair. Seen in daylight, he was better looking than I'd thought he'd be with wide-set eyes and a wide mouth. He had a strong chin with only the faintest stubble showing.

"Lash what?" I asked. Was it the way that people greeted each other in the morning in these strange lands?

"It's a hot drink. It keeps you awake." I saw him staring at the water flask beside the fire. He shook his head. "Never mind. Water it is." He stretched and stood, and almost tripped over the wood I'd gathered for the fire. I shook my head. If he insisted on trying to make his way alone, he wasn't going to last out the day.

*   *   *

CHAPTER 6

PROBLEMS OF THE WILD

Saffron seemed to be done with treating me like a captive or a criminal. We ate breakfast and chatted and I drew a map for her about which road to follow to reach Torvald. I also tried to give her a dozen warnings about what to do and what not to do. By the time I was ready to take my leave from her, the sun had vanished behind heavy clouds. The wet, damp smell of rain hung in the air. I was almost sorry to part ways with Saffron. I now felt more like a traveling companion, almost a friend.

Real friends don't tie you up.

I rubbed the red marks on my wrists. There was that, but somehow the feeling persisted that I knew this girl. I should have been furious for how she had treated me, but I just couldn't work up the anger. She had skills enough to hunt her own meat, and a wicked knife, and that meant she could have killed me if she'd wished. There was also her determination to make her own way—and her interest in dragons. Those things had me thinking she had a good heart underneath that spiky exterior.

But that exterior was going to be a problem in Torvald.

I wasn't signing on for going back. But I worried about her. What if she ended up asking others in the city about dragons? What if she tangled with the Iron Guards? That wasn't going to go well for her. I wanted to try and talk her out of her plan, but what could say?

I know how dangerous it is to talk about dragons because I have books on dragons and that alone was enough to have the king's Iron Guard come after me?

What would I say after that? I would end up telling her my entire life story and she might not even believe me.

She would just have to cope on her own, somehow.

Just as I would have to out here.

Looking over the few belongings I had in my bag, I let out a breath. Saffron had given me some of the rabbit meat. I had given her a few coins. Now we each had to make our own way. I packed my books and caught Saffron eyeing them as if she wanted to sit down and read one. Standing, I hefted up my bags. It was, to my best guess, about late morning and still we hadn't moved from the ruins. The gray clouds looked ready to drop a hard wetting. I looked up at them and wondered if I would be able to reach a farm house or an inn—or even a cave before I got soaked.

Glancing around, I searched for Saffron so I could at least wish her good luck.

She stepped from the woods, leading what looked a balking, young horse. The horse looked odd to me—it was a lot taller than any horse I'd ever seen and for an instant, I could almost swear it had a sinuous, long neck…and the shadow of wings. I squeezed my eyes closed, knowing it was impossible for horses to have wings—or a blue-green hue to their coats. When I opened my eyes again, I saw it was just a horse. Tall, yes, but the blue-green came from the sheen off a dappled black coat.

The horse did seem to be looking oddly at me, almost as if it had an air of interest in me that I'd never before seen in a horse.

Saffron didn't have so much as a rope around the horse's neck—clearly this was a very well-trained horse.

"This is Jaydra." Saffron waved at the horse. Saffron's cheeks colored and she gave a short laugh. "I've…uh, known her forever. You might say we grew up together. I had her tethered in the woods.

"With what?" I glanced around for a rope.

Saffron just shrugged and waved a hand. "Well...you know."

"I don't know that much about horses. When we had money enough to have stables, we also had stable boys who looked after them. I just rode." Bending down, I pulled up a hank of grass and offered it.

The horse—a mare I noticed—stared at me, head high, snorted and stamped a hoof, then swung around to give me a view of a wide rump and a long, swishing tail.

"And she doesn't like grass," Saffron said.

"A horse that doesn't like grass? Now I have seen everything the world has to offer."

Saffron was looking at me with eyes narrowed and her head tipped slightly to one side as if she was doing sums in her head. Or thinking really hard and trying to decipher a new text. "She's a different breed of horse than you would have ever known before."

I turned away from the horse, moving back a step so I was well out of kicking range—just in case. I gave Saffron a smile. "Well—if you're not actually going to tie me up or kill me and steal my goods or anything else dire, I guess I'll be on my way."

"Are you sure you won't help me find my way into this city of yours?" Her forehead bunched and she chewed on her lower lip. She looked younger now and freckles stood out on her cheeks. My chest tightened. I wanted to help her, but she really had no idea just what she was asking from me.

"I'm sorry, Saffron. I can't. The city...you're going to be disappointed by it, I promise. It's dangerous and dirty and—"

I tried to tell her, but I could see the ripple of annoyance across her face as she snorted and shook her head.

"Fine. Go." She turned to her horse and draped an arm over its back. The horse glanced at her and shook its head from side to side, as if it had something to say and Saffron wasn't listening. Saffron leaned her back against the horse's side, folded her arms and frowned at me, a line now tightened between red-gold eyebrows. "I hope you don't get eaten by bears or something worse."

I gave a laugh. "Bears? Since when do bears live this close to the road?"

She rolled her eyes. "Don't you know anything? A bear is big enough to live wherever it wants. And go wherever it wants—that includes roads."

I glanced at the woods around us. Were there really bears around? That didn't match what I had read about such animals. I picked up my case of books and my pack. "I may be safer with bears than I was with you jumping me. Good…well, good luck to you. In Torvald, you'll need it."

And good riddance.

I pressed my lips tight. Yes, good riddance. I didn't need her help. I had read about the woods beyond Torvald. I knew I wanted to head to the King's Village so I would keep to the road and that would guide me there. If nothing else, there would be signs.

But already the bags dragged at my shoulders. I walked away from the ruins and Saffron and her odd horse, anyway. And I was not going to think that I'd heard a grumble that had sounded almost like words coming from Jaydra, Saffron's odd horse.

*   *   *

I'd once read that of the many problems with the wilds, the biggest one was that they were in essence wild. I'd had no idea of the meaning of that, but after walking for an hour, weaving in and out of the woods, I now knew exactly what it foretold.

The road had been easy to find—but it also had the disadvantage of travelers on the move, although there were few of them, and soldiers, of which there were far too many. I didn't mind the one, but the other could end with me dragged back to Torvald. Parting with the road yet again, I headed for the trees. They'd been cool and shady at first, and easy to duck into to hide myself. Birdsong had greeted me. I'd wandered a little deeper, certain I could keep the road in sight. That had become impossible.

Now I wasn't certain where I was.

The trees all looked the same, roots tried to snag my feet and tripped me, and branches swatted at my face and pulled at my hair and cloak. Trees should not be allowed to grow their roots above ground like this—it was messy and unsightly. Roots were supposed to be kept underground, as they were with the trees in the city. Branches should grow up high—or had they all just been trimmed within Torvald?

And I wasn't going to think about the stones that bruised my feet or the mud making my boots heavy, or how the sounds of the animals had changed from birdsong to growls and roars that kept stopping my stride so I could search for the source of such noise.

Sitting down on the ground, I dropped my bags and pulled my cloak tight. The hem was now muddy and heavy. I let out a long sigh. My shoulders ached, as did my calves and thighs and feet.

I had thought of my time with Byers, learning to drive a wagon, helping her haul water and harness her mules and find firewood had toughened me. I'd been ready for the life of a wandering adventurer—or so I'd thought. I'd been utterly wrong.

In the past hour, I'd acquired scratches on my face, bruises on my shins and my bags were rubbing my fingers raw.

It seemed unfair that the wilds should be so very wild. I would just have to make my way back to the road and try to find a friendly farmer who might give me a ride on his wagon.

But that would require me to get to my feet—and perhaps I could just sit a few minutes longer. That left me facing an unpleasant possibility—what if I didn't have what it took to be an adventurer?

I frowned at the idea, picked up a stick and began drawing in the damp dirt. Idle sketches to pass the time while my feet rested.

Perhaps I should have stuck with Saffron—maybe worked harder to change her mind so that she came with me to King's Village? Or perhaps I'd been rash to leave Byers? But, no, that would have meant leaning on others, as I had done all my life. This was a chance to prove myself—and I had my books with me to provide me with company.

I patted the reassuring weight of the case with my books. They were the hope for the future—they were my hope. Perhaps I would come across traveling Gypsies and we would exchange stories—tales of dragons…and even odd horses.

The drawing I'd made in the dirt started to look more like Saffron's very tall horse with the blue-black coat. I crossed it out and tried to draw the dragon I thought I'd seen last night.

I'd only glimpsed it, but it had looked so real. Even given all my reading about dragons, I don't think I could have dreamed of a dragon that looked like the one I thought I'd seen. After all, I had read of the large crimson red dragons and the blues.

This dragon of last night had been blue-green, the color of moss, or the sea on a sunny day. In the firelight, its scales had seemed to shimmer and change color, depending on the flickering light. It had a softer, shorter snout.

I looked at what I had drawn in the dirt and dragged the stick through the image to cross it out.

Just one of the reasons why it must have been an illusion!

There were no such dragons in any of the books I had read. I'd been tired, and talking about dragons had mixed up the traits of half a dozen or so of the images I knew to create an entirely new breed out of long-dead stories.

But, oh, how a dragon would have made this traveling about so much easier.

"Time to get moving," I muttered, needing to hear someone talk, even if it was just myself. I pushed off the large, hard stone and brushed the cold off my backside.

A crack in the woods north of me had me catching a breath and holding still. A twig had broken—but what broke it? Another branch or twig broke, leaves crackled, and I heard a deep, snuffling sound coming closer.

"Saffron? Is that you and your horse?" My voice sounded too high. I cleared my throat and called out, "You haven't fooled me, you know. And I really don't want to be kidnapped a second time." I lifted my bag—it was not much of a weapon—and I put a hand on the knife on my belt. The knife suddenly seemed far too small and slight. I called out, "If you wish to join me I'm heading for King's Village and you're welcome to come along."

More branches cracked—large ones by the sound of it. My heart thudded up into my throat and I wet my lips and drew my knife. "I'm just going to go on my way—and I won't be waiting for you!"

The crunching of leaves and the snuffling drew closer. Neither a horse nor a girl could be making that sound.

A guttural, throaty snarl shook the woods.

Cold flooded down my spine. The sound had come from behind me.

Did I really want to turn and see what had made such a growl?

I had to. The urge to look was undeniable, like drinking water when parched or pulling in air after being too long underwater. Pulse fast and hard, my breath coming in shallow gasps, I turned ever so slowly.

The noise behind me had stopped—but that was even worse.

There are no bears out here.

I told myself that over and over again. The king's army patrolled these roads and woods, and no bear had been seen in years. Or that's what the books I'd read had always told me.

But just how many of the king's patrols had I seen coming since parting company with the road?

In truth, even on the road, I'd seen only two patrols. I had a new perspective on the supposed wealth of the Middle Kingdom since leaving the capital, and it looked to me as though little to nothing went to the upkeep of the roads or the people.

None of that, however, would help me right now. I was on my own—without a road, or a patrol or even a friend's help.

I looked behind me.

For an instant, I saw nothing but trees and dark forest. The tall pines blocked what little sunshine could make its way past the gathering clouds. And then something moved—something large with glittering eyes. It growled again, and long, white fangs flashed in the pale sunlight. My heart banged into my chest, but I forced myself to hold still.

The bear's patchy, black fur left it able to hide in the woods and deeper, reddish stripes the color of the flags that had once hung over the gates of Torvald marked its hide. It was unlike any picture of any bears I'd ever seen in my books. It boasted two sets of long fans or tusks, one pair on the upper jaw and one on the lower jaw. A low forehead sloped back from the face and small, black eyes stared at me. It lifted its snout and snuffled the air, as if it could not see very well. Still snuffling, it rose to stand on all fours, staring in my direction.

My throat and mouth dried. I was shaking inside. This could be no ordinary bear. It looked as if it could be a bear that had gone to the soldier's guild and had been thrown out for being too good at killing people. Maybe it was some strange new breed no one else knew about.

Maybe I'm the first human to see it.

For an instant, that thought left me excited and grinning. But the bear let out another growl, and it struck me that seeing this bear might be the last thing I ever did.

I took a slow and careful step backwards and stepped on a dried twig. The snap reverberated around the little clearing and up my spine.

The mangy bear sank down on all four paws and roared.

I knew I would soon be dead if I didn't move.

Turning, I ran. I never knew I had that much speed in me. Behind me, I could hear the bear crashing through the woods. I dodged around trees, swung myself over boulders. I didn't know if I could outrun the animal, but I had to try.

I willed myself to go faster, putting everything I had into the sprint. My lungs burned and my side ached. I ducked under low branches and sprinted around huge trees. And I could hear the bear's crashing, its heaving breath—I could smell the stench of rotten meat coming from it.

Ahead, the sliver of glinting light broke through the trees. It had to be the road. Oh, please, that had to be the end of the woods and the road. That had to be safety and sanity again—and maybe help.

I burst out of the trees and into bright daylight that left my eyes stinging. Squinting, I made for the hardened-packed stone road. I jumped over the ditch on the side of the road, a deep one used to drain water from the roadway. I thought that maybe, just maybe I had made it to safety and relief surged through me. Risking a glance back, I leaned over to brace my hands on my knees. The bear crash out of the trees. It was even bigger than I had thought, its black eyes glowed red, and its hair hung off it in unhealthy, loose hunks. Bits of bone clung to its fur—and bits of other things.

It gave another bellow and charged me.

Instead of leaping over the ditch, it tumbled blindly into the deep gash beside the road. It really couldn't see all that well. Stones sprayed up as the bear struggled to right itself. I didn't wait for it to get free. It was panting with exertion and white foam dripped from its face.

I was just as exhausted, but fear pushed me on. I jumped over the bear and headed back to the woods. Behind me, the scrabbling of rocks told me the bear was climbing out of the ditch. It roared again and started after me.

Heading into the woods, I slashed at the smaller branches that blocked my path. I was going to die like this, killed by a mangy, half-mad, blind bear. But I wouldn't die without a fight.

Turning, chest heaving, hands and face cold, I faced my doom.

The huge bear roared and lunged for me. And I could no longer face it—squeezing my eyes closed, I braced for it to strike me and tear me apart.

Something hit my chest with a hard thump, almost like a shove of someone's hand. Air rushed from my lungs and more air swooshed past me. I tumbled head over heels. It was painful, but it didn't feel like claws or teeth were ripping me apart. The world spun. My stomach gave a hard flip. Branches and leaves tore at me and past me. And then

I smacked into something hard. Grabbing for it, I clung to rough bark. I could hear the rustle of leaves. I opened my eyes. My feet dangled, but I had my arms wrapped around a thick, oak branch.

Below, the bear snuffled, searching for my scent, I was sure, and lifted its head to give an angry roar.

A hand fell on my shoulder and I glanced to one side to see Saffron. I was expecting to see a rope in her hand—surely she had used one to pull me up here. For an instant, I wondered if she'd somehow slammed me up here with a punch. But that was impossible.

However, Saffron simply straddled the branch I was hanging onto, smiling at me as if there was some joke in all this.

I looked down at my chest. The tightness had gone, almost as if something had let go of me. How had I gotten here? How had Saffron managed to pick me up with what seemed to be an invisible force? I opened my mouth to say something, but I couldn't think what, and the words fell out. "I'm in a tree."

"Better than being on the ground right now." Saffron glanced down at the bear. It roared again, and pawed at the ground, as if it thought I'd somehow buried myself.

"I've heard them called grim-bears. They're pretty stupid by what I've seen. Creatures of instinct really, but they are bad tempered. And there are a lot of them around."

"But…I am in a tree! How did I get here? I'm not entirely sure what—"

Saffron put her fingers over my mouth and leaned close to whisper, "Hush. Someone's coming!"

*   *   *

Chapter 7

Dragon Tricks

A simple dragon trick allowed me to make Jaydra seem like a horse. Of course, she could hide herself, but I didn't want Bower bumping into her. It had seemed likely he might.

By what I could tell, Bower and the few people I'd met so far in this strange land were more primitive to me than any dragon-clutch or island village. They didn't know any dragon tricks. I had thought they would be able to shape fire or call light, but I'd done that once and had been called a witch. It didn't take long to realize these people couldn't make themselves quiet so that they became almost invisible, a skill that I had learned alongside Jaydra. And they didn't know how to shape light to change the shape of what someone saw.

It was easy enough to do.

I breathed deep, let my thoughts slip into the sky, and concentrated only on my breathing. I spread myself into the calls of the birds, to the crackle of the leaves on the branches, the creaks of tree limbs, and to the distant noises of the forest.

Then I looked at Jaydra and saw the light around her, and shifted that into the light coming off a long-legged, tall horse with a blue-black coat.

Okay, so a little green got in there, too.

She still looked more horse than dragon, unless you knew how to see past the light around her.

She wasn't happy about that—she wasn't happy about Bower leaving us, either.

Watching Bower walk away from the ruins where we'd spent the night, I had to admit it was a lot like watching a dragon dive to its death in stormy waters. My chest tightened and a churning in my stomach told me I had made the wrong choice. But he was going one way and I was heading another.

Saffron cannot leave Bower, Jaydra said in my mind. She swished her tail—it made a louder sound than a horse tail should, but I couldn't do anything with light to disguise that.

I let out a sigh. "Yeah, I know. If I can jump him so easily, I don't know what he'd do out there on his own. But his path is in a different direction."

No. Bower is connected. The bond tugs on me...and you. Jaydra sounded quite certain of this, but I wasn't.

Zenema would say we have a duty to find out why there is a bond.

I sighed and could almost hear our den mother's voice in Jaydra's thoughts.

Zenema was always telling us to go after the things that scared us, after the things we didn't understand, or the things that could help us understand better. It was her who encouraged me to find out about my past, after all. She said it was like learning to fly.

No hatchling wants to fly, until they do. You are always scared, but you will never know just what you really are until you try. When you fly, you find out more than you expected.

Kicking at the grass Bower had tried to feed to Jaydra, I wondered if we were meant to go after Bower. It wasn't in my plans, but I was here to find things out. So, we would just have to see what happened next. I glanced over at Jaydra. "You're going to have to stay looking like a horse."

Jaydra growled, which was a disconcerting sound to have come out of a gangly horse.

"When you fly, you'll have to be invisible. A flying horse could just get shot down. By what we've seen, this whole world is out to fight something. Everyone has metal weapons and high walls around the towns. And you heard Bower—he thinks his own city is dangerous."

City! No dragon would ever build such a thing. Jaydra gave a snort. That was a better sound to have coming from a horse.

I patted her neck, feeling scales under the illusion of her looking like a horse. "You're right about that. But dragons don't need walls—your scales are your defenses, and you have claws and fire. But you have to admit that some of the things we've seen—buildings almost like mountains, and houses with steam coming out of brick chimneys, and lines of people all marching down a road—are pretty impressive."

Jaydra gave another snort. *Not as pretty as the ocean and white surf on the sand, and not as nice as a good, warm cave.*

I had to grin. Jaydra was right—and the images she sent me left me longing to go back to our clutch and the islands. Before I could do that, I had to learn how to control my magic. A simple dragon trick was not a threat to anyone— but I could feel my magic under my skin, itching to leak out. The urge to use it was growing stronger every day, and if I didn't learn to manage it, it might burst out in a way that would harm not just those around me, but me as well.

Jaydra sensed my worry. She gave a deep, rattling purr that reverberated even through my chest.

Saffron, my den-sister, Jaydra thought at me, buffeting me with her fierce loyalty and bumping me with her nose. I was humbled.

She had stuck by me on this. She didn't have to come. She could have stayed on the islands, fishing in the seas and scaring the villagers and tumbling and playing with her clutch-brothers and sisters.

Putting my arms around her neck and breathing in the scent of pine on her, I said, "And Jaydra is mine. "Now come on, we must find that oaf of a boy before he manages to break his neck. And you're going to have to be a horse for a time—or invisible."

Jaydra huffed a breath of smoke and shook herself. The horse standing before me changed back into a young dragon. She shook herself again. Her scales began to look more like the leaves of the forest, and her bright eyes gleamed like sunlight on water droplets. She shifted on her legs and they became tree trunks. Spreading her wings, they changed from huge dragon wings into seeming to be odd colored clouds.

Slowly she vanished.

She was there, but she looked so much a part of the world that most would look right past her. I knew the trick, too.

Breathe in, breathe out. Feel the environment around you.

The same trick came as naturally to me as swimming…or riding a dragon. I slipped onto Jaydra's back now, and I knew I was just as difficult to see as she was.

Anyone looking at us would see the forest, they would hear the birds, the hum of the insects and the sigh of the wind in the branches. The world would be just as they expected—and glances would slide past Jaydra and me.

I liked this merging into other things—becoming so much a part of the world that I was no longer a person but a part of the sounds and the woods. The world flowed together to form one mosaic.

For we are all one really. I am a part of this forest just as is Jaydra.

In fact, the only thing that was not really part of this forest had to be Bower. Even from this distance I could hear the thump of his books and his grumbling. I knew when he left the road to head into the forest, and when he passed other travelers.

No one noticed me or Jaydra.

It wasn't really magic. Not like what the old Hermit had once told me about. It wasn't making someone float or teleporting or even reading someone's mind. This was more a natural talent that many wild creatures had, along with unerringly finding their way home, or appearing fiercer and bigger than they were. It was all about focus or the lack of it.

That was the real trick.

I had never really thought about it before. But chatting with Bower had made me think about the difference between us. Growing up with dragons and on an island, I had always felt as if I belonged to the dragons and to the islands. Bower wasn't like that. He looked different and seemed to act different from anyone I had met here.

There was something special about him.

He had almost seen Jaydra, after all, and he shouldn't have. And Jaydra had felt some sort of connection with him. I couldn't help but think there was a whole lot he missed and that he was disconnected from himself and the world around him.

But that had me thinking about my own lack of connections—wasn't I seeking those things here?

Climbing up on Jaydra's back, I settled myself. With a quick, pouncing move and a surge of strength, Jaydra lifted into the air and spread her wings.

My heart beat faster to be on Jaydra's back again. Wind stung my cheeks. I grinned.

I was riding on a dragon, skimming above the canopy of trees. A part of me kept thinking this is just as everything should be.

But everything wasn't quite so smooth.

I wasn't sure what I was going to tell Bower—that I was following him, that I didn't think he could handle the wilderness on his own, or that I wasn't letting him out of my sight until he agreed to take me to Torvald? None of those seemed like good things, so I asked Jaydra just to circle high overhead where we could keep an eye on Bower and I could think.

But Jaydra's worry interrupted my own. *Trouble*, Jaydra thought at me.

Glancing down, it wasn't hard to spot Bower. He burst out of the woods at a run. Behind him one of the bear creatures that seemed to be everywhere came out of the woods.

"We have to help him, Jaydra. Dive lower." I pointed to where the sweep of a road cut through the valley like a knife. Ditches lined either side of the road. Bower jumped across and stopped—as if that was a good idea.

Jaydra dove lower, and the bear lunged at Bower. Thankfully, the bear fell into the ditch, but I knew Bower wasn't out of trouble.

"Fly, Jaydra, fly!" I told her.

She gave a rumble and picked up speed.

Bower had seemed to realize he was still in danger. The bear was climbing out of the ditch—and Bower was running again for the woods.

A band tightened around my chest. I hunched over Jaydra's neck. I feared even Jaydra wouldn't get there in time to save Bower. I was going to have to use magic.

But I couldn't—what if it went wrong? What if I killed Bower?

Bear plans to kill Bower anyway, Jaydra thought at me.

She was right. And I had to act fast. Bower and the bear were back in the woods and Bower wasn't as fast as the bear.

This isn't magic. This is just a forest trick.

I tried to hang onto that idea. Maybe if I wasn't so worried about what I was doing it would go better.

Extending my mind toward Bower I tried to think of this as being like how Jaydra could extend her claws to catch a fish in the sea. We were close now—almost hovering right above the trees and Bower and the bear.

My head pounded. Sweat sprung up on my forehead. I stretched out my mental talons and slammed them into

Bower. In my mind, I saw him fly into the air, away from the bear. But he was still in danger.

Tightening my hand, the invisible talons that existed in my mind closed around Bower.

Jaydra swung around and I jumped from her back and grabbed the nearest tree branch. I clung there, struggling to bring Bower up next to me. Instead, I was crashing him around through the branches, scraping leaves into him. With a gasp, I focused only on him—on my mental talons that had hold of him.

Suddenly, it almost felt like a natural, simple movement.

He thudded down on the branch next to me. I leaned back, breathing hard, sweat cold on my skin, shaking now.

Bear waits for Bower and now Saffron to come down, Jaydra thought at me. *Jaydra likes bear meat.*

I could feel her annoyance at not having the chance to attack the mutant bear-creature, but she also understood my earlier insistence that I protect her from them. I didn't know enough about this land to say just what these creatures were capable of. Were they poisonous to dragons? Would Jaydra get sick if she ate one?

No! We can't risk that. This bear doesn't look right and we don't know enough to say if it's sick and could make you sick. I thought the words to her. Her annoyance at not having the chance at a fight came back to me. But I could at least give her something to do that might make her feel better. Can you find Bower's books and things? He doesn't have them with him.

Jaydra has Bower's scent. She sent me an image of being able to track Bower—or his things—anywhere.

Bower seemed dazed. I put a hand on his shoulder and he looked at me, eyes wide and twigs stuck in his hair. "I'm in a tree!"

He looked a mess—his hair tumbled and his cloak torn—and he frowned at me. I dreaded to think just what he must be thinking. Would he call me a witch now? Would I have to tell him about my tricks—and about Jaydra? My heart was pounding, and we had to rid of that bear before it decided to try and climb the tree. Jaydra wasn't really big enough yet to hold both of us— and fly far.

I gave a shrug for an answer and said, "Better than being on the ground right now." Looking down at the bear, I wondered how long it would hang around. It roared again and pawed at the ground. "I've heard them called grim-bears. They're pretty stupid by what I've seen. Creatures of instinct really, but they are bad-tempered. And there are a lot of them around."

"But...I am in a tree! How did I get here? I'm not entirely sure what—"

Leaning close, I slapped my hand over his mouth. Jaydra had breathed one word into my mind—*Riders.* She let me share her sensations—she could smell horses and humans and hear the clop of their hooves and the jangle of their harnesses.

I leaned close to Bower to whisper, "Hush. Someone coming."

To my surprise he actually took heed of my warning.

Within moments, I heard the riders with my own ears and not just with Jaydra's dragon senses. The bear, too, stopped snuffling and lifted its head. It let out a low, long growl.

The beat of hooves on the hard road faltered. A shout rose up. From high up where we sat in the tree, I could just glimpse what looked like banners on spears and I counted five of them. Then a sword, raised high, glinted in the sunlight.

"What is it?" Bower muttered beside me, his words muffled by my hand.

I pulled my fingers away. "Soldiers. Five, I think."

His face paled. He gulped and struggled to climb up on the limb. I had to help him, but the bear ignored us now. It had turned to face the road and gave another roar that sounded like a challenge to me. I sent my thoughts to Jaydra for her to stay hidden and safe—we were safe as well as long as the soldiers didn't look up. But just in case, I used the trick to make us seem nothing more than leaves and branches—we were just part of the forest.

Below us, the soldiers marched into the woods, their armor clanking. I heard a horse whinny and muttered orders were given—someone was being left to hold the horses. Then the soldiers tromped forward again, making enough noise to scare away every bird and forest creature.

But not the bear. It bellowed again and clawed at the earth, leaving huge gouges in the fallen leaves and dark dirt.

Four soldiers stepped from the trees in a rough semi-circle. All of them wore helmets that hid their faces and armor with a mark on the front that I had learned meant they were the king's soldiers. Three of them carried spears with fluttering banners attached. One swung up a wicked longsword. He pointed at the bear with his sword and called out. "You know the orders. Bring the beast down—it's half mad already."

The two soldiers to his right stepped forward.

The bear reared up on its back legs. The man with the sword called out, "Attack!"

The two soldiers ran forward, thrusting their spears into the bear's mangy side.

The bear swung a huge paw and broke one of the spears, slammed a paw at the other soldier and knocked him back.

Roaring now, the bear spun and started into the woods, the soldiers all chasing after it.

"We have to help," Bower said, glancing around him as if looking for a way down from the tree. He looked pale and his hands shook—on the verge of doing something stupid.

I grabbed his arm. "Wait. Those are soldiers, and if I have learned anything of late it is that it's wise to know who is a friend before you offer anything."

His mouth twisted down. "Meaning, you jump someone first and ask questions later." He let out a breath. "Maybe you're right. Maybe those aren't nice men. But they need help." He reached for a tree limb to start down.

I let him go.

Listen to your blood, Jaydra thought at me.

Zenema had once said that—but what did it mean? Muttering about stupid idiots, I followed Bower. I hadn't gone through all this rescuing just to see him get into more trouble. My head still pounded and climbing took all my concentration.

In the woods nearby, I could hear the fight—the bear's roaring, the soldiers' shouts and cries, the man with the sword calling out orders. And then it all went quiet. A moment later a shout went up from the soldiers.

I grabbed Bower's shoulder and fisted my hand into the material of his tunic, stopping him. My hands were starting to shake, too, now, and I wasn't sure just how much more rescuing I could do. "Bower, for now, we have to stay hidden—I'm certain of it. At least until we find out more about these soldiers. And it doesn't sound like they need your help or mine."

To his credit, Bower glanced up at me and gave a nod.

The smell of smoke rose in the woods. For a moment, I had no idea what that could mean, but Bower said, his voice low and rough, "They're going to burn the body. They would only do that if the animal was diseased or something unnatural."

I frowned and tugged on Bower to come back up to a higher branch. "They're coming back." Bower climbed back up onto the thick branch where I stood.

A gruff voice carried up to us, and I recognized it was the man with the sword talking. "...another this week. I tell you, Lichter, these monsters are getting worse, coming this far south."

Another voice, this one higher and younger-sounding, answered. "Grim-bears!" I heard the hack of a man spitting. "A plague they are. I've heard it said they're magi—"

"Watch what you say, Lichter."

The younger voice went even higher. "I'm just saying, they only really started turning after the king—"

"Do you intend an insult to the king?"

Glancing down, I saw the man with the sword face to face with young Lichter. The man with the sword had his helmet off and blood had spattered his armor and sword. Even from up in the tree I could tell that it wasn't a threat the man with the sword was giving—he didn't hold his sword poised for an attack and he leaned in close as if giving a warning.

I was left wondering why these soldiers worried so much about what the king might hear from this far away from any castle or city.

Is this the same king Bower seems to fear?

From nearby, Jaydra asked with her thoughts, *Why would men with swords and weapons fear a king? All men can be killed—even a king.*

Yes, but kings are different, I thought back. *Kings are like…. den-mothers. They are surrounded by others who will protect them and they have power.*

Jaydra seemed to think this over and thought back to me, *den-mothers do their own killing. They don't send out others to do it for them.*

You're right there.

The smell of smoke became the stink of burning hair and meat—the dead bear had been put on a funeral pyre. Below us, the man with the sword wiped off his blade on a rag and sheathed it. "We're not here to chase grim-bears. What about those tracks we were following, Lichter? Didn't the boot prints lead this way?"

"They did, sir. After the traitor left the wagon he turned into the woods, met up with someone at some ruins, parted company and headed this way. By the look of it, he may have tangled with that grim-bear. Might even be in its belly by now and made into cinders along with the bear."

"Or he might not have."

"Captain!" A new man came into sight, leading five horses. "Found this near the road." He held up a knife. The blade glinted in the light and so did a silver medallion on the hilt.

"That's mine!" Bower whispered. "I must have dropped it." He didn't sound happy about it—and I wondered what kind of idiot dropped his knife when he had a bear chasing him.

The captain took the knife and turned it over once. "It's marked with House Daris coat of arms. He came this way, right enough." The captain glanced around, his eyes narrowed.

Don't look up, I thought to him and held my breath.

He shook his head slightly. "To me it almost seems like…" He let the words trail off.

I reacted the only way that I knew how—flinging up my hand, breathing out quickly through my nose, remembering how the dragons could convince the world they were not there.

"Stay still!" I whispered to Bower. We were bits of branches and bark. Nothing but russet and yellowing leaves. Nothing but sky.

The captain glanced up, and I could feel his gaze sweep over us. He stared straight through us and past. For a moment, he frowned and narrowed his eyes. I knew my trick was weakening. I held my breath.

He flipped the knife in his hand, catching it by the hilt. He tucked it into his belt. "Back to the road. We may pick up fresh tracks there or some sign of where this traitor has hidden himself. If nothing else, we may find some other rebels to arrest and take back to the king. If we fail in that, it'll be ourselves thrown into prison."

The captain gave orders to mount up and the soldiers rode away, single file, leaving behind greasy smoke, their horses pushing a path through the trees.

I looked at Bower. His face seemed very pale but he managed a shaky, lopsided smile. That, however, wasn't making me happy with him. I stared into his dark eyes and told him, "Whatever you did, friend, it was bad enough to have those men chasing after you. So why did they call you a traitor?"

*   *   *

CHAPTER 8

DECISIONS

The sound of the soldiers' horses, cantering down the road faded away. Swallowing hard, I stared back at Saffron. Could I really trust her? She had saved my life just now—but she had also threatened me.

I lifted my chin. "And whatever *you* just did…it wasn't natural. Those soldiers looked straight at us. I even felt that captain's eyes connect with mine, and then his gaze slid off as if his mind—or something else—had told him that he saw nothing."

"What did you do?" I asked again.

Saffron simply slid off the branch, catching the next one down with one hand, allowing her weight to swing her to the next branch after that. She landed lightly on the ground with a small thump. She moved like something out of those old books I had been reading. I glanced down. It seemed a very long way away. Gingerly, I eased myself off the branch and got the tips of my boots onto the one beneath me.

Feeling more confident, I leaned over to wave at Saffron, to make it seem that I must climb up and down trees all the time.

The soft sole of my boot slipped. I grabbed for a handhold, caught a slim branch that cracked and snapped. I crashed down, hitting one of the larger branches with my shoulder. The limb creaked but I managed to snag a handful of leaves. I kept sliding. The smell of sap bloomed. The leaves came off in my hand, and I fell again and landed on my back on the forest floor with a painful thump.

Saffron stood over me. "That's a funny way to climb down from a tree." She offered me her hand.

I waved her away. "I'm fine. You must have weakened the branch when you were coming down."

She scowled at me, snatched her hand back and turned away to walk toward the road.

"Wait! I'm sorry." Getting up, I hurried to catch up with her and snagged her sleeve. "And... thank you." Leaning down, I swatted at the worst of the dirt and leaves that clung to my breeches and tunic. "For saving my life. Twice now. Those, uh, those guards—"

"Didn't seem as though they liked you." Saffron had stopped walking. She put one hand on one hip and looked up, muttering, "Where has she got to now?" She turned, heading for the road—or where I thought the road was—once more.

Looking around, I could see black smoke rising up in a column above the trees from the fire the soldiers had built. I was going to hope they knew not to set the woods ablaze—Byers and even Saffron had built their fire in a ring of stones. Birds were slowly drifting back—I could hear their wings fluttering, but couldn't see them. I decided to catch up with Saffron, I turned and strode after her and asked, "You're looking for your steed? Are you sure it didn't run away? Maybe the grim-bear—"

"My *steed?*" Saffron smothered a laugh. "She would hate to be called that. But my steed, she never strays too far, but she is *very willful.*" She said the last two words loudly, as if speaking not to me but to some invisible companion.

"Look—uh, I mean it. Thank you."

Saffron paused and glanced sideways at me. "You were in trouble with that bear. And those soldiers didn't seem to be the nicest men I've met."

"Well, you did a lot—and you didn't have to."

She gave me another look, her eyes bright and her hair almost a halo around her face.

There was something about her that left me uneasy. She was almost like a force of nature—like a storm about to release bolts of lightning. She charged the air around her as if she was a vivid, red-gold cloud. "What you did back there—that was magic, wasn't it?"

She looked away, clapped her hands and gave one, sharp whistle, calling for her steed, I would guess.

I stumbled over a bare root, hopped a step, and told her, "I knew it. Magic!"

Saffron didn't look at me, but a fresh flush of pink bloomed on her face. "Did you hit your head when you fell out of that tree?"

"It all makes sense now. Why you were so cautious when I wandered close to your camp…why you attacked me. I've …" It was my turn to fall silent. I left my mouth hanging open and my face heated.

Could I tell her I had read the old sagas?

She already knew I read books about dragons, but the rest of it—she could be tried for just knowing what I knew.

"I've read books," I said quietly. "But I never ever thought magic could be real. I thought the world had lost it all." I glanced around. "My books—I dropped them. I've lost them."

We had reached the edge of the woods and stepped out of the shadows of the trees and into fading sunlight. I hadn't realized so much time had passed.

Saffron faced me and poked a finger into my chest. "You're not just delusional, you're careless. Books like that have to be worth a fortune. You shouldn't even be allowed out."

I spread my hands wide. "Okay, then how did you snatch me up like that into the tree? You didn't have a rope—you don't have one now. That was magic, too. I felt something around my chest, I remember flying through the air, and suddenly finding myself in the tree, next to you. If that wasn't magic, what was it?"

"I'm not some kind of witch." Saffron said, a note of threat to her voice. She took a step closer to me. "So just stop it."

I couldn't stop. I knew I was close to the truth. "I've read about such things. Where did you learn it?"

Turning away, Saffron shook her head. Her shoulders slumped and her hands fell to her sides. "I—I didn't. It's just…" She let the words trail off and waved a hand.

"It just comes to you. Of course. That makes sense. I've read about some people who were born with special abilities, and others had their magic manifest itself in later life. But it always had something to do with dragons." I tapped a finger on my lips and tried to remember. "Some families have inherited special traits because their ancestors were great dragon-friends or there is a blood connection to dragons in some deep way. Isn't that how the old stories always go?"

She glanced at me and hunched a shoulder. "You're asking me that? I don't even know the stories you're talking about."

I looked around again. I could see the road, but no sign of my bags and I couldn't remember where I had dropped my things. "I wish I had my books. I might be able to look a few up for you. There's only scattered bits of information, of course. So much has been lost over the decades, and it seems to me that no one has ever conducted a thorough study. You mention dragons these days or magic and it's either prison or worse for you. It's just so frustrating—but if I had my books, I—"

The rustling of trees behind us interrupted me. Jumping back, I almost fell. I staggered away from the trees. Was it another grim-bear or had the soldiers returned, sneaking up on us from the woods?

Turning to look into the tall trees, Saffron spoke to someone I couldn't see. "There you are."

I peered into the shadows between the pines and oaks. I could still hear branches snapping. Trees swayed. For an instant, the trunks seemed to blur, and become a massive, blue-green scaled leg with long claws.

No! What?

I shook my head, squeezed my eyes shut and opened them again. This time I saw Saffron's impossibly large horse calmly stepping out of the trees with one of my bags around its neck and the handle of my satchel of books gripped in its mouth. The horse swishing its tail almost as if pleased with herself.

"She has my books…my things." I stuttered the words. Just how smart was Saffron's horse?

Scowling, Saffron crossed her arms over her chest. Her horse pranced a few steps closer. I couldn't blame the horse for being nervous, so close to the funeral pyre of a grim-bear. I grinned, delighted to see my books again. Apparently, Saffron wasn't so pleased.

"Well, yes, thank you very much, I *did* sort it all out on my own," she snapped. What she meant was beyond me. Saffron nodded to me. "Him? Oh, you were right. He's a bit daft, but—"

"Excuse me!" I straightened and pushed back my shoulders.

Saffron glanced at me. "Are you going to tell me it was smart to lose your knife? Or to get into the path of a grim-bear?"

"I didn't put myself into the path of anything, and if you're running for your life you tend to drop everything."

The horse gave a snort and dropped my books. Going over to her, I picked up my satchel. I reached out to pat its neck, but the horse danced away from my touch. I noticed how its eyes seemed strangely colored for a horse, with flecks of gold and a glinting green in them. Bumps rose on my skin. There was something here I wasn't seeing.

I'd had this feeling before. In fact, over the years I'd often gotten an odd sensation of something being wrong. Of late, it had gotten stronger. Now, the hairs on the back of my neck rose. My head ached. I shut my eyes, hoping the sensation would go away, but it clung to me like a wet cloak hanging off my shoulders. The world seemed blurry.

Saffron was saying something. I looked at her and saw that she had taken my bag off her horse's neck.

Jaydra.

The word popped in my head. I frowned over that. "She's just a horse," Saffron said, finishing whatever she had been telling me.

I nodded. "Of course, I just haven't ever seen any horse quite so large."

"You said you knew I'm not from around here," Saffron said, somewhat indignantly. "We hail from the isles to the west of here. Far, far west."

"The Western Isles. Yes, I know of them. King Enric maintains there is little more than savages out there, and that half of the things said of the isles is nothing but myths."

Saffron rolled her eyes. "So I'm a myth now? Or a savage? Or a savage myth?"

"Well, not a complete one—but you did jump me. Is that why you know magic? Does everyone in the Western Isles know magic?" I asked, a little breathless over such an exciting idea.

"What? No! And it isn't magic. Well, not exactly. It's just, tricks. Ways of seeing and doing things." Saffron pulled a face, her mouth tugging down. "And, no. No one in the isles can do what I do, or not many anyway."

She glanced sharply at her horse as if the horse had said something. The two locked stares. Saffron lifted an eyebrow, and the horse tossed its head as if it had found something to be funny. Was that even possible?

Looking at me, Saffron asked, "So are you still intent on going your own way?" Saffron nodded at the road.

I followed her stare. I had no idea which direction the soldiers had taken. And I had no idea if they would come back this way again. Next time, I might not be quite so lucky as to avoid them.

I gave a sigh.

The air still smelled foul from the smoke. A touch of rain hung in the wind as well. And the simple fact was that Saffron had saved my life. I owed her a great deal. I also couldn't resist the idea that she had used magic.

Perhaps it was nothing like the magic mentioned in books, but here was a chance to find out a few truths for myself.

Hadn't I fled the city determined to discover the truth of the world, and here I was standing right next to someone who knew magic. Or tricks as she called them. If magic existed, why not dragons, too?

I started to smile, but another thought occurred to me. Was Saffron really a dangerous rebel who did have some tricks?

Well, if she was, I was a dangerous traitor as well.

Shifting my hand to take a better grip on my satchel of books, I said, "I'm coming with you. You will never even get into the city gates without being arrested. The least I can do for you is guide you to Torvald."

My stomach knotted at the very idea. I couldn't believe I had just agreed to go back to my home. On the other hand, if the soldiers were outside Torvald searching for me, perhaps inside the city walls might be the safest place for me—the place where I wasn't expected to be. I would just have to hope that proved to be true.

Saffron's eyes widened and she stood straighter to face me. "You can get us into the city then? All of us?" She waved at her horse.

I didn't know why it was so important that her horse come with us, but I nodded. "I know of a way in. But let me warn you that you may not care much for it."

A frown tightened her forehead, but cleared in an instant. She shook her head. "I have a need to see this city near mountains. I will go no matter what."

Holding up a hand, I knew I must give her every warning I could so she was at least making a decision based on some knowledge. "Someone with your…talents may find Torvald a great danger. Magic is not just frowned upon; it is considered to be criminal fraud."

She shrugged. "What will they do? Call me a witch and throw stones at me?"

"If anyone names you witch, the king's Iron Guard will come to drag you to prison and your horse will be sold to cover your fines and I doubt you will ever be seen again. I have…excuse me, I had some say at court, but that is gone. I would not be able to help you."

Again, she shrugged and waved off my words. "So I will not be discovered. I intend to do the discovering anyway."

I let out a long breath. I had done all I could.

She had at least hidden her skills from me, and they only came out because she used them to save me from the grim-bear and the soldiers. Maybe, if she was not threatened, she would have no need to use her powers

"Very well, we'll go."

She stepped closer and smiled. "Thank you for your warnings, but we will take our chances as we find them."

I thought it a bit presumptuous for her to say 'we' as if I would agree to everything she wanted to do without fail. I glanced over at her horse, which seemed to be staring at me, and unhappy with me as well. I tried to shake off the feeling—but was Saffron using 'we' for herself and her horse? I could not think so.

"Just get us to this city and find us a way inside and we will be forever in your debt," she said, her tone grand and formal. She had an odd way of speaking at times, as if her and her horse were nobles from the days of old.

Hefting my books again. "I can do more than that. If it's information you want, I know where books—more than the few I carry with me—might be found. If it's mountains and cities you want to know about, that's something I can help with."

Jaydra, the horse, gave what seemed to be a smoky snort and nudged my chest with her nose, almost knocking me off my feet. And now she seemed happy with me.

Something wasn't quite right with this horse, but I was done arguing about anything for now with Saffron.

*   *   *

We headed in the direction Bower had come from, and I hoped he really could find his way back to this city of his. I wasn't certain he could, but I was glad to have his help. The stench of the burning bear fat was terrible. I didn't have to urge him to walk faster to get away from that. As we walked, with Jaydra still looking like a horse and now carrying Bower's bags, she asked, her voice echoing in my head, *Saffron should like Bower.*

I glanced back at Bower. He was starting to slow his pace after only a short walk.

I do…apart from the obvious, Jaydra thought at me. I heard her give a soft, laughing nicker.

He may be slow, but you're the one who is a horse. And I am not going to try to explain that I can't ride you. Jaydra knew as well as I did that if I mounted her, the illusion that she was a horse would not hold for long. Where I touched, Bower would start to see blue-green scales and Jaydra's wings.

Ridiculous disguise! What happens when Bower sees me flying?

He won't see you fly because we won't be flying to this city. You have to walk like any other horse.

Jaydra snorted.

She was annoyed with this deception. That came through clearly in her thoughts. Like all dragons, she could be a little arrogant.

Not arrogant. She gave an annoyed huff. *Realistic. I am a dragon. Biggest, strongest, smartest creature around.* She snickered again and slapped me with her tail. I turned to thump her on her snout.

"Hey!" Bower hurried to catch up with us. He looked alarmed at my apparent intended cruelty.

Bower can see you were about to do something incredibly stupid! The dragon-horse whinnied and turned a mournful look at Bower. *Look at Jaydra the mistreated.*

For a moment, Bower's eyes widened. His eyebrows shot up and lines marred his forehead. Was it possible he might have heard the words she had projected? I had heard Jaydra, but only another dragon should have heard her. His mouth pulled down and he looked away with a small shake his head.

Bower muttered, "Your horse is odd. At times I get the curious notions it is trying to tell me something."

I gave a laugh, but his words unsettled me. Walking a little faster—which made Bower have to stride out to keep up with me—I said, "My horse is trying to talk to you? Do you have talking horses in this city of yours?"

Jaydra said Bower special. Saffron has no idea how special. Jaydra nudged me with her nose.

I swatted at her again and thought to her that she had best behave.

Bower glanced at me, mumbling something about the notion being worth forgetting.

Lifting her head, Jaydra sent me an image that she was hungry. I was as well. It was coming on dark and I'd not eaten all day. I was used to going without food for a day or so, but I could hear Bower's stomach grumbling. And now Jaydra was mentally grumbling, too.

Not going to start eating grass and you wouldn't let Jaydra eat bear. If anyone thinks to put heels into my side, best think again.

I sighed. With the daylight fading it seemed wise to leave the road for the safety of the woods. Bower didn't seem to think that wise. "What about grim-bears?" he asked.

Shaking my head, I told him, "We'll look for a spot that won't attract a bear."

"You can do that?"

It didn't take long to find an old overgrown trail that led up to a hilltop. A scattering of ruined cottages stood here, their roofs caved in and the windows smashed and the doors gone. Gardens had gone wild, but they would have plants we could eat. It looked like it might have once been a beautiful place to live, before whatever had happened to force those who lived here to abandon it.

Jaydra didn't like the destruction and ruin. *Bad happened here.*

I agreed with her, so we found a spot on the hill that gave us a view down to the road. The trees would give us some shelter, but it was a mild enough night. I gathered firewood and Bower set out rocks for a fire ring—at least he knew something.

Resisting the urge to use some magic to make the fire—I wasn't sure I wouldn't launch a fireball that could singe the clothes off our skin—I settled instead for using flint and stones. I soon had a small blaze going—not so big that anyone would take much notice.

"Why would anyone leave this place?" Bower asked. He sat on the ground and pulled his cloak tight around him. I had harvested some of the plants to eat—we had a feast of beans, fresh greens, and sweet peas to eat. Jaydra had left to go hunting and she had thought back to me that she would bring fish, too, if she found a lake or a river.

Glancing over at Bower, I watched the firelight play over his face. He had fine bones and looked made for a city and not for these wild lands. "There are places like that all over that I've seen in my travels. Ruined towns and ruined villages. I had always heard the mainland was supposed to be... I don't know...richer than all of this." I picked up a stick and poked at the fire. A knot had formed in my chest. I didn't tell Bower how I'd thought the mainland would be teeming with dragons and dragon riders, just like the drawings on the cave. I'd thought it would be easy to find the mountains with dragons—shouldn't everyone know where they were. Instead, I had learned at once not to ask questions, to keep moving, and now that I seemed to be close to finding a city near a great mountain... it all seemed as if perhaps I was too late to find anything that would help me understand where I came from and how I could better control my magic.

Bower nodded and pulled his cloak tighter. "The realm is in a bad way." He cleared his throat and looked over at me. "It wasn't always like this. I've read stories...oh, such stories. The Middle Kingdom was once the greatest land of all. People traveled from the whole world over to come to the court at Torvald. There was art and music, and the city...why it was said to be so white and brilliant and beautiful that some travelers fell on their knees at the first sight of it and wept."

"What happened? Do your books tell you that?" I leaned forward, my face warmed by the fire.

Bower looked different when he spoke about his stories and his books. He went from being a skinny young man who seemed to know nothing to his eyes lighting with fire and his voice becoming strong and warm. I could glimpse the man he might become—someone strong and thoughtful and serious.

From nearby I heard Jaydra's thoughts as she snickered. She gulped down a fish.

Quiet! I threw up a few walls in my mind so I might concentrate on what Bower was saying.

He stared into the fire as if seeing into a far distance. "It's a long story—or it should be. No one really speaks of it anymore, and I think few know, for hardly anyone reads. But it starts in the old times." His voice softened, and I settled back to listen to his words.

"There were once five great cities, and Torvald, the greatest of them all. Towns and villages dotted the roads, all the way to the coast and from the mountains in the north to the southern border. The Middle Kingdom used to be one of the most powerful kingdoms under the sun. Even the hot southern lands with all of their rare spices and clothes couldn't come close to us."

"The hot southern lands? I never heard about them. There's so much I still had to learn about the world." I frowned and poked at the fire. Anger itched under my skin and my face heated. Why hadn't den-mother Zenema taught me more? Did she not know? Or had she thought I wasn't ready for teaching?

Bower smiled. He ate a handful of peas and said, "Don't they teach you very much in the isles?" Bower shrugged. "Well, that's a lot like it is here. We once had great schools and academies, but they're all gone now. But I've read of the lands far to the south where the land gets hotter and hotter, and the ground becomes drier for the rains only come once a year for a month. There are seas made of golden sand and these seas are as large as a whole country. The people live in rocky areas that have deep wells and there are—or were—a dozen different princes who each controlled a different part of the land. Many of the people also travel—and there were once southern dragons there."

My skin started to tingle. "And dragon riders?"

Bower nodded. "At one time, bandits and raiders from the south would cross our borders to steal from the rich lands. They'd take sheep or crops or anything they could. And there were Wildmen in the north. But Torvald had Dragon Riders." He frowned and pressed his lips tight, then looked over his shoulder as if he was afraid someone might have heard him say these words.

"Tell me about them?" My heart was beating faster and I knew these had to be the people riding dragons that I had seen on the cave drawings. Jaydra sensed my excitement. I felt her edge closer to us. She had found a spot in the woods where she could be a dragon again, with her belly almost full. She hadn't brought any fish back to share, for there was hardly enough for her, but she was happy to sit close, sniffing the air to smell for danger and listen to Bower's stories.

"I've said too much," Bower said. "Forget I said that." He hunched a shoulder. "They're just stories, but it can cost you your life to say such things in Torvald. They do terrible things there."

I threw a stick into the fire. "What do you mean? And I've already seen your books." I waved at his case that carried his books. "They're all true stories, aren't they? The city in those drawings—they're all of Torvald."

Bower frowned. He rubbed at one eyebrow and forced the words through his teeth. "Yes. No. Maybe."

Humans. Never know what you feel! Jaydra thought to me.

Ignoring her, I demanded, "Well, which is it?"

Sitting straighter, Bower looked at me, his eyes almost glowing as they reflected the firelight. "It is true. At least I believe it is the truth, but no one else in the city does, and I've been told—warned as I've warned you—not to fill my mind with old tales. But almost everyone I've ever known believes that Torvald was once a terrible place, that everyone's lives were hard, and that those who lived in Torvald were in terrible danger for all the generations before the Maddox line took the throne to save us all."

"What's a Maddox line?" I asked. "That word seems oddly familiar."

"It should be. The Maddox became the kings of Torvald—they are the ruling dynasty. Hacon Maddox saved the city from a dreadful disaster that was going to rip apart the kingdom. He discovered traitors in the royal court, and the people chose Hacon Maddox as the new successor to the throne because of it. By all that's known, they've been regarded as heroes for generations."

Forehead tight, I said, "I find it strange how your words don't match up with the look on your face. Do you like this Maddox line or not?"

Bower glanced behind him again as if someone might hear us talking out here in the middle of the wilds. "It isn't my place to like or dislike—I've been told that most of my life. But all is not well, not in the citadel nor in the rest of the kingdom it seems. The current king—King Enric—has always told us how powerful he is and how safe the kingdom is, but that's not what I keep seeing now. And things in the city…they have changed. There are things that you cannot say, cannot talk about. This conversation would end with both of us in irons. And yet people don't seem to notice the troubles. Sometimes I fear it is because something is blinding them."

I shook my head. "They could try to put irons on me!"

Bower smiled but shook his head. "You have not seen the king's Iron Guard. I have heard they travel out of the city, but these days I think they stay close to the king. They're not really men—they're something else. And they give King Enric his power. No one can defeat the Iron

Guard. No one can stand up to them. And King Enric doesn't believe that Torvald was once the center of all dragon activity in the world. That is, according to the king's own laws, heresy and lies spread to try and undermine the proper place of humans as rulers of this land."

"Ugh…really?" I picked up another stick and started to draw in the dirt. "Why would the king think that?"

"Oh, the king thinks anything to do with dragons and magic and sorcerers is a lie that will break the spirit of any true soul and make us less than human. Those fairy stories are meant to frighten children and such tales can lead to an unjust world and the subversion of his rule. For years, books have been burned and scrolls destroyed. The king's laws have been around for a very long time, and now there are only a handful of books left from that ancient time."

"That sounds terrible!"

"It was. It is." Bower leaned forward again, resting his elbows on his crossed legs. "Torvald, from what I have been piecing together, used to be a friendly, open place. Travelers would come from far and wide to see the dragons that wheeled overhead or to talk with learned men and women who lived with them. If what the old books say is true, Torvald was rich and happy. Now, there are parts of the city that have been left to rot and ruin. People fend for themselves as best they can and struggle to keep up with their taxes. I very much fear the king fears rebellion and so the laws grow worse every day. Anyone who so much as makes a joke against the king can be thrown in prison."

Frowning, I stared at Bower. I still couldn't understand this. "But how can anyone deny that dragons exist? That is like saying the sky has no stars or the sun does not rise in the east."

This place thinks differently of dragons, Jaydra thought to me. She, too, was uneasy with such an idea.

Bower tipped his head to the side and gave me a measuring stare. "I never thought I'd ever find anyone who believed in dragons. Why are you so certain they exist?"

I bit my lip, but I was too annoyed to stay silent. "Why would anyone be certain they don't? And why wouldn't anyone want to have dragons around?"

Bower lifted one hand and dropped it again. "It's not just about the dragons, it's everything that has anything to do with the past. It's magic and history and everything."

Chin dropping down, Bower gave me a long look. "Are you certain you must visit Torvald?"

I huffed out a breath. "Didn't we settle this already?"

"We did, but I'm still worried."

"It sounds as if you do too much of that." An odd knot of emotions tightened around my chest like the claws of a dragon that were squeezing too tight. "I've gotten used to hiding what I can do," I said, the words almost too quiet.

Bower was silent for a moment. He stood up, walked around to my side of the fire and sat down next to me. "I know about that. When my parents were alive, they encouraged me to read. But then…well, once I was on my own, I learned all too quickly that I'd best keep everything I knew about the past to myself. I could not tell anyone— not my friends or the few servants in my household."

Leaning back, I stared up at the stars. They seemed too peaceful—sharp and glittering and splashed over the sky like a river. I knew that I shouldn't say anything more and I searched for something else to talk about.

What if I told Bower about Jaydra and he acted like so many others we had first met—running away in terror or even falling limp to the ground in a faint? What if he changed his mind about helping us? It was one thing to think a fantasy dragon was an amazing idea, but it was another to actually see something so big—and Jaydra was still a small dragon.

Remember what Zenema said. Jaydra's thoughts echoed in my mind. I heard her shift her weight in the nearby woods, her scales sliding over the dirt and leaves and her claws clicking against stones. *Follow what is in your blood. Follow your heart.*

She was wise, was Zenema. All dragons were—when they wanted to be. Even young, fierce Jaydra had a way of looking at the world that made it all seem to make more sense.

Sitting upright, I glanced at Bower. "My parents abandoned me out in the Western Isles."

Mouth dropping open, Bower stared at me. I wanted to punch him. He snapped his mouth shut, glanced away and then asked, "Why would they do that?"

"I don't know. That's one of the things I need to find out. Maybe they were scared for me. Or maybe they were scared of what I could do…the tricks." I licked my lips.

The band around my chest eased. Now that I had finally started to speak of myself, it seemed surprisingly easy. "The tricks are easy, but…well, I need to learn when to use it and how to stop. My…well, Zenema, who raised me as her own child, she said my parents came from the Middle Kingdom. She judged that by…by some cave drawings and by my clothes. And there was an old hermit out there who taught me my words and to read a little. I would like to think my folks wanted really to save me or hide me, but the truth is that I don't know. And it is time for me to discover who my family was…who I am."

"Why didn't this hermit ever try to help you find your folks?" Bower asked.

I shook my head. "He was a hermit. He never left his hut, let alone his island."

I was suddenly at a loss for words. A tide of despair swelled in my chest. Maybe it was all a ridiculous quest to find out who my parents had been, and who I was, where my magic had come from. What if Zenema had just really sent me away because she didn't want me to hurt the rest of the clutch with my erratic magic? But would she have allowed Jaydra to come with me if that was true?

How could I know what the truth was?

Bower frowned, but he gave a nod as if he understood. "Well, it sounds like this hermit did what he could, teaching you a few things you had to know. I've read there are villages in the Western Isles. We import something from the sea-- rare herbs and shells and sometimes fish."

I nodded. "They're more like those savages you mentioned. They build simple huts and hunt with spears and dress in cloth made of pounded roots and paint their skin. I didn't like them and they really didn't like me." I didn't want to mention how the villagers treated me as if I was a young dragon—with wary respect and suspicion, as if I wanted only to raid their fishing nets.

"Sounds like you were alone," Bower said.

Saffron never alone! Jaydra snorted.

I shot a frown in her direction—she'd sounded more like a dragon and nothing like a horse giving a snort. Turning to Bower, I told him, "Not completely alone. I had Jaydra...and Zenema and other friends. But..." I couldn't add that they were all dragons.

Picking up a stick, Bower tossed it into the fire. A shower of sparks rose up in a spray of golden embers. "I thought I had it bad, but I never had a power or an ability that set me apart from anyone. I really did have people around me. But I know what it's like to want to know more."

Tell Bower, Jaydra thought at me. *He managed to flee his nest. He wants to learn. He may seem a fledgling, but Bower has a strength deep inside.*

Biting my lower lip, I decided that maybe it was getting a little too difficult to keep so many secrets. A part of me also wanted to tell Bower everything. At least Jaydra could then act like a real dragon in front of him, instead of trying to be a very large horse. But it was such a risk.

Clearing my throat, I wet my lips and tried for a calm voice. "Bower? I'm going to tell you something that might change how you see the entire world."

He glanced at me, his forehead bunched with lines and his eyebrows lifted. He was probably imagining that I was about to tell him some other piece of a terrible past. I swallowed the lump in my throat.

The corner of Bower's mouth lifted. "Don't worry. I would hope I have tolerance enough to hear anything you might say. And I won't tell. No matter what, I would never tell on you."

"We'll see about that." I muttered. Louder, I said, "There is another reason, I think, why we met each other out in the road. And yet another reason why it is for Torvald that I am bound."

He waved a hand. "You told me. You need to find a fortress city made out of and on a mountain."

I shook my head. "Yes, there's that. But…" I let the words fade and took a deep breath. This moment was like that of the one before I took a plunge off a cliff.

Oh well. Follow the truth in the blood, as Zenema says.

"I was never raised by any human hand. Zenema—my adopted mother—was something far more."

Bower's eyebrows drew low and flat. He was staring at me like I had started to speak another language. "And Jaydra is more than she seems," I said.

I heard Jaydra shift and she thought to me, *Now?*

Now. I thought the word back to her.

Jaydra stepped into the clearing. For a moment, she still seemed to be a horse—a large, tall horse with a long tail and shades of blue in her deep, black coat. I sketched a small set of hand gestures in the air that I knew from experimenting would clear all vision. My awareness of the world sharpened, as if a thin mist had been suddenly blown away. The sky seemed clearer, the wood smoke seemed warmer and stung my nose, the air on my back seemed colder, the ground I sat upon seemed harder.

Bower and I were no longer two humans and a very large horse before us—instead, a blue-green dragon stood on the edge of the firelight, her eyes glinting with gold and green and brown. Jaydra lifted her head higher on her sinuous neck. She curled her tail around her. Her scales shimmered.

Mouth falling open, Bower stared. For a moment, it seemed as if he could not even move. Then he jumped up with a strangled shout, staggered backwards, tripped over a rock and fell on his backside, his arms outstretched.

Luckily, he hadn't fallen into the fire. His cloak tangled his legs and he fumbled to pull it away and free himself.

Standing, I moved over to put a hand on Jaydra's warm scales. "I am going to Torvald to find my human family, but that is not my only family. And Jaydra is not my horse. She is my den-sister, my dragon kin, and my friend."

"By the name of the First!" Bower muttered. He got his cloak untangled and stood up again. He was still staring at Jaydra, his eyes huge.

Jaydra blew smoke from her nose. *Has Bower never seen a dragon before?*

I caught the humor in her thoughts and told her with my mind, *Go easy on him—he hasn't!*

Turning back to Bower, I studied his pale face. Was he shaking—and was that from fear or excitement? "Bower, you don't have to worry—" I stopped myself. Of course he should worry. Jaydra was a dragon and he was a mere human. Unleashed from her horse-illusion, Jaydra seemed taller, larger and far fiercer with gleaming, pointed teeth, sharp claws and wings that she now spread and fluttered, stirring a breeze. "She isn't about to eat you," I said.

Bower straightened and pushed his cloak back over one shoulder. "Of course not. Dragons rarely eat people, unless they are wild—the dragons, that is. Or that's what I've read." His words tumbled out in a rush and I realized from his tone that it wasn't terror he was feeling. He laughed and spoke to me, but without dragging his stare from Jaydra. "You really were raised by dragons? That's amazing. I've never read that before. And the horse is a dragon?" He laughed again, clapped his hands together and rubbed them roughly. "How do you do that? Is it an illusion? Or does she really become a horse? She is a she still, yes? Or can she change her entire form and shape? Can she look like a human?"

With a shake of my head and a shrug, I said, "It's just something we can do. It's a dragon trick. It's like how a fish hides in the rushes and weeds. Jaydra only looked like a horse. It's just a twisting of light and what's around you. You can almost see that something is wrong, but unless you know how to look past the trick to the reality, you just see the trick. But that's not important. What matters is that I saw drawings of dragons and a mountain and a city. That is why I have to get to Torvald. I think it might be the same place as the one on those drawings. The drawings that my parents made. I have to know why they did what they did. I have to know—"

"Why you are the way you are," Bower said, finishing my thought.

I nodded. "Why we are the way we all are. I am not certain any of us knows what happened to us—why are there no dragon riders?"

Bower stood a little straighter. "You're right. We all need to know what happened to the dragon riders."

*   *   *

PART 3

TO THE CITY

CHAPTER 9

INTO DANGER

I couldn't keep my eyes off her—the dragon that is. Jaydra had to be the most amazing thing I'd ever seen. She surpassed all the drawings in any books I had ever read. She was an amazing dragon, even more so than the ones with mammoth size, or those with four wings instead of two. Those dragons had seemed like something from a dream, but Jaydra looked so real and solid. She even smelled like a dragon.

Well, in truth, she smelled of fish and a touch of sooty smoke. Her scales seemed to shimmer with amazing shades of blue and green.

The next morning—after Jaydra had brought us fish to share for our morning meal—I asked Saffron to allow Jaydra to stay in her dragon form. "She only has to hide as a horse when we hear others on the road. Even that though, was a mystery to me.

I still didn't understand how a dragon could look like something else. It had to be magic of a kind. Nowhere in the books I'd read was there mention of dragons pretending to be any other creature.

Physically, it seemed impossible for Jaydra to take the shape of a horse. As a dragon, she was as long as two houses and half as tall as a pine. And Saffron said Jaydra wasn't yet full grown. So, her looking like a horse had to be illusion. Jaydra could fold her wings tight to her side. She also had small flares along the length of her tail that Saffron said helped her to fly.

It seemed to me that Jaydra used her tail as much for communication as anything—it would flick when she was irritated or could curl up around her if she was pleased or thump the ground with irritation. Her eyes were also expressive, and her snout shorter than others types of dragons I had seen pictured. It seemed to me as though she was well adapted to swimming and diving.

Were all dragon species so specialized?

Pelting Saffron with questions, I learned more about dragons in a few minutes than I had in years of searching for information.

It was clear they adored fish—and I mean *adored*! Or at least Jaydra did.

We kept mostly to the woods, avoiding the roads and possible encounters with soldiers. At the sound of water—the splash of a river or creek—Jaydra would slip away, amazingly silent for such a big creature to investigate. We usually followed and would find Jaydra sitting on the riverbank, her tail swishing, her stare fixed on the flashes of silvery fish in the water. She would sweep the fish out with a claw, and after lunching on fish as well as having had fish for breakfast, I could tell I would soon tire of such a diet. But I could never tire of watching Jaydra.

The illustrations in my books hadn't done justice to the way sunlight seemed to glow from her scales when she got them wet in a river, or how deep and multi-colored her eyes were when she looked at you.

When we took a rest after eating our midday meal—for a change Saffron had trapped a rabbit to skin, roast and eat—I pulled out some scraps of paper from the back of one of my books and started scribbling notes.

An Encounter with Dragons, By Bower of House Daris

Of all of the strange things about my current situation, the strangest is probably the swiftness with which a sense of normality has been reached. As we travel toward the city of my birth—the place that may both answer our questions and seek to silence them forever—it seems that we have fallen into an easy rhythm. I walk side by side with the girl, Saffron, and usually behind us there trails the female dragon, Jaydra. Occasionally, Saffron will take the lead to scout ahead, for we must be ever watchful for the patrols which seem to be ever more numerous. I pulled back to walk beside the dragon and it felt to me like walking beside an old friend.

I wonder if this is one of the many odd affects dragons have on humans. Is it an aura they radiate due to their size or warmth? Or perhaps they inspire us to be even better humans by the fact that they are so good at being dragons? It seems to me that our species were destined to be friends. In all my reading of the old books, I recall clearest the constant references to dragon riders and dragon friends. Perhaps there is a kinship between us that neither species can properly fathom?

But what then of all I have been taught? Why do so many think dragons are nothing but stories of monsters meant to frighten children? And what of the official tales that dragons eat people, spread disease, and are frightening phantoms? Certainly, the story that there are no dragons is a lie, so it must follow the rest is untrue as well. But perhaps Jaydra is an exceptional dragon? She certainly exhibits an ease with me that is far more like that of a friend, and not that of a pet or companion animal.

However, no friendship that I have with this one representative of dragon kind is anything compared to the connection between the dragon and her 'den-sister' which I take to mean some kind of familial relationship.

From what little I have pieced together, the society and culture of these dragons is structured with dens and clutches. The den you might regard as your home, the territory which you live within and protect. The clutch refers to the place where the eggs are laid and those born and raised together. A clutch-sister grows up from the same batch of eggs under the den-mother. So Saffron regards herself as a den-sister, but not a clutch-sister to Jaydra the dragon. This means she was raised in the same nest by the same mother who they call Zenema.

As Saffron has explained, her den is actually inside a long-extinct volcano. This snow-capped peak rising high over what Saffron has called their home island, and the volcano itself offers several den caves to more than a few den-mothers, but no dragon is as old or highly regarded as Zenema. I can just imagine how this impressive peak must pierce the sky like a dragon's snout, standing head and shoulders over a lush, green jungle forest below. The way Saffron talks about it makes it sound as if the hillside is riddled with holes and tunnels. This is just one peak, and it seems the island dragons have many such dens throughout the Western Isles. This has led me to wonder if that is the original reason why the citadel of Torvald sits on Mount Hammal? Was Mount Hammal once taller? Or once home to dragons and dragon dens Mount Hammal certainly exploded at one point—the evidence of past upheaval is plain in scars that are still not fully healed or reforested.

As with every bit of knowledge I discover, more questions are posed to me.

But the question that puzzles me most is that of the connection between Saffron and the dragon. Saffron claims she actually talks to Jaydra, but from the dragon I can hear nothing but yips, snorts, chirrups, whistles and rumblings. Perhaps Saffron can understand this strange dragon language? Or, even though Jaydra's lips cannot form or manipulate our words, it might just be the familiarity of growing up together that leaves them able to communicate. But could it be true that part of the bond between dragon friend and dragon is the ability to share thoughts, or even to share minds?

I can see how this might frighten some—for in sharing is there not always the risk of losing something of oneself?

"Come on, now!" Saffron laughed and poked at my shoulder. "Why spend all your time with your nose to a page when you can take a look around you instead?" She turned and spread her arms. I glanced up.

We had strayed higher into the forest and hills, up to where a river wound down the hillside. Below us, we could see the valley and the main road, which wound its way to Torvald. In the distance, the villages around Torvald cast up a haze of smoke from cooking fires. It was a chill day and I could almost wish to be beside one of those fires. But I could also see the movement of the king's army in the distance—and the fires from their camps seemed to cast an even greater haze into the sky. It was odd the king should have so many of his troops so close to Torvald and not out protecting our borders, but there must be a reason for it.

In the far distance loomed the hazy shape of Mount Hammal, and below it glittered the towers of Torvald and the king's palace. It was easy to see why anyone might regard Torvald as impressive. The city was large enough to be a triangular scar upon the land, and the buildings and towers rose up into the clouds. The woods to the east seemed a hazy blue, and the grayish smudge of cooking fires, factories and chimneys gave the city an almost dream-like haze. Although I couldn't see any details, I knew all too well the many terraces of Torvald, of the winding streets, the wooden houses of the poor districts and the large, stone houses of those rich enough to build with white marble brought to the city along the rivers that wound nearby. The entire city stood proud in the gently rolling landscape of the farmlands that surrounded it, as if it had been dropped here just to be a sparkling jewel.

But there were troubling signs, too. I'd not been gone all that long from the city, but now it seemed as if the king's soldiers camped around the city, almost as if they were ready for a battle. But who would they fight—the people of Torvald? The idea left my skin cold and I did not even want to think of such a thing. But then I also remembered the ruins of villages we had spotted in these hillsides, much like the one where we had stayed last night. What had happened to those villages? Had the people been taken away? Killed? Had their houses been burned just because they had harbored—or might have harbored—Salamander rebels?

I could not believe such a thing. King Enric had ruled for so very long—as long as I could remember. He had to be secure on his throne. Perhaps the villagers had simply moved to Torvald to find work in the factories or to be under the protection of the Iron Guard. And yet still the idea lingered and left me uneasy. What if we were walking into a city soon to be plunged into disaster?

Pushing my shoulders back, I decided if that was the case then I had best be inside the city walls where I might be able to do at least a little good for the citizens there.

Almost as if she sensed my unease, Jaydra burst out with an excited chirrup. Saffron spun around and stared at her dragon.

"Everything well?" I asked. "Does the dragon sense anything coming?" Jaydra was always the first to sense anything coming our way, from birds in the sky to army patrols.

Saffron shook her head and leaned against her dragon with one arm draped over Jaydra's neck. Her face had paled and worry had darkened her eyes.

I put my pages away and stood. "What is wrong?"

Straightening, Saffron scanned the horizon. "Jaydra can smell dragon."

Frowning, I shaded my eyes and stared out at the valley and the distant mountain behind Torvald. "There aren't any dragons within a hundred leagues, and I don't think there could have been any dragons around Torvald for close onto a hundred years. At least, that's what everything I've read indicates."

Saffron closed her eyes, which I thought was an odd way to sense something. She took in a deep breath and I noticed that Jaydra did the same thing at the same time. After a moment, she said, her voice soft, "There were. A lot of them." She opened her eyes and fixed her stare straight at the peak behind Torvald. "They lived there, near that city. Jaydra can sense them. There were families and broods and dens and many, many clutches. The sky would have been thick with dragons."

My breathing quickened. "The old stories really are true. I've read them over and over again. All about the great flights of dragons and their riders. There are ruins behind Torvald—some say it was once a great teaching academy, but others hold it was a place of bad luck and is still plagued by sprits who wish ill on the living. But I've read of the vast dragon enclosure where the gigantic brood mothers lived. I've imagined what the sky would have looked like as flights of dragons swept in and out." I looked up at the empty sky—filled only with scudding clouds that looked to be bringing rain.

"What have we lost?" I muttered. My heart gave a lurch.

And then Jaydra lifted her head and let out a low, rumbling roar. A shiver puckered my skin, and I realized I'd spoken the wrong words.

What are we about to recover?

*   *   *

CHAPTER 10

WILD IN THE CITY

Bower said we could reach the city in three days if we kept to the roads, but he disliked the number of soldiers who seemed to be camped around the city. So, we kept to the woods and deer trails and it took five more sunrises and sunsets before we came close to the city walls. Bower said we should be glad not to have met any of the Iron Guard, but I didn't understand why they were such a problem.

The weather turned cold on the fifth day, with huge clouds that hung low in the sky threatening rain or even snow. I'd been snaring rabbits for our meals. I'd also taught Bower how to find sweet berries to eat, although there were few of them left this time of year. But Jaydra and I showed him how to dig up the Yar roots we'd found, which could be boiled in a skin and made into a good soup. That helped hold off the cold. It also was good to have Jaydra in her dragon form—we slept each night sheltered under her wing, leaning against her warm body.

Looking up at the tall clouds now, dark on the bottom and white and fluffy on the top, I judged winter would soon be here. The air smelled of rain. A longing for the islands and their warm weather swept through me, but I had to see my quest to its end. I had to learn how to control my magic and it was time to learn the truth about my family.

Both a sort of wary excitement warred within me—wary due to how Bower seemed to become more nervous the closer we came to Torvald and excited that I might at last find out if this city would reveal the secrets of how to use magic and let me discover why my parents had left me. I didn't know which I should feel, but the sense that we were close to learning something stayed close to me. This had to be the place—for it was a place where dragons had once lived.

A chill wind blew from the mountain today and Jaydra couldn't contain her interest. She pushed her nose in the air and thought to me, *Dragons. Many dragons. Not island dragons. Not clutch-family. Some bigger than den-mother. Much bigger. Some not good. Different, changed.*

I listened to her rambling without question, but I caught her mood. Some of the scents captivated her interest, others she disliked and some she distrusted. I could not blame her for starting to be more wary and cautious.

This was entirely new territory for both of us. I had only ever been around sea dragons and I had no idea what to expect from any dragons that still might live here. The area around the city, too, seemed crowded, the roads choked with what seemed like more people going in than were going out, and even Bower had started to wonder about how we were going to get past the army camps to get to the city gates.

With all her dragon senses, Jaydra knew little more than I did about this place—her senses were allowing her to slowly piece together the past. *They lived there. On the mountain. Many dens all sharing the same mountain.*

"Impossible!" I said and ignored Bower's strange look at me. On the islands, the dragons all wanted their own spaces—I couldn't imagine a lot of dragons sharing one den. Bower still wasn't used to me talking to Jaydra, and I felt sometimes as if he thought I was speaking my thoughts aloud.

Mighty, mighty magic must have been here. Special place. Many dragon and human dragon-friends. Jaydra kept sniffing the air, even rising up on her back legs now and then as if ready to pounce into flight.

When I saw her start to spread her wings, I shouted, "Wait! You can't just fly over there without any idea of what's underneath you. You've heard what Bower's been telling us. You've seen how those in this land react to you."

Jaydra doesn't want to be a horse again. She emitted a short plume of flame. *Jaydra fly and hide in the sky.*

I huffed out a breath and stepped over to pat her neck, her scales warm under my touch. "I know. I know you can do that. But what if some archer thinks you're a bird and an easy practice target—and then finds out you aren't that at all? We have to use some stealth." I could feel Jaydra starting to pout, so I added, "How about one good flight, stretch out your wings, before we have to keep to the ground for a time?"

A fast and furious flight would cheer her up. She was like me in that respect—she liked new experiences and adventure.

Stepping closer, Bower asked, his eyes wide, "You're going to fly?"

He had such amazement in his voice that I had to grin. "What did you think that these wings were for? Decoration?" I tugged on Jaydra's nearest wing and she spread it out. "Come on. We're going to need you with us to tell us the names of everything we see. Besides, this is the best way to get past the soldiers that are camped around the city. We can use the clouds to hide, and you can tell us the best spot to land near the gates. Then we can slip into the city."

Bower's mouth fell open. He shut it with a snap and then stammered, "To do what? Where? Up there?" He pointed to Jaydra's back.

Where did Bower think flying usually happened? Jaydra gave a chirp and knelt down, lowering her shoulders so we could step up on her foreleg and swing onto her back, sitting just in front of her wings.

Taking a step back, Bower put up both hands, palms facing me. "I'm not sure. I mean—am I ready for this? Maybe I should stay on the ground and sketch what I can of the process?"

I gave him the sort of stern look I would expect from den-mother Zenema. "Get your stuff packed up now. Use your cloak to tie the handles of your bags together, then swing up behind me and use your bags sort of like a saddle. Now!"

Bower moved to tie his bags together. He dragged his feet over it, but he did as I asked. As soon as we had his bags secured, he put his hand on Jaydra's side. He looked ready to jump back if she so much as sneezed.

I gave a laugh and pushed him. "You won't hurt her—she won't let you. Not even with those giant paddles you call feet."

He frowned and glanced down at his booted feet—they were big, even for a tall, skinny boy like him. With a sour glance at me, he climbed up onto Jaydra's back, only slipping once. He settled into a seat behind his bags. And he just sat there—not holding on, feet dangling and looking as if he'd slide off the second Jaydra took to the air.

I sighed. He knew nothing about how to ride a dragon. Climbing up, I settled myself in front of him. "Hold on to me. Grip with your thighs and lean into any turn. Think of it like—"

Like riding a horse, Jaydra thought to me. She snorted out a cloud of smoke."

Bower coughed but he put his hands on my sides. "Please tell me you can ride a horse, Bower."

"Jaydra is not a horse," Bower said, his tone tense and stiff.

Too right, Bower, Jaydra thought to me.

She stretched out her wings, took a few steps and began to beat at the air with her wings. Her feet lifted, Bower clutched my sides and gave a gasp.

And then we were above the trees and rising into the clouds.

Cold air rushed past my face. I could feel Jaydra use the dragon trick to make herself seem only a shadow on the cloud, but I was just glad to be on her back and flying again.

There really is no time when you feel freer than this, or more alive.

Jaydra's powerful wings spread even wider. She rose higher with each wing beat. Underneath me I could feel her muscles work, and in my mind I could sense her delight. The world below fell away, vanishing into clouds. We rose above the sounds of the soldiers and their clanking armor and weapons, above the smells of the villages and their fires, and far up until all I could hear was the beat of Jaydra's wings.

Jaydra soared up into the sunlight above the clouds. The warmth was welcome after the chill below. She lifted her head and turned in a great circle. I loved flying, but my joy could not compare to the delight a dragon savored. Flying completed them—it made them what they were. I wished now that Jaydra would not have to hide as an earth-bound horse again.

Only a short time, Jaydra thought to me.

She pulled her wings in close, put her head down and plummeted toward the ground. I gave a laugh. Bower's hands gripped my sides tightly, his fingers digging into my skin. The wind tore at my face, rushed past my ears and forced tears out of my eyes.

With a whoop, I urged Jaydra on. The clouds slipped past. I lived for these moments when everything else faded and we were not two different creatures but were one in a fierce, electric moment.

Jaydra rolled and her speed kept Bower and me on her back. She unfurled her wings, letting a sudden catch of air lift her up into the clouds again. All dragons were master fliers, but I had always thought Jaydra one of the best.

Glancing back at Bower, I expected to see him frozen with fear. Instead, his face shone red and he was grinning. He gave a shout and Jaydra answered with satisfied agreement. This was fun.

Jaydra had taken us closer to the mountain. The clouds thinned and I could make out wide streets and tall buildings. Far to the north, I glimpsed mountains and dark green forests. To the east, water gleamed silver in a wide lake.

Fish, Jaydra thought to me.

I wondered if we should show Bower how Jaydra liked to go fishing, but Bower was tugging at my tunic.

Leaning closer, Bower shouted, "Too close."

I shook my head and yelled back, "Jaydra is an expert flier. She can get much closer than this to the ground."

He let go of me and pointed down with one hand. "No, too close to the city! They've not seen a dragon in generations."

Then let us show them, Saffron, what a dragon can do! Jaydra thought and dipped one wing to circle overhead.

No, Jaydra, there could be panic. People could be hurt.

Jaydra ignored me, and I caught the mischief she was feeling. She just wanted to play a little, but this was not a game.

Bower had already made it clear that the people below us did not believe in dragons. If they saw Jaydra now, who knew what might happen.

Without thinking, I stretched out a hand. The power deep inside me stirred. I closed my eyes and sketched a symbol in the air ahead—something I knew without knowing.

For a moment nothing happened.

And then the power burst out with a crack like thunder.

Lightning split the sky. The clouds closed over us and rain pelted us, freezing cold.

Bower gasped, as did I. Opening my eyes, I saw Jaydra soar over the shoulder of the mountain and past stony ruins. Lightning flashed again, but the sky had darkened with so many clouds it seemed almost night. No one could see us—but I feared the lightning might strike Jaydra.

"Land. Behind the city, on the far side of the mountain," Bower shouted.

I nodded. We needed to get out of this storm I had called—it was far more than I'd meant to do and it could get us killed.

Jaydra, you have brought us farther and faster than I had ever thought that you could do, please land, now. The compliment was the surest way to get a dragon to do as you wanted.

Jaydra let out a roar that sounded with the rumble of more thunder. She glided down from the dark clouds until we found a clearing. Rain was still pelting down as Jaydra's feet touched the ground.

Sliding off her back, I patted her and told her that she might as well fish the lake. The thunder and lightning hung over the city now, so we were safe for a moment, if almost as wet as if we had been swimming.

Bower dragged his bags off Jaydra and climbed down, and she flew off to fish the lake. Bower and I scrambled up to a thicket of trees that gave us a little shelter from the rain.

Collapsing on the ground, Bower grinned and said, "I never expected in my wildest of dreams for anything to be so wonderful!"

I could only smile and nod. I was cold now and shivering. Bower put his cloak over me and went to gather wood. We soon had a fire going. Jaydra came back with fish for supper. After we'd eaten, I turned to Bower and asked, "So, how do we get into this unfriendly city of yours?"

*　　*　　*

Jaydra reluctantly allowed me to shift her into the illusion of a horse. But the trick didn't want to work at first. It took me three tries, and I could almost think calling up the storm to hide us—as I'd done by accident, intending to call up no more than a cloud—had somehow drained me. At last, a tall horse stood before us. I glanced at Bower and he nodded—if he saw her as a horse, so would others. But I worried. It seemed to me that the illusion was shimmering and a little blurry, almost as if a fog also surrounded Jaydra.

The good news was that night had fallen, and Bower had a plan.

"If we come around the city and come in from the lower heights, we'll enter into the poorer section of the city. There's not so much traffic there, and should be fewer guards."

I hoped he was right.

It took most of the night to travel down to the gate Bower wanted to use, and Jaydra grumped about how she could fly there in minutes.

As Bower had said, the gates at this end of the city seemed to be left permanently open. Even as late as it was, a steady stream of people traveled into the city, most of them with handcarts filled with wood or with food carried in baskets and brought in from the farms. The king's troops camped on all sides of the city, it seemed, but this night they stayed in their tents, out of the cold mud. Sometimes snatches of songs lifted up or shouts from a game being played, but the few guards left on duty looked cold and ignored us.

Closer to the city, Bower used a few coins—money he called it—to buy himself a turban head wrap and he traded his cloak for a battered, leather tunic. He glanced at me and told me I should be wearing a dress. I didn't see why, but after he bought me such a garment—in a soft purple—I gave in and pulled it on over my tunic and breeches. He frowned at that, but I wasn't giving up my own clothes.

Glancing at Jaydra, Bower asked, "Can you have her limp? As a disguise. That will explain why we aren't riding her, and we can tell everyone we're looking for a blacksmith."

Jaydra thought to me that no one had best try to put iron shoes on her.

"Not going to happen," I told her.

Bower glanced at us and hefted the bags in his hands. "Keep your eyes on the ground. Keep walking. If anyone asks any questions, let me talk. Your accent will give you away as a stranger, and that might not end well."

I gave a shrug and followed him and a caravan going into the city, but I had to sneak glances up and around us.

More people were going into the city and no one was leaving. I heard some talking of a fair the king was planning on holding, of games and prizes and food to be offered up next month and for the whole month long to celebrate the anniversary of the Maddox line coming to rescue Torvald and accepting the throne. That certainly would account for the crowd coming into the city.

Never before I had been around so many people. No two were alike. Some were large, others small, some far older than I'd ever seen. It was funny to see how some men held children on their shoulders, and the women all seemed to wear long dresses. Their clothes came in every color and style—a few wore rich garments, but most seemed dressed in rough linen such as I had seen in other villages on the mainland.

The gates seemed to be undefended, but then I saw what looked like two large, metal men—but they weren't men. They seemed to be almost statues made of metal of some kind. But that wasn't right, either. They were larger than any man I had seen and much wider, and looked identical. Both wore helmets and armor. Despite Bower's warning to look down, I had to glance at them. I had the strangest feeling from them…almost as if I could sense life of some kind inside that metal.

Bower stepped on my foot.

I turned to snarl and slap him, but he grabbed my wrist and tugged me around to the far side of a caravan going into the city and out sight of the metal statues. These had to be the Iron Guard Bower had talked about.

The tribes that lived in the Western Isles sometimes carved figures from wood—and then claimed a spirit could enter the carving. Was this the same? I didn't know, and I realized I would have to listen more to Bower and try to observe more and not get myself into trouble. There was so much I didn't know.

Bower urged us into the first narrow alleyway we came across. Jaydra followed us, limping as Bower had asked. We made another turn and kept climbing the steep streets. I risked another glance up to see crooked buildings leaning against each other. I was surprised by how much dirt there seemed to be here—it darkened windows, it choked the street drains, it hung in the air and I choked on soot and ash.

I'd had it in my head that a city would be cleaner than any village or the wilds, but the opposite was true. Discarded rags, broken shoes, bits of broken pots, bottles and food scraps littered the streets. Scraggly cats and dogs skittered out of our way, carrying dead rats or refuse. Jaydra gave an offended sniff and turned up her nose. Her hooves clattered on the cobblestone, and my boots slipped on them. The stones seemed hard, and why would you want them instead of the earth of a nice cave. But the buildings amazed me.

There were so many different kinds. Some looked made of wood, some of stone, some of things I could not name. Not all of them looked to be in use—many had darkened windows or caved-in roofs.

Why build them if they cannot be used? Or why not tear them down? Why live in such a crowded place.

As if to prove me right, the very next turn brought us to a narrow alley that seemed crammed full of wooden crates and blankets put up like the army tents I had seen. It seemed odd to me that people would live here when just a short distance away stood empty houses.

I glanced at Bower.

He nodded and lifted one hand. "I told you Torvald is not what it once was. This is Monger's Lane."

"Should I know what that is?" I asked.

Before Bower could answer, a man crawled out of one of the tents and stepped up to Bower. "Lord Daris? Bower of House Daris?"

Lips pressed tight and heart now pounding, I glanced at Bower. Bower was a lord? He had never told me his family was important.

Bower held up a hand to stop my questions, and he faced the man who had come up to him. Skinny and bald, the man's age was impossible to guess. His clothes looked to be little more than aged rags, brown and patched. The bones on his face and hands stood out—did people not feed their own kind here in this city. "Jakson, is it not?" Bower said, his tone making the words not much of a question really.

"Yes, m'lord. Glad I am to see you well. Been hearing some terrible things." The man wiped away a bit of scurf from his face and scratched at his chest.

A few others peeked out of the tents, but mothers pulled their children back. However, some of the older folks who lived here came forward. I tensed, but they offered Bower smiles and nods.

Soon others approached. They seemed a ragtag collection the likes of which I had never before seen. No one in the Western Isles allowed anyone to go hungry. Every family looked after its own—I'd see that in every island village. Even the disagreeing, the angry or the ill ones were cared for, and food and clothing was left out for the few hermits who took to living on their own.

What sort of place left its people to live in tents in all this dirt and trash?

A few hands stretched out to touch Bower's sleeves and I heard murmurs of Daris...House Daris. Bower put down his bags, pulled a few coins from his pockets and handed them out, and I could see now why they treated him with such respect.

I had assumed he'd come from wealth—who else would carry books with him, and his clothes, while dusty, had been of fine fabric. But I had never thought him to be a lord. It seemed he was far more than I had known.

Bower knows the meaning of den-family. Jaydra's thoughts carried approval, and I agreed. Bower even appeared noble at that moment—no longer the awkward youth, but a generous soul, seeking to look after his den. His city.

"How is your family, Jakson?" Bower asked. The others who had taken his coins had scurried off, back to their tents.

"Some good and some not so good." Jakson waggled his hand like a dragon might waggle its wings. "My littlest has the cough, but we've no coin for a doctor. But we'll have food from the fair the king is planning. She'll get better, tough little thing that she is."

Bower shook his head. "I've a coin left. Take it. I...I also must leave my books with someone. Will you take them Jakson, and if I do not return for them, sell them for whatever you can get to whoever will pay you and not ask questions. Can you do that?"

"M'lord, you've not heard?" Jakson grimaced. "It's all anyone could talk of amongst us anyway, seeing as we knew you and your family. The old lord was such a kind man."

"Thank you," Bower said. "But what is this talk?"

"The proclamation went out that House Daris has been cast off the Noble Rolls. Struck from the charts, from all duties at court and all privileges. You'll be knowing what that means," Jakson muttered, his face growing even more lined with worry.

Bower let out a long breath. He patted one hand against Jakson's chest. "Ah well, it was only a matter of time before that happened."

Jakson shook his head and wiped a hand over the stubble on his chin. "You can't go home, m'lord. They'll be out looking for you. They'll have a watch on your house, m'lord. Might be best as you should stay with us. We can get you out. There's some people—"

"Friend, I only just got back into the city. But here is where they are least likely to be looking for me now. Don't worry about me. I'll be able to hide in plain sight, and I shall be fine." Bower didn't *look* fine, however—in fact, he looked positively *not* fine to my eyes.

Even in the flickering fires of this camp, I could see new creases marked lines around his eyes and mouth. His shoulders sagged. He scrubbed a hand through his hair and I shared Jaydra's worry for him.

Jakson gave a nod. "Most of us knew your father and he was good to us back in the day. As you have been. We'll look after your things, m'lord, but no talk of selling them will I hear. We'll keep them safe for your return." The old man leaned close. "There's a flame within. Don't be forgetting that."

Bower's head jerked up. I didn't know what the words meant, but they meant something to Bower. Jakson headed back to his tent, and I tugged at Bower's sleeve.

"Let's leave this spot," I told him. Jaydra added her opinion, pawing at the cobbles with a clatter.

Jaydra was right. This place stank of foul things.

Bower turned from the tents to walk with me, Jaydra in step behind us. I glanced at him and asked, "Are you worried about the guards finding you?"

Pointing ahead to a nearby bridge, Bower whispered that we must keep our heads down. The iron men stood guard on either side of this bridge, and there were no crowds crossing it that might hide us.

I glanced at the iron men, wondering if they could see—would they notice Jaydra was a horse or not? One metal head seemed to turn our way, and I caught a breath.

A shout rose up behind us—someone calling out thief and robber.

The iron men moved with startling speed, changing in an instant from seeming like statues to being clanking monsters that stomped past us, heading over to look into whatever crime was being committed in the street behind us.

Bower tugged on my arm, and we crossed over the bridge and into wider and cleaner streets. I let out a breath and I could even feel Jaydra's relief at being away from the filth and the empty houses.

It was almost like stepping into another world.

The houses seemed bigger. Lanterns lit the outside stone structures and more lights glowed from within, spilling out of big windows. The people here wore thick cloaks and some even rode horses. Music came out of some of the houses, sweet and lively. I almost wanted to stop at these inns and taverns as Bower called them, but he kept pulling me with him. Every now and then we came across an empty, dark house and I wondered why it had been left to ruin. But it seemed that no one in this part of the city lived on the streets.

"How far must we go?" I asked. I worried a little that Jaydra was not going to want to stay a horse much longer. I could feel her impatience—and she was getting hungry. So was I.

Bower shrugged. "To House Daris, not far. But…well, it may be wise first to have a look to see if anyone is watching it." After glancing at me, Bower shook his head.

"Who was Nev?" I asked.

His shoulders seemed to sag. "My father, Nev of House Daris, was good to the poor and I tried to keep up that tradition. But too often it felt like a bucket of water thrown onto a raging fire- it never seemed to do much good. He… I never really knew what happened to him after he was taken away by the king's Iron Guard." His voice had become clipped and hard, and I wondered about that.

I thought it bad my parents had left me, but Bower's father had been killed by another. It surprised me that he wasn't angrier—but perhaps he was and just hid it better.

He stopped, and I did as well.

Ahead of us, the road opened into what seemed like a small bit of woodlands with trees and grass. The buildings here seemed even bigger than any I had ever seen, and the streets were wide enough to allow fancy wagons with doors and tops that carried nice smelling people around. The horses all shied away from Jaydra as if they knew she wasn't another horse.

Turning to me, Bower smiled. "Some luck at last. My friend Vic is here. That's his carriage over there—I recognize the coat of arms on the door. He'll be at the Small Goose Theatre over on the other side of the square for tonight's entertainments."

I frowned. "Your friend, can we trust him?"

Bower glanced at me and frowned. "Just wait here with Jaydra. The carriage drivers are here, so you'll just look like another horse for a carriage or a noble, and the servant set to keep watch." He left me in the wooded area in the center of the square of buildings. As he had said, other men and women—each dressed in what looked a fancy uniform with gold embroidery on their chest that matched one on the carriage door near them or on the horse's harness, loitered here. Some alone, and some talking to each other. I stepped closer to Jaydra and tried to look like we both were bored and belonged here, but I feared that neither was true.

My heart thumped against my chest and sweat stuck my tunic to my back. It was warm in the city. And Torvald was not what I had expected.

From what I had heard in other villages, it was supposed to be wonderful. I thought it crowded and noisy. To me, it seemed as if everyone I had glimpsed was either scared or ignoring those around them. It made me doubt I would learn anything useful about magic or my family.

All I'd wanted to discover was who I really was and how to control my magic. I had thought I might find a new home here, but now I didn't want that to be the case. None of this felt like the sort of place where I would ever fit in.

*   *   *

"Fortunes read. Fortunes told!" a man called out. He didn't shout, but his voice was clear enough to cut across the noise of wheels and horses and people strolling around me.

I'd grown tired of waiting for Bower. Now, from where I stood with Jaydra, I watched a man weave his way through the people strolling across the square.

I had thought magic was forbidden. Hadn't Bower told me that?

Zenema could read fortunes, I thought to Jaydra. The man was heading our way. He wore tan robes that swept down to his ankles and walked with a heavy staff made of ash. Under a drab cloak that looked dull brown, I could just make out a belt around his waist, and from it bits of metal flashed. It seemed impossible to place his age. His hair and beard were gray and long, but his face did not seem lined. He offered everyone a good-natured smile as if nothing in the world could ever disturb him.

And he's confident too—just like Zenema, I thought to Jaydra. *The old hermit once told me it's the mark of a powerful sorcerer to be able to read the future and be calm even when in danger.*

Jaydra snorted. *Den-mother Zenema didn't need to see fortunes. She knew Saffron and could see what Saffron would do.* Her thoughts carried an edge of impatience, and dismissal.

But if this man really can do magic that means that there are others in the city like me, I thought to her. Zenema had told me to follow the magic inside me and to go to the place where my parents had come from. Maybe this was the place and here was one person who had magic. It had to be a sign.

I watched the magician come closer, his steps halting. He tapped in front of him with his staff and I realized he was poor sighted. White clouded his eyes.

I nudged an elbow into Jaydra's side and whispered, "Look, he has white eyes just like Zenema.

Saffron's eyes not white, Jaydra thought to me.

I frowned at her, but the magician had come closer, so I reached out and touched his arm.

He stopped and fixed me with a white-misted stare. "Yes? Who stops me?"

"I'm sorry." I pulled my hand back.

"You've come to have your fortune read, haven't you, girl? Want to see if you are to marry a pretty man? A rich man?" He thumped the ground with the tip of his staff. "Well, if you have a coin I'll read your fortune. What's your name?"

I had no coins—I hadn't found a use for them. I had traded for anything I'd ever needed. I patted the pouch at my side, wondering what I might trade. I had the fold of cloth with my mother's name on it, a dragon's baby tooth, a few shells and some of the colored rocks from the island's many caves. I fished out one of the colored rocks for others had liked them. "I have these. I've always thought them prettier than coins. Will this do?"

He reached out and took the stone, frowning. Then he brought the stone very close to his eyes and muttered, "An uncut emerald. You surprise me, child. What did you say your name was?"

I frowned. I wasn't sure I should tell him, so I said, "I don't want to know about any future marriage. I need to discover the truth about my family."

The man tucked the stone into a pouch that hung from his belt, and then he stroked his beard. "You are a strange one and no mistake. Emeralds and family. Are you a runaway from one of the orphanages?"

"What's an orphanage?" I asked.

Jaydra's voice brushed against my mind. *Be careful with our secrets.*

She had a point. We did not know what might happen to us in this city. We didn't know who was a friend or not. I glanced around. No one else seemed to be paying us any mind, so I asked the man, "How come you're not afraid as are so many others here?"

The man blinked. "Afraid of what? You?"

"Of…what happens to those who break the law. Afraid of the guards, I guess."

"The Iron Guard? You mean because of my gifts?"

Leaning closer, I whispered, "Isn't magic against the law? So fortune telling could get you into trouble."

The man's mustache twitched. He smoothed his gray beard again and the hairs frizzed as if charged by lightning in the air. "You are in the right of things, but do you see any Iron Guard? Do you feel their metal nearby, hard upon the senses, leaving the air smelling of copper? My magic tells me where I am safe. It even led me to talk with you. A powerful feeling pulled me to this spot, to this rich neighborhood where I do not often visit. It was the magic you see. It can call to you like that."

I thought about the times I'd felt my powers bubble up, how it suddenly flooded my senses so I had no choice but to answer it. I nodded. "It controls you then?" I pushed out a breath. If he couldn't control his magic as old as he was, what hope did I have?

He gave a soft laugh. "No, I control it. The magic is alive within me, but I make the choice to listen to it or not. I made peace with it long ago and it has become my friend."

I frowned at that. What did he mean make peace with it? Make it a friend? I wanted to master my magic, control it and make it work for me.

Dragons not controlled by others, Jaydra thought to me.

I glanced at her horse face. She gleamed with a touch of blue in her black coat in the light of the lanterns hung from the buildings. And she stared back, a little smug that this magician had not seen through the illusion that made her appear to be a horse.

There are all kinds of magic, I told her with my mind and looked back to the magician.

He pushed his shoulders back and looked both wiser and nobler than he had before. "There are so few of us left. So few who can control the power inside. Have you ever heard of any others like me?"

I opened my mouth to say something about dragons and myself, but Jaydra gave me a powerful mental shove. *Saffron, be wise with secrets, and Saffron has no control.*

I won't tell him the whole truth, I thought to her, irritated I couldn't speak more plainly. This was a chance to learn about magic. Pulling out the fragment of stitching that bore my mother's name, I held it open before me and asked him, "What can you tell me of this?"

"Amelia." The man touched a finger to the letter. "This is your mother? An aunt?"

"I want to find my family, if they are from here. Can you do that?"

"Ah..." He frowned, bushy eyebrows flattening over his white eyes and he stroked his beard again.

My chest tightened and so did my throat. My heart beat faster. What if I had insulted this last magician by asking him to do some petty, little magic. I fished the last colored stone I had and shoved it into his hand. "Take this. And please help me."

From across the way, Bower called out, "Saffron?"

The magician held the stone in his palm, passed one hand over the other. The stone vanished and in its place appeared a flower. "A yellow flower for a yellow-named girl. He glanced again at the scrap of cloth and murmured, "Amelia."

Bower stepped up to my side, frowning and pushing a little between me and the magician. "What's going on? Is this man threatening you?"

As if I could not take care of a threat. I gave Bower a stare. I don't know what was funnier—the idea that an old man could be a danger to me or that Bower might rescue me when he'd been unable to take care of himself in the woods. I shook my head and jabbed an elbow into Bower's side. He was going to offend the magician for a certainty. "Bower, show some respect. This man has magic."

"Bower, you say?" The man squinted at Bower, his white-filmed eyes seeing something perhaps that normal eyes could not.

"Saffron, I don't like this," Bower muttered. "I glimpsed Vic in the theater and the entertainment is about to end. We must be ready to leave." Leaning close, he whispered, "This old man cannot be like you."

"The girl has paid for my services, Bower of House Daris!" the magician said, his voice suddenly grave and loud.

Bower glanced around us and his frown deepened, pulling lines to his forehead.

"He knows your real name, and he made my rocks vanish."

Bower crossed his arms over his chest. "And half the city has heard about House Daris—a wild guess means nothing."

"Do not be alarmed, Bower of House Daris." The old magician stood taller now. His voice deepened. The gray in his beard turned white in the lights and his eyes almost seemed to clear. To my eyes, he looked ten years younger. He really *was* a magician—this proved it. He gave Bower a smile. "Your identity is safe with me. The girl has paid for me to find her parents, and I will do so. I have a name to work with so let the hunt begin. But I need somewhere quiet to work the most sensitive of spells. You have a mansion nearby…with a library."

Bower dropped his arms to his side. His eyes narrowed. "More guesses. And why should I take you to House Daris? So, you might rob it of what little is left?"

I pressed my lips tight and wanted to punch Bower, but the magician nodded and said, "Of course, m'lord. I understand your concerns. We live in dangerous times and one cannot be too careful. But I can offer you proof of my skills."

He thrust his arms wide and his staff seemed to glow. His cloak fell back and a sudden puff of black feathers showered to the ground as if he had shrugged them off his skin. His cloak shimmered in a deep, scintillating red, almost like dragon scales.

I gasped and clapped a hand over my mouth.

Bower did not seem so easily pleased. He shook his head and gave a snort. "You'll have to do a lot better than that. You could have secret panels in your cloak and strings attached to your wrists or fingers to pull them."

"Bower," I hissed the word at him. If he wasn't careful, he would offend the magician and I would lose this chance to find my family. I glanced at the magician.

He didn't seem insulted by Bower's doubts. He lifted his chin and stroked his now white beard. "Then I shall show you another of my skills." He pulled a plain, silver ring from what seemed to be out of the air. A simple square had been carved into the metal. "This is the Adamant Ring. It has the ability to freeze a man solid and leave him unable to move. Do you dare try it?"

Bower huffed out a breath. "We have no time for this nonsense. Saffron, come on—we're going…"

"I'll try it," I said. My stomach ached with the need to prove to Bower this man was what he said he was. I had to have his help—and Bower had to know that, too.

"You are indeed a brave girl." The magician dropped the silver ring into my outstretched palm. I slipped it onto one finger. It fit snugly and seemed cold to me. It didn't feel magical—I could sense nothing from it. Even Jaydra snuffled at it and turned her nose away as if uninterested.

Tipping my head to one side, I asked, "Are you sure this is working?"

"I haven't said the magic words yet, child." He raised his staff and passed one end over my fingers, muttering strange words I couldn't understand. I didn't feel any wave of power. Bower's eyebrows lifted high. I shrugged.

"Only I know the command to activate the ring's powers." The magician pointed to a nearby metal railing that seemed meant to keep anyone from walking across the grass. "Grab that with your free hand."

I did so. The ring clicked against the railing and the metal felt scratchy and cool on my skin. A lump lodged in my throat. Was Bower right—was this just an old man who knew a few tricks?

The magician lifted his staff again and muttered something.

Growing tired of this, I tried to pull my hand away, but something had stuck my fingers to the railing. It held me fast. My fingers tingled as did the ring.

Den-sister? Jaydra sent me her worry. I thought to her, *Doesn't hurt, just feels tingly.* "She's hardly frozen. And I've seen suggestion work like this before," Bower growled.

The magician shook his head, and touched my hand with the tip of his staff. A sharp jolt of energy spread over my skin. I pulled my hand off the railing. My heart was racing. I flexed my fingers and gave the ring back to the magician. But how I wished I could keep it to study its power.

"Please, great magician, tell me where to find my parents!"

"Of course, child. But as I said, I need space and quiet to work my spells of finding."

I turned to Bower who stepped between me and the magician. He grabbed the ring from the magician's hand. "Try now to make me freeze? Can you do so without my touching metal? Can you? Saffron wasn't frozen."

I tugged at Bower's hand to get him to give back the ring. "What under the skies are you doing?"

"Magnetism," Bower said. "That was how you did it—magnetism." Bower pushed the ring back into the magician's hand. "I've read of such a thing—how metal can be made to stick to metal. It was once something used to make a compass work, and the dra—and riders used it. It is forbidden as are all the sciences from the old days."

The magician stepped back. He turned to me. "If that is how you feel, I will leave. Magic cannot work where there is no faith."

He turned and strode away from us, vanishing into the crowd now stepping from one of the huge buildings that surrounded the grassy square.

I turned and thumped a fist into Bower's chest. "Look what you've done! I've lost my chance to find my family."

Bower shook his head. "I am so sorry, Saffron. He was not a real magician."

"But he made my stones disappear. He knew your real, full name. He stuck my hand to the railings." A hollowness formed in the pit of my stomach. What if Bower was right? But he could not be. Magic was real.

Bower waved a hand. "There are rare metals that fell to earth from the skies and have been thrown out of ancient volcanoes. They attract other metals. By using the right combination of metals, you can make metals stick to each other or repel."

"It sounds like magic to me," I muttered. I was angry with Bower. I wanted to run after the magician, but I was certain that Bower had insulted him so much that he would never help me.

The cloth with the name Amelia had fluttered to the ground. Bending down, I grabbed it up and pushed it back into my pouch, the hint of lavender still lingering in the air.

"I really am sorry," Bower said

Turning away from him, I stuffed my cloth back into my pouch. "I don't want to talk about it. Now where is this friend of yours?"

*   *   *

We didn't have to wait long before a young man with curly hair, a narrow long face and in a fine tunic made of soft fabric and fine black breeches strolled over to where we were waiting. He saw us and one hand dropped to the short sword he wore at his hip.

Saffron? Jaydra gave a low nicker. I could feel her tense. Putting a hand on my knife hilt, I stiffened, ready to defend us should I have to.

Bower stepped from the shadows. "Vic, it's me. Don't be a fool."

"Daris?" He glanced around and waved us toward a waiting carriage. "Get in. Quick before anyone sees you with me."

I stood my ground. "What of my horse?"

The youth—Vic—glanced at me. He shook his head. "Tie it to the back."

Den-sister? Jaydra sent me a warning dislike of this Vic.

Be calm, Jaydra. This is Bower's friend. Follow us.

She gave a loud, not-very-horse-like snort. Vic turned away to talk to a man who had to be his driver, for the man had already mounted to the top seat and was focused on steadying the nervous horses. They weren't too pleased to have a strange, giant horse stepping up so close to them.

Bower helped me into the carriage—it had steps, unlike any wagon I'd seen, and inside fabric covered the benches, making them soft. It even smelled good—like leather and soap.

Vic climbed in after us, slammed the door and clasped Bower's arms. "You look a Gypsy," Vic said and grinned. I thought they looked complete opposites with Vic in fine garments of black and Bower in a simple tunic, breeches and boots and his turban. Vic wore no hat, but jewels glinted at his throat and on his fingers.

"Bower, you've grown some muscles." Vic smiled, but his good humor didn't reach his eyes.

Leaning back against the soft seat, I crossed my arms. Right now I wasn't happy with Bower or his friend.

Voice low and urgent, Bower said, "We really need your help."

Vic turned to look at me in a way that made my skin crawl. I had only seen the oldest and wildest dragons ever look at me like that before they remembered I was actually a den-sister and not prey. "Who is this lovely vision, Bower?"

Disgust swirled up in my stomach, knotting it. Jaydra's rising anger bled into my mind as she sensed my own annoyance.

"This is... Lady Saffron," Bower said.

Eyebrows pulled tight, I shot Bower a sideways look. What did he think he was doing, naming me a lady?

Vic's smile widened. "What House do you hail from? None of the older families, I am sure or else I would remember meeting such a charming lady."

I clenched a fist and resisted the urge to put it into action. Chin lifting, I told him, "I hail from the Western Isles." There, that wasn't a lie. Weren't the dragons the oldest creatures on the islands? And the noblest?

Fluttering a silk kerchief to his mouth as if to wipe away his widening smile, Vic said, "I never knew there were any…good families that far west."

Bower interrupted with an impatient wave of his hand. "There'll be time to work out lineages later. For now, we need something to eat and a place to stay."

For a moment, Vic kept staring at me. I stared back, giving him my fierce glare.

Vic was the one to break away, turning to Bower. "Of course I'll do everything in my power to help you, but you have to help yourself as well. You don't realize how difficult things have become. The king has called for your head. House Daris is finished. I have no idea what good I can do for you. And you could not have appeared at a worse time. Torvald is teaming with Iron Guard as the king readies for his great fair to celebrate his reign."

Bower frowned. "A fair? King Enric's never held such a thing before. Why now?"

Waving a hand, Vic said, "The proclamation that went out simply said the king expects to usher in a new epoch— and will celebrate new safety and security for the realm."

Bower's mouth pulled down even more. He shook his head once and said in a tight voice, "That does not sound promising to me, but just get us past the Iron Guards who may be guarding the streets around House Daris."

Face going pale, Vic clenched his silk scarf in one hand. "I was going that way anyway. But…well, I suppose I could take you to the old park, just behind your house. But what if there are guards?"

Leaning back in his seat, Bower glanced out the window. "I can find a way in." He glanced at me and smiled. "I told you I would get you into the city. Now Vic will get us to House Daris and we'll find food, rest, and what you need."

I forced a stiff smile and I could not help but wonder if Bower's friend's help might have a hidden cost.

*   *   *

CHAPTER 11

THE PAINTING

I wasn't sure I could trust Vic to be honest, but a phrase I had read floated up in memory—*I don't have to trust him, I just have to trust him to be him.* The one thing Vic would hate is any fuss caused by him calling on Iron Guard. Vic would not want the responsibility.

He was also obviously a bit taken with Saffron. That annoyed me, but it was something to our advantage. Besides, Saffron could look after herself. It was a little sad that Saffron—someone I barely knew—could prove more trustworthy than could someone I had known since childhood.

Vic had his carriage take the lanes around the back that led to the park behind House Daris. He seemed torn between wanting to remain near Saffron and wanting to put as much distance between himself and me as he could. Caution won out over his interest in Saffron, for he stayed in the carriage, doing nothing more than handing Saffron from the coach with a gallant smile and a promise that he would be pleased to show her all the best parts of Torvald. I had to bite the inside of my cheek to avoid telling Vic not to be such a ninny and that Saffron could manage better without him. I feared we were both better off without the little help he was offering.

His carriage moved off, leaving Saffron and I standing under a large sycamore tree that was starting to shed its leaves. Below us in the lower tiers of Torvald, lanterns gleamed and around us this neighborhood seemed quiet with only the sound of a dog barking in the distance. I had mixed feelings about being so close to home again—I had left never expecting to return, and now my muscles seemed knotted with tension for fear of the Iron Guard being on watch and a reluctance to see what had happened to House Daris.

"These are all your houses?" Saffron asked. She spun around in a slow circle and then leaned her shoulder against Jaydra.

I managed a small smile. "No, this is a neighborhood of mansions, most of which have fallen on hard times like House Daris. Either the noble families that had once lived in them have moved or died out. House Daris stands at the end of the avenue." I pointed to the old family house, but didn't move. Was that a shadow by the front gate, under the decorative portcullis or a guard?

"There's someone there," Saffron said, her voice low. Laying a hand on my arm, she nodded at the front gate. I sucked in a sharp breath and let it out. I thought everyone in the city must hear it. A match flared and lit the face of a guard. He lit a pipe and doused the match, falling again back into shadow.

"How did you know he was there?" I whispered to Saffron.

She shrugged and glanced at Jaydra, as if the horse-dragon had told her someone stood watch in the darkness.

"How do we get in?" Saffron asked. She glanced at Jaydra. "And no, we are not flying up to the roof—that's going to get us noticed for a certainty."

I started to tell her I was not going to suggest flying, but maybe the dragon really had thought up that idea. I told Saffron, "My house—if I can really claim it to be mine still—is made of stone, with a wall that's overhung by the trees. The garden stretches into the park. There's a place where ivy vines are thick and lead up to the trees. We can climb over the wall and then slip in an upstairs window." I glanced at Jaydra. "I don't think your horse can climb—but can she stand watch for us?"

"Do you have stables?"

I nodded. "They've not been in use in years, but they're still standing and you can slip into them from the park."

Saffron nodded and swapped stares with Jaydra.

Jaydra snorted, tossed her head, but followed us as we headed for House Daris. The horse-dragon trotted into the shadows behind my house that led to the stables, almost seeming to disappear.

Saffron shot me a quick grin. "She'll use her own tricks so as not to be seen. One of the few good things about the fact that this city doesn't believe in dragons is that it makes it easier for us to hide."

We walked over to the back of my house.

Seeing it again stirred an uncomfortable sense of unease within me, as if my skin no longer fit.

After seeing Jakson, I had started to remember my old life—and it had felt right to help those people down there in Monger's Lane. This city wasn't a bad or an evil place. Deep down it was like what Saffron had talked about…. A den…a family. But now, staring up at the walls to a house that was no longer my home, I realized this was no longer my den. I would never be welcome here again. I was starting to think that my earlier idealism to try and make a difference within my city was just a childish dream. We climbed the ivy with ease—I had done this for many years as a boy and the actions brought back memories of better days when my parents had still been alive and the world seemed a simple place. Reaching the top of the wall and the trees, I motioned for Saffron to follow me. She made a face at me as if I was asking the obvious. Up we went, on thick, oak branches. The trees shivered a little, but we reached the top floor and the window with the latch that never fully caught. But I had no need to try and open it. The little window was smashed and broken open. It made it easy for me to climb in, heaving myself over the sill and slipping inside.

I'd had a worry that the servants might still occupy the house—or guards might be inside. I need not have feared such a thing. The house had been wrecked.

Glancing around the room, my heart stuttered and anger swelled in my chest. What few furnishings had been here had been smashed—not even taken for use elsewhere but hacked to bits. The statues that had been too large to move and sell lay as rubble scattered across the floors, which looked scarred by metal boots. With a tightness in my chest, I made for the library, trying not to see the destruction around me.

In the library, moonlight flooded the room through holes punched in the roof. The room wasn't just ruined by rain that had gotten in, it had been deliberately destroyed.

Every shelf had been torn from the walls. Water had puddled and soaked the floorboards. Worse of all, whoever had done this had smashed the walls to uncover the secret room. I put a shaking hand on the wall and stared at the destruction.

Words written more than five hundred years ago lay in scattered scraps, strewn across the floor. Some of the books had been torn apart and trampled underfoot. The books I'd left now looked like a pile of debris. Whoever had done this had taken great delight in this destruction of knowledge. It wasn't just accidental or even the work of petty vandals.

This was a deliberate act of savage ignorance and hatred.

Gernigan had done this. I was willing to wager on such a thing. My heart thudded hard against my ribs and I clenched my jaw. How could he have? But he had given me up to the Iron Guard. He had decided that I had caused the fall of the House Daris. He had hated my interest in books and the past.

I could have spat I was so angry. I turned away, unable to even look at Saffron.

"Someone doesn't like you much," she said. "Why would anyone ever do this? All these books…" She reached out to touch the spine of one book, hidden within the pile of damp pages. "Where I grew up, only the old hermit had books—and he only had a few and he treasured them." She glanced at me. "We'll show them they were wrong. That this knowledge meant something."

Hands clenched, I nodded. "Thank you. But we still must find out about your family."

Saffron shook her head and rubbed her arms with her hands. "How do you know you will have anything in here about them? It's all lost to us anyway."

Pushing my shoulders back, I glanced around. I also pulled off the turban I'd been wearing and tossed it aside.

"Unlike much of living in the wilds, or even handling a sword—which I know little of—there is one thing I do know. And that is books. There has to be some scraps or pages I can salvage. A book buried or overlooked. There will be something to save. Go explore the rest of the house. Give me a shout if you see anyone."

A smile curved Saffron's lips. "Are you sure of that?"

"Why not? The guard thinks the house empty. If we are quiet, he will go on thinking that. Take any room that still has a bed to sleep in tonight—there was always a nice room at the southern end, up in the tower. My parents always saved that room for guests, and you surely count as a guest of the House Daris. Go on, and I'll see what I can find in here."

She hesitated a moment more and then said, "I'll see if I can find the kitchen and any food, too." She slipped away.

I turned back to the wreckage and let out a long breath.

An abandoned girl. Born eighteen or twenty years ago? Frizzy, red hair…the family had to flee to the Western Isles. And a wreck of a library.

It was going to be a puzzle, but if I could find it, I knew exactly the book that might hold a few answers.

*   *   *

I had never seen any building as big as this one. No village in the Western Isle used stone for construction and nothing was ever bigger than a good-sized lodge, which couldn't even hold a dragon. The dragon caves, of course, were big, but those had been carved by nature. And the dragons always liked to find small alcoves for sleeping, because they were the warmest. I couldn't understand why anyone would even want to live in a place like this.

I followed a narrow room that had doors that opened into more rooms, and then went down a wide stairway to a space with a black and white floor and really tall ceilings very much like a cave. A faint smell of dust and rotting wood clung to every room. More doorways led into what looked to be feasting halls and at last I found a stairway that led down to the kitchens. From here, the windows looked onto the gardens, but they were all smashed. The garden looked as if it had gone wild, but I thought I might find something for us to eat there, so I went outside.

Den-sister? Jaydra's thoughts brushed against mine. Through our connection, I could sense she stood in the garden, which looked to be even bigger than the park behind the house.

Jaydra! Why are you hiding out here?" I asked her with my thoughts. I didn't want the guard to hear us. *Weren't you going to hide in the stables?*

She sent me an image of jumping over the wall—with just a little use of her wings to glide over the top.

Frowning, I glanced around. Jaydra sent me her senses—how the guard slowly walked around the house once every hour, but for now he was leaning against the front door, tucked in tight to stay warm against the cooling night. Pulling of the dress Bower had bought for me, I left it in the house and headed into the garden at the back of the house. I smoothed my own skin tunic and breeches, glad to just have them on again. *Jaydra tires of being a horse—and now, behind walls, why should there be a need to hide?* Jaydra's horse form shimmered and for a moment I could see her wings and her long neck.

I patted her nose. *If you wish to leave me, you can fly high over the rooftops and go see the mountain, or even go back to the Western Isle. But, den-sister, my quest is not finished. I must stay a little longer.* Leaning against her, my heart seemed to be heavy in my chest. *These are odd people with strange, closed-minded ways, but I still must know what Zenema sent me to learn.*

Jaydra butted me with her head and thought, *Jaydra came with Saffron and goes where Saffron goes.*

Then we have to put up with this just a little bit longer. Think of it as enemy territory—we need to be watchful until we know where all the dangers lay.

Jaydra fight any enemy! She snorted and I saw the hair on her black horsehide ripple as she almost broke the illusion of being a horse.

Jaydra, when this is done, we will fly far away and you will never have to be a horse again. For this night, will you stay in the stables?

She swished her tail, but nodded. I didn't want her flying again, so we walked to the back walk in the garden and found a wooden gate still barred with a heavy iron latch. Once it was open, Jaydra led me to the House Daris stables, which stood behind the main house. The place smelled of straw—a dry odor—but the stalls all stood empty and silent.

Jaydra sniffed and glanced at me with her wise, ancient eyes. *Saffron and Jaydra should leave soon. This is a bad place.*

I patted her neck. "Soon," I whispered. "Zenema said I have to find my blood kin. The answer to all of my questions lies in my blood."

Jaydra shook her head and blew her nose at the hay that she did not want to eat. *What if Saffron never finds them? Never learns to control her magic?'*

I took a step back. Never had Jaydra spoken to me so directly. This was an idea I could not even consider. "I will find out. I will. But for tonight…tonight I am going to have one night in a house with a bed just like a human girl."

The words spilled out of me. Face hot, I bit down on my lower lip. Jaydra looked at me as if I had refused an offer of fish. Gulping down a breath, I stammered, "I—I didn't mean that I don't also want to still live with dragons."

Jaydra snorted in annoyance, but thought to me, *Saffron is a human girl, not dragon. Den-sister…but not clutch-sister.*

She pulled her thoughts away from me and then turned away as well. I tried to reach out with my mind to her only to find she had closed herself off to me.

Chest tight, I headed out of the stables and walked back to the garden. I barred the gate again and leaned my forehead against the polished wood.

Now I've hurt my closest friend in all the world. She must think that all I want to do is to run off to live a human life. That's not true!

But would it end up being true? Would my quest lead me to a place I didn't want to be? It had led me to this city, and I had no idea where it might lead me next. I almost wanted to fly away with Jaydra—but Zenema had said I must find my answers. And the truth was my magic was still a danger to Jaydra and anyone else around me. What if I lost my temper? What if I tried to make fire and instead set a forest ablaze? I had to find my answers.

Turning, I trudged back to the house, no longer quite as excited as I had been about exploring it. How could I explain to Jaydra that she and Zenema and the others were all the family I had ever wanted, but they were not what I needed? Zenema seemed to know this, but Jaydra was so young in so many ways. How could I explain to Jaydra that the magic inside me scared me sometimes? She seemed to think she could take on anything—but I could still remember how I had almost killed her back at the cliffs.

I knew then that if I could not learn to control my magic, I would have to become like the old hermit. I would have to leave everyone and everything behind and live alone. I would have to make certain I kept those I loved safe.

But I was not yet ready to face that future.

Inside, the house seemed almost too quiet. It still smelled musty and tired—I felt that way, too. I had meant to find some food in the garden or the kitchen, but I was no longer hungry. I didn't even want to hunt up some water.

Wandering from room to room, I found most of them empty. Moonlight streamed in through broken windows. I kept my steps light and made no sound. Mice skittered out of my path, surprised by me walking around like a ghost. I was starting to wonder if even a bed had been left behind. It seemed like anything that could be taken away had been. Turning, I headed back up the stairs again.

Maybe I am doomed to be an outsider?

I wandered down yet another long, narrow room, this one with cracked windows on one side and one huge painting on the other wall. That wall showed pale marks where other things had once been. I began to see that only the heaviest things had not been swept away.

At the other end of the long room, more doorways opened into other rooms. I found a bed at last, or at least a mattress. The bed was so big it had not been able to fit through the door, but all the bedding had been taken away. I was starting to think a night in the stables with Jaydra would be more comfortable.

Going back to the long, narrow room, I stopped in front of the painting again, wondering who this was.

The man had been painted riding a white horse. He held a sword up as if ready to strike down an enemy. It wasn't the best painting I'd ever seen—but then I had seen so few. The hermit had had one painting of a mountain that I had thought beautiful for it looked just like a snow-covered peak. And I had seen several paintings up for sale in one village I'd traveled through—most of them of flowers or animals, and I'd almost wished someone would paint Jaydra and Zenema for me. I wasn't certain I liked the man that had been painted here. He looked to me to have a narrow face and hard eyes. His mouth turned up a little at the corners as if he knew a secret and didn't ever intend to tell anyone what that might be. He wasn't a handsome man—the lines on his face were too strong for that. But there was something about him that seemed familiar to me. Stepping closer, I brushed a hand over the dust on the painting.

I could see why no one had taken the painting with them. When I brushed at it, my fingers tingled. Magic held this here—I was certain of it. But what kind of magic? Leaning even closer just made the painting become slashes of paint in dark and light colors, so I stepped back. And saw something odd.

It seemed to me that the man had a black mark on the side of his neck. It was in an odd shape, almost like a cloud—like a storm.

And it was a mark I had seen before.

Lifting a hand to my shoulder, I pulled down my shirt and glanced at the mark on my collarbone. It, too, was like a black cloud. I'd had this my entire life, but no one had ever been able to tell me what it was.

Behind me, I heard a gasp. I turned to see Bower staring at me, eyes wide. Quickly, I pulled my shirt back in place and turned to face him. He just stood where he was, a half-crumbling book in his arms and his mouth hanging open.

Crossing my arms and careful to keep my voice low so the guard outside would not hear, I muttered, "What? Did you find something?"

Bower shook his head slowly and pointed with one hand to the painting. "No. You did. Your coloring—your eyes. I should have seen it before. That...that is a painting of the most famous Maddox—Hacon Maddox. It's hung in this house since Hacon gave it to my family and made them promise never to remove it from House Daris. "I think..." He cut off his words and swallowed hard. "I think that man in the painting is your ancestor. He was a king. The king, in fact, of Torvald. Which means you are related to King Enric, which is why you have the mark of the storms on you—the mark of the Maddox line."

Now my mouth fell open and I stared at Bower. My throat seemed too tight for me to swallow and my breath was coming in short, shallow gulps. Was he mad? I could not be related to a king...and certainly not to one who hated dragons. I blinked and could think of nothing to say. No, this could not be. I pulled my shirt collar closed even tighter, but my glance slid back to the man in the painting, the one with the hard eyes and the secret curving his mouth. The man who had become king of the Middle Kingdom.

And to the mark that looked like a storm cloud that stood out on his neck.

If I was not related to him, then why did I have the same mark?

I gave a soft groan and faced Bower again. This was worse than not finding the right answers—I had found an answer I didn't want to hear.

*   *   *

CHAPTER 12

SCIONS

Saffron was staring at me, her face pale and her words seemingly stuck in her throat.

I clutched the copy of *The Peerage of Torvald*, which I'd been able to salvage from the ruins of the other books. It was the sort of book that was difficult to burn or destroy, thick and heavy with hundreds of pages and thousands of entries. The book had been handed down through my family, and my mother had said this copy dated right back to the times when the abandoned ruin on Mount Hammal was in use as a monastery.

Glancing at the painting of Hacon Maddox, I could almost wish it had been taken away or destroyed. But I knew that Hacon Maddox had given it to the House Daris as both a gift and a reminder that House Daris owed their fortunes to him. He had said it must hang here forever, and so it still hung. As a child, I had feared the face staring down from that painting—he had looked cruel and bad-tempered to me. Even now, I did not want to stand in front of him any longer than I must.

Walking over to Saffron, I took her hand and pulled her with me. Just the fact that she came with me told me she was in more shock than I had imagined.

I led her up to my room on the top floor—the upper floors were always the warmest, and the heavy furniture in my room had been left intact. Or at least a chair and the bed still stood in the room. I had no idea where my clothing had all gone. I had Saffron sit and I put the book on the bed and faced her.

She was rubbing her collarbone, but she pulled her hand down as if it had been burned and said, "It can't be true."

I rubbed the back of my neck. "It could be a coincidence that you share…well, the same mark. But…there are other indications as well."

Sitting on her fingertips as if to warm them, Saffron glared at me.

I held up a hand. "Hear me out." Walking over to the bed, I took up the book and carefully paged through it. I'd been thankful to find it—and three others—still intact. I would have to see if I could get these to Jakson for safekeeping along with my other books.

The pages listed each family with drawings of their flags, their coat of arms, and some held listings including illustrated family trees, the portraits done as very clever colored sketches.

Wetting my lips, I told Saffron, "Torvald has had many noble families over the centuries. As well as a lot of kings and wars. Some family lines ended when the name died out, or changed due to marriage or other intention, such as…"

"Get on with it, Bower," Saffron growled.

Swallowing hard, I turned the next page. There it was—the Maddox line. It was to be found toward the end of the book, and after that only a few listings were present. No one had been keeping track of the current nobles. I glanced at the names and dates, so carefully inscribed.

"Every family works hard to track our ancestors—or the families used to, at least. The birth of every noble child was once cause for a huge celebration, but it all changed with Hacon Maddox."

Saffron shook her head. "Why should I believe that I am a princess or something? It makes no sense. Why did my parents leave me in the wilds if my family is so powerful?"

I winced. "The House Maddox hasn't been the most beloved of all of the monarchs of the Middle Kingdom. They also, by all the stories, haven't gotten along with each other all that well. There is a reason only King Enric came to the throne, and why no other Maddox is here to challenge him, or even to be named his successor. I don't know for sure why you came to be in the Western Isles, but I do know some of the story of the Maddox line. Every noble in the city probably knows a little bit. We have to know it, you see. That is all that is left of our history."

Coming over to Saffron, I settled the book in her lap. "Here is the line of House Maddox. The founder Hacon Maddox is listed, but he thought so little of his wife that he did not include her, nor does he include his father."

Saffron peered at the book and pointed at the illustrations inked onto the page. "Are those drawings of the Iron Guard?"

"They are. They came to Torvald with Hacon Maddox and they fought for him to liberate the city from the terrible dragon-kings. Or so the history goes. Much of the history from that time is…dubious. It was said that Hacon Maddox viewed himself as a hero, but that he also killed half the population of the city. Those who supported the old ways died and those who bowed to King Hacon lived."

Saffron glanced at me, her eyes narrowed. "And your family lived—what does that say of them?"

I took the book back from her. "You don't have to be so hotheaded."

She stood. "Why not? If this king is so bad, why don't you fight instead of all cowering? And if he's good, then fight for him."

I stared at Saffron. Her hair had come undone around her face and right now it seemed almost a fire around her. Sparks flashed in her eyes. She was almost as grand as Jaydra when she was in her dragon form.

And suddenly it all made sense to me.

The Salamanders—their emblem of a dragon's tail, not a lizard. It was not that everyone who opposed House Maddox had died—they had been smarter than that. They'd become a force within the kingdom—the flame within. They must believe House Maddox could be overthrown and the rightful dragon-friends of Torvald put back on the throne. But who was their leader? We needed King Enric to have order and control, but I could see now why King Enric had become so harsh with his laws—he feared the Salamanders. He didn't want anyone studying the past in case the city turned against him. But I was starting to worry that perhaps King Enric had turned against Torvald.

Saffron thumped a hand onto the book. "You have not given me proof of anything. You've just told me my great-great-whatever used those metal soldiers to drive away the dragons. Dragons like Jaydra! Well, I don't believe it." She huffed out a breath and half turned away.

I stepped in front of her again. "Saffron, that is all in the past. But this is what you have to look at now." Opening the book again, I pointed to a broken family branch and one name that stood out

I tapped the name. "Vance Maddox was, by all that is known, the younger brother to Hacon. Legend has it that he was seduced by the dragon-friends of Torvald and ended up betraying his own brother during the liberation of Torvald, as it's often called. Some said Vance was put to death, but other stories hold that his brother cursed him with misfortune. This book is one of the oldest in the kingdom and has been kept accurate by my family for centuries, and look at what is written."

The page was smeared and blurry due to the poor treatment my library had met with, but next to Vance Maddox's name someone had written in the name Iris and under that was the note of a girl child named Amelia. "Wasn't that your mother's name?" I asked.

Saffron glanced at the book and her face paled. She sat down with a thump and put her face in her hands. Looking up at me, she asked, "Nothing is well. What am I going to tell Jaydra? How can I ever meet my real blood-kin family knowing what they did? And how can I go back to the Western Isle?" Tears shimmered in her eyes.

I put a hand on her shoulder. "Saffron, maybe this is a chance for all of us to do better. What if you've come here to convince King Enric that dragons are good? What if, because of you, peace comes to the land? This is a chance for House Maddox to become something far better than it has been."

Shaking her head, she stood. "Is it? I thought I would be pleased to find out about my family. Instead, I find they are nothing that I want. It's like with this city—it's dirty and not what anyone said. What if I'm the one who only brings trouble with me? You just don't understand what I needed from my family—and now…now how can I ever ask them for anything!" With a deep sob, she turned and ran from the room.

I thought about following her, but another thought popped into my head.

Better to leave Saffron to settle.

It was an odd thought, for it didn't feel like my own.

Heading back to the library—books, or the few I had at least, were one thing that brought me comfort—I settled to the task of trying to rescue all the pages I could.

This had to be difficult for Saffron and it wouldn't surprise me if she left tomorrow and never returned. But if she stayed, perhaps she could change King Enric's mind about dragons.

Even such a thought made my head whirl. We might see a whole new history begin. And then I looked at the torn pages, the books ripped into shreds. All ruined and for what—just to keep history unknown?

Settling into sorting out the pages gave me not just comfort, but I also thought of my time away from the city. It had not been that long, but at one time if someone had asked me what the kingdom would do without King Enric I would have been horrified. It was unthinkable. Now I began to wonder if Saffron could change him—and if she could not, then perhaps the Salamanders should be given the power to put King Enric off the throne.

However, there was still the Iron Guard—they would protect King Enric at all cost. It seemed an impossible idea to even consider the king stepping down willingly for the good of the kingdom.

But what if I left with Saffron and her dragon?

Outside in the stables right now there was a living dragon, capable of the most amazing things. Looking down at the ruined books, they seemed far less important to me. I had been flying on a dragon.

I smoothed another rumpled page that could be salvaged. Someone else someday would need this knowledge. For me, it was all stored in my head.

I don't need these books—I can't hide behind them anymore.

Taking the pages I could save, I found a discarded chest, folded the pages into an oilskin that had been left in the kitchen. In the garden, I pried loose a rock and tucked the pages away under that. Someone else would find this treasure and sort it out. It was time for me to stop reading about adventures and start living them.

Going back up to the library, I took the three books that were still mostly intact. I would take them to Jakson in the morning. For tonight, I would spend a little more time with my old friends.

I stroked a hand over my copy of *Erp's Tales*, an ancient and faded book of stories my father had once read to me. It had been a favorite book, and I was glad to see it had survived when so little else had. Perhaps it had for it looked worn and not worth very much.

The warm glow of memory spread through me. I rubbed my hand over its familiar, board cover. Sitting down, I decided to read just one story—the story of the dog-eared boy who discovered he was actually really an enchanted dog.

I settled back to flick through its pages, using only bright moonlight to read the text.

A fold of thick paper fell out, fluttering to the floor.

Wondering what this could be, I scooped up the page and unfolded it. My chest tightened and my hands numbed.

My father's strong, slanted handwriting marched across the paper—two embossed seals at the bottom marking this as not just from House Daris—but also from another famed house—House Flamma.

My skin prickled. That was a name from legend. But why was this here?

Shaking now, I almost didn't want to read the note. The old anger flared—why had my father not been more cautious? Why had he not begged the king for pardon? Part of me wanted to put away this note, but my curiosity drove me, as it always had. My father had hidden this away before he had been taken away from us and executed. I had to know what he'd written.

Unfolding the page, I read the few lines there.

My son,

If the time has come for you to read this, I have passed beyond this world's troubles. For that, and for not being there to guide you, I offer my heartfelt apologies. But you have already shown, in your few years, the makings of a courageous heart and so at least some of my sadness is comforted. Now I must pass on the terrible burden that you must keep and a trust that you must follow.

King Enric is one of the many reasons why I have chosen to hide this and sought to keep you safe by keeping you ignorant of the truth. So few families of the old regime are alive, and even fewer of those who can be trusted. It was once said that the greatest, next to the kings of Torvald, was the House Flamma. Never forget this.

'Never a Flamma far from her dragon' was the old saying. Your mother and I hoped to secure you a future. However, that was not to be. We were betrayed and so this truth must come to you with these few words.

The House Maddox is not the rightful kings of Torvald. They usurped the throne from the House Flamma-Torvald, dragon-friends and Dragon Riders. The House Flamma-Torvald oversaw the Dragon Academy on Mount Hammal.

Hacon Maddox stole the throne and sought to destroy all dragons. This was not done without one of the oldest of dragons giving this prophecy to the Dragon Riders. Memorize these words and keep Torvald safe.

Old and young will unite to rule the land from above. Upon the dragon's breath comes the return of the True King. It will be his to rebuild the glory of Torvald.

The last word looked hurriedly scrawled and blurred as if my father had not had time for the ink to dry before he had folded this and hidden it.

I leaned my back against the wall, the letter crumpling in my hand.

Everything I thought I'd known about my father suddenly seemed to not be what I'd thought it was.

I'd thought him just a simple man, trying to help others. I'd thought he'd broken the law and had been arrested.

Now I was left wondering. And worried. Why had my father thought this prophecy was the most important thing to leave me? Why had he hidden it? Was this the prophecy the Salamanders thought to use to throw House Maddox from the throne?

I knew but two things now—Saffron was of the House Maddox, and her family had killed mine.

I could only sit and stare at the letter and wonder if I should burn it.

*　　　*　　　*

CHAPTER 13

THE RULER OF TORVALD

Saffron? Jaydra's voice in my head woke me up a fraction before the shadow loomed over my face. I opened my eyes to see red and silver metal—a soldier's helmet. Early dawn glinted across the metal face.

A hand gloved in red metal shot out to almost clasp my arm. But Jaydra had warned me. I was already rolling off the bed where I'd collapsed last night. My boots hit the floor and anger bubbled up, hot and dark.

I can destroy them.

The thought came on a rising wave of fury—at Bower for telling me I was a Maddox, at my family for what they had done, at the world for being so unjust. I let the power surge through me like the front of a storm. Fragments of words and dragon-fire sizzled in my chest. I thought of Jaydra's golden eyes when she was angry and Zenema's powerful teeth and claws. I called on the force within me and the world turned white.

Saffron! Jaydra called out again to me with desperate need, a roar in my mind. *I am losing you—come back to me!*

I realized I'd almost snapped my connection with Jaydra. This had happened before when I'd been angry and had summoned the magic within me. It was too much like the time I almost plummeted to my doom on the cliffs.

Gulping a breath, I tried to focus on the world around me. I dodged another metal hand as the giant guard in the room reached for me. His fingers raked the wall. I turned for the window, intending to throw myself out of it. I would get to Jaydra and then come back and burn this silly city to the ground.

A dull voice ground out one word: "Stop." This time the metal hand caught me by the shoulder. It was like being held by a mountain, the grip seemed unbreakable, but I feared my bones might break under such a force. The Iron Guard held me fast.

Jaydra was roaring in my mind. The Iron Guard spun me away from the window and I saw a small man in a uniform.

The small man stepped up to me. As soon as he spoke I realized he was the one who had ordered me to stop—he was controlling the Iron Guard.

Thin lipped, he looked as if he'd smelled something sour. He told me, "Don't resist if you want your friend to live."

A muffled thump sounded from outside the room and a shout that sounded like Bower.

I shivered in the cold dawn and tried to pull free of the grip on my arm and shouted at the guard, "Don't hurt him."

The guard stepped closer to me. "You do not give the orders. One word from me and you will be torn limb from limb." The Iron Guard grabbed my other arm and began to pull. I yelled. My shirt slipped down from my shoulder and the man in front of me stepped back his eyes widening.

I knew then what I must do. "Harm me, and the king himself will have your head."

Eyes narrowing, the guard stepped up to me and touched the black mark on my collarbone as if it was dirt that could be scrubbed away. He frowned and nodded to the Iron Guard. "Take her. The other traitor, too. We'll sort this out at the palace."

I threw my thoughts at Jaydra, afraid she would leap into this and be hurt. I was not yet certain if she was a match for these Iron Guards, but I knew I was too angry to control myself or my magic. Jaydra was much the same. I could imagine her smashing this house and the others around it in search of me, or setting fire to the entire neighborhood. "Jaydra. Hide."

Den-sisters fight together! I could sense Jaydra shifting back into her dragon form. It would only be a short leap until she flew up to the floor where I was being held.

No, Jaydra! I need you safe—I need Bower to be safe. I focused on how worried I was for Bower.

I knew it was harsh to use her liking for Bower against her, but if these Iron Guard had once driven all the dragons from this city, they might know how to kill a single dragon. I also focused on my thoughts that perhaps Bower was right and I could change the king's mind. *Jaydra, I have to meet my people and this Iron Guard will take me to them.*

I might not be very clever in the ways of the world, but I knew that if I wanted everyone in Torvald to see the beauty and loyalty of a dragon they must see a dragon at its best and not in a rage.

Jaydra sent back to me a rage so strong it knocked me back on my heels. I let the Iron Guard drag me from the room and kept my focus on Jaydra.

Hide, I urged her. *Use your dragon tricks here. As soon as you can, fly away. Go back to the Western Isles. Tell den-mother Zenema what happened here. She'll know what to do.*

Reluctantly, Jaydra's anger faded. She withdrew from my mind before I could tell if she would do as I asked. I could still feel her annoyance. If something did happen and she felt me in pain and distress, I feared she would tear the city apart to get to my side.

It was comforting to have a dragon on my side. That let me push back my shoulders and nurse my anger instead of giving into fear.

We marched down the stairs and into the biggest room on the first floor. Bower lay on the floor and one of the Iron Guard stood over his immobile and silent body. For a moment, I feared Bower must be dead, but he gave a groan. His face looked cut and blood dripped from the corner of his mouth. I struggled to slip from the grasp of the Iron Guard, but he would not release me, so I slanted a look at the human guard. "Let me go, or face the king's wrath when I tell him what has been done this day."

The man's mouth pulled down. He hesitated, but at last gave a nod. The Iron Guard released his hold, and I knelt next to Bower and touched a finger to his forehead. His skin seemed so hot.

"Saffron," Bower gasped.

"At least you are alive. Oh, the trouble you seem to find for yourself—and for me as well."

"Enough. Put them in irons," The guard stepped out of the front door and spoke to someone standing there. "Your information proved true. The king will remember you for this."

"And the reward? There was a reward mentioned."

My skin chilled at the sound of that voice.

"Vic," Bower snarled. He struggled to push up from the floor. I helped him to stand, but the Iron Guard clamped shackles onto our ankles and wrists. "I was your friend."

Vic Cassus glanced into the house, eyes wide and startled. A plain, heavy traveling cloak swept from his head down to his booted ankles. Probably trying to hide his identity, I thought.

I stared back at him, wondering if I could accuse him of something that would have him arrested. But I glanced at Bower and saw the sorrow in his eyes—even now, he thought of this man as his friend.

"Sorry, Bower. I'm not sure you understand how things work now in the city. This is not your realm of olden tales." Vic lifted a hand. "You know well that if my family does not have the king's good grace—and money to keep the old house going—we shall perish. Just as did House Daris. King Enric's word is law, and King Enric has vowed to reward all who are loyal to him. I for one am loyal."

"And why will he ever trust you since you have proven you will betray a friend?" I spat at him. "You may profit in the short run, but in the long, you will find you have no friends."

He had the decency to look away from me, refusing to meet my stare. Bower was dragged into an enclosed wagon and the Iron Guard pushed me in as well.

For a moment, I listened for Jaydra's voice—but I could not hear her. I could not reassure her that everything was going to be well. She was gone. Relief eased my shoulders for a moment. After all, how could I reassure her that Bower and I would be safe when I had no idea if that was the truth.

*   *   *

Slumped against the wooden wall of the enclosed wagon, I could only hold my aching ribs and wince as the wheels rumbled over the cobblestones. Saffron's chains clanked and so did mine. The wagon smelled of stale urine, sweat and fear. My only consolation was that I had hidden away my books and the letter from my father with the prophecy—but I wanted to kick myself for trusting Vic.

I'd thought he would be himself—the man who watched the shows at the courthouse but who did not involve himself. I had thought him too good a friend to ever take coins to betray someone. He was right in one respect—I had not known before this how much things had changed. If the king had everyone frightened enough to sell out the very people who were supposed to be their best friends, then life here had become intolerable.

But outside the wagon the sounds of a fair starting up could be heard—music and vendors calling out. The wagon rumbled on past those sounds and started to climb—to the palace.

Worst of all—I had let Saffron down. I might as well have betrayed her myself, for I was the one who had trusted Vic.

I had never felt so tired, so low or in as much pain as this. Closing my eyes, I listened to the city, wondering that life could go on seemingly without a protest over two innocents being swept up to be taken to what would probably be their deaths.

And I had been one of those who had turned away from such things.

I could remember Master Julian's scream still—and how I had wanted to help. But I hadn't acted in time. Again, I had been slow—I had not gotten us away from House Daris. No, I'd wanted my books saved and for Saffron to sleep in a bed, and all that would now cost us dearly.

From outside the wagon, I heard the guard shout to make way for the king's Iron Guard.

I wondered if the guard thought I was the leader of the rebellious Salamanders or the most dangerous criminal in all of Torvald?

For some reason, they thought me deadly. That was the least true thing possible.

I let out a sigh. What would the king do with me if he ever saw that letter from my father—the one with the prophecy that was supposed to lead to his downfall? The answer was obvious. He would do what every king had done when faced with a threat to the throne—he would have the Iron Guard tear me apart. Just as King Enric had done to others. I turned my face into the wall.

"Bower? Bower, will you stop sulking? We must talk and I fear we don't have much time."

I turned my head to see Saffron sitting opposite me, a chain hanging between her ankles and one between her hands. "I'm such a fool."

She frowned. "For trusting that Vic? Yes, you are. But that is not to the point."

I winced and tried to sit straighter. "What is to the point? My head feels like a broken melon, my sides were trampled upon by an Iron Guard, and it is a miracle we are not yet the both of us dead."

"It's not a miracle. It's my mark." She gestured to her collarbone. "I told them I must see the king. I am going to try what you suggested—I am going to convince him dragons are good and that he does need to fear them."

Letting my head fall back against the wagon wall, I took a shallow breath that almost did not make my sides ache. "Saffron, I was wrong. I was wrong about Vic. I fear I was wrong about the king. I don't think he will listen to reason, and I fear if you try you will die." I lifted a hand and touched the corner of my mouth. I had the taste of copper blood on my tongue and was one of my teeth loose?

Saffron's frown deepened. "Stop acting like that. You did what you said. You helped me find my family. Now I have to do the next part."

I glanced at her. "Which is?"

She shook her head. "I can't tell you—I shouldn't. Jaydra said I have to be careful with my secrets and I should have paid more attention to her counsel before this."

"Little late for that," I muttered. I fixed a hard stare on Saffron. "If you want counsel, listen to mine. Everyone hates dragons—and they do so because of King Enric. Do not give him a reason to want you dead—do not threaten him in any way."

"I have to try—and your idea was a good one. Why are you so ready to quit?"

"Because Vic was right—I have been living with a head full of stories!"

"And how is that bad?" Saffron asked, glaring at me

The wagon rocked to a halt. Wherever we were, it stank of sewage and I feared we would not be kept anywhere comfortable tonight.

Leaning forward, I told Saffron, "Tell them nothing. Pretend you are just a traveler—you are that. Do not let the king know who you really are! Use that whatever it is thing you do to make yourself vanish and save yourself."

Saffron's mouth took on a mulish downturn. She shook her head. "I'm kin to this king of yours? He'll have to listen to me. I will make him."

I opened my mouth to tell her that was a daft idea. Before I could get the words out, the door to the wagon opened and an Iron Guard yanked me out by my chains. I hit the ground and lay there moaning until I was pulled upright by the guards.

I groaned, but Saffron stepped out of the wagon looking very much like a princess, despite the chains on her ankles and wrists and the skins she wore. She kept her head up and glanced at the guards as if daring them to touch her.

I could only hope she would listen to me and that she and Jaydra would get out of this alive.

We should never have come back.

"Move," the guard shouted.

The Iron Guard dragged me up a few steps and into a circular room. My head was ringing and my sides ached—I wanted to throw up. Instead, I squinted around me, wondering where we were.

It was only then that I recognized the chambers of the courthouse.

The Iron Guard dragged me and pushed Saffron into the main chamber, the very one in which I had seen Master Julian sentenced to his doom. I glanced around at the raised tiers of seats and the galleries of wooden benches, the podium and the tall wooden cabinets. It was supposed to be a fine building, full of pride, honor and grandeur.

Instead, it held only one man—King Enric Maddox.

*   *   *

CHAPTER 14

THE KINDNESS OF KINGS

Saffron stood next to me and it was all I could do not to lean on her. King Enric looked as he had the last time I had seen him—young, tall and elegant in finely embroidered robes of gold and purple. His hair seemed darker and his face—was that a shimmer I saw? One that was not unlike the one I'd first glimpsed on Jaydra when I'd thought I'd seen a horse—or a dragon?

I narrowed my eyes, but I could not quite bring the king's face into focus. I glanced at Saffron. Was she doing something? Was she trying to help us escape?

I turned to look at her, only to see her frowning and staring hard at the king. Was she sensing the same thing I was? Or was she searching for a family resemblance. Certainly the strong chin, the straight nose and the high cheekbones were the same—but I thought Saffron's eyes were larger and held more intelligence. The king I thought only looked cunning.

King Enric glanced at us, his expression a touch bored. He signaled for us to be dragged before him. The Iron Guards stood close, one behind me and one behind Saffron. The king smiled, as if my anger amused him. He brushed an invisible touch of lint from the sleeve of his robe.

The guard fell to one knee, his head bowed. "Sire, these are the traitors Vic of House Cassus informed on."

Despite my wish to remain defiant, I myself oddly entranced. There was something mesmerizing about the young king. Was it the too smooth skin? The piercing blue eyes perhaps? Or the fine robes that swayed as he moved? I couldn't look away from the king as he walked in front of us. He was the ruler of all the Middle Kingdom, the most powerful man in the world. I had been frightened by him and what he represented for so long that it was hard to think of him as being a real person.

Standing in front of him, I realized I had been a Salamander in truth for years—I was one of those dissidents the king had been after. I had defied him with my books, my reading the forbidden, and I had made friends with a dragon. And I was proud of it all.

But another emotion tugged at me.

Behind the king's silks and his back hair and smooth skin, I sensed a power that reminded me a little of the dragon magic I had seen at work with Jaydra who had made herself into a horse. Could Saffron sense it too? It was as if my mind was trying to tell me something, but it could not quite allow the truth to surface.

The king stepped closer and I caught a scent of something. Was that the smell of overripe fruit? Of flowers starting to turn and die?

Suddenly, the king grabbed Saffron's shirt and yanked it down, exposing the mark upon her collarbone.

I gave a low growl, but the Iron Guard slammed a hand down upon my shoulder, and I fell to my knees.

Saffron glanced down at me. The king let her go and stepped in front of me. "Bower, I know who you are." He paused as if he searching for something, almost as if he was scenting the air and sniffing out some truth hidden to me.

My heart seemed to clench and stop. I had always thought the king uncannily powerful, but now I wondered if he could even read minds? Or was there some other secret he knew?

"You are Bower …" He paused again and his stare traveled over my face, searching. I realized he waited for me to betray myself but I had nothing to tell him. Did he want to pull the prophecy from me? My head swam for a moment, but I met his stare. "Of House Daris," he said. Turning away, he smiled at Saffron. "Just as I know who you are—Saffron of House Maddox."

*   *   *

Not my real name…my name is Saffron. Just Saffron.

My mind was whirling as the king's gaze seemed to search into me. His wasn't an unkind face, I thought. In fact, some would think him handsome were it not for the glittering, intense concentration in his eyes. If a dragon ever looked at me like that, I would be certain it had the dragon sickness or was about to eat me.

I stared back at him, trying to see some resemblance between us. Was there something in the set of his eyes and cheekbones that I recognized from having seen my own reflection in the waters of home?

The king put a hand on my birthmark. His touch was cold, and yet a bolt of recognition shot through me. He was connected to me just as I was to him. Something in our blood spoke to each other.

The king gave a nod. "I know exactly who you are."

For a moment, a giddy delight flooded me. I had found someone who knew magic at last. And then I pulled back, staring at him in confusion. I didn't know what to feel— angry still at the poor treatment we'd been given, outraged by his Iron Guard, a touch frightened. But if we were kin, he must listen to me.

I am Saffron Maddox, but I am also Saffron dragon-friend. A spark of magic warmed my chest.

"Guards, take Bower of House Daris to the dungeons." Turning from me, the king lifted a hand to dismiss the guards.

"No," I said and had to clear my throat to keep my voice steady. "You cannot."

The king glanced at me, his eyebrows raised. "Cannot? That is not a word to use with a king."

He stepped in front of me again. "You may be a Maddox, but you do not yet know what that means. You will learn."

I shook my head. I could not allow Bower to be hurt because of me. Bower had come back to the city for my sake—so I might find my people. Well, I had done that. And Bower was not going to suffer for having helped me.

Summoning the spark of dragon magic, I allowed my fear and anger to twist inside of me until it was like a storm beating against the shore. I threw it against the king.

For an instant, he staggered back. His image seemed to wobble. And then anger sparked in his eyes. And my magic went wild.

A thunderous crack split the room. I went flying out of the Iron Guard's hold and smacked into a stone wall. The air smelled of smoke, singed wood and lightning. My head was ringing. When I could open my eyes, the king bent over me. He glanced to the side, so did I. An Iron Guard had been rent by my magic. Half of the metal body tried to move and twist, but it could only flop about.

There was nothing inside of it.

Exhausted, I closed my eyes and let the world fade away.

*   *   *

PART 4

AMONGST KINGS

CHAPTER 15

YOUR RIGHTFUL PLACE

You must follow the truth in your blood!

Zenema's voice seemed to be coming from the mouth of a woman with short, frizzy hair tied back. She stared at me with sorrowful eyes and wrapped a blanket around me to protect me against the cold of a dangerous sea journey.

Mother?

I thought the word to her but she couldn't seem to hear my thoughts. She kept looking at me with pity, despair and a wild hope in her eyes. They were the sort of eyes a dragon might have—a deep, golden green, flecked with glittering silver.

You have to wake up, Saffron.

The voice coming from the woman changed again, it was not a human voice nor was it Zenema's.

"Jaydra?" I whispered.

Who are you really, Saffron?

This time the voice seemed to belong to an old man.

I don't know. Surely this woman; my mother should know who I was. "Why did you leave me? I asked, tears stinging my eyes.

I never left you, Saffron. You had to hide. You have to hide.

The woman's skin changed, becoming ridged, hard like a dragon's scales. Her neck elongated and her body widened and wings sprouted. Was I looking at Zenema or Jaydra? I could no longer tell. My family was human. My dragons my family. The woman-dragon regarded me with fear, worry and a challenge.

Was this the dragon inside me—the part of me where Jaydra's mind and mine touched?

"Who are you?"

"I am Saffron," I mumbled. I knew no other answer.

You have to wake up, Saffron.

Why was she or they so insistent? *"Who are you?*

"I am Saffron dragon-friend, Saffron den-sister to Jaydra and den-daughter to Zenema."

Wrong! Who are you?

"I—I don't know!" I found myself wailing the words. "Who do you think I am? Who do you want me to be?"

Saffron—you have to wake up now!

I coughed and sat bolt upright. I lay on something soft. A knocking continued. Jaydra had been trying to wake me up, aware I was asleep or unconscious and in danger. I heard a click and turned to see a door open.

I reached for my belt knife only to realize I was not wearing it. Glancing down I saw I was not wearing an awful lot. A gown of white linen with heavy embroidering around the neck and hem covered me. I looked up. The bed had a blue canopy over the top and blue curtains around it and four huge dark posts.

I had no recollection of how I'd gotten here or even where here was.

The room seemed large, with a small, wooden cabinet that gleamed. A standing mirror stood to one side of one high, thin window slit. Tapestries on the wall showed a man I now recognized as Hacon Maddox leading a charge of Iron Guards across a battlefield.

"My lady?"

Looking over, I saw the intruder Jaydra had been trying to warn me about.

She looked to be a girl no older than me, dressed in a blue gown. She carried a silver tray with bowls of steaming water, scented soaps, and what smelled like roast meat. I was suddenly starving. She looked to be near that, for she was as thin as a sapling.

"What lady?" I said and frowned at her.

"Sorry, ma'am. Did I say it wrong? Should it be princess? Your highness?" The skinny girl reached a hand up to touch blonde hair she had scraped back into a knot. Her face paled and her hands started to shake.

Rubbing at my head, I said, "Come in and shut the door. I'm just not used …" I let the words trail off and waved a hand. I wasn't used to any of this.

"Yes my…ma'am." She came in, shut the door with a kick, and said, "I'm to help you wash and dress, and have brought breakfast, ma'am." She put the tray on the bed and stood with her eyes downcast and her hands folded in front of her.

Feeling the ache in my shoulders, I remembered my magic had thrown me against some wood…or a wall. I looked at the tapestries again. "Is this… the palace?" I asked. Wasn't that where everyone had said the king lived?

"Yes, ma'am." She looked up, her eyes bright. "Breakfast first?"

"Why didn't the king throw me in the dungeons?"

"Ma'am?" The girl's face paled. She blinked several times and swallowed hard.

"What are you not allowed to have a thought of your own? Or an opinion?"

"King Enric is great and terrible, my lady," she said the words clear and slow, as if they were a magic formula that kept her safe.

I swung my legs out of the bed and stood, trying to stretch the aches and knots from my muscles. The girl was staring at me, eyes wide and her mouth open.

Walking over to the window I judged the room too high to leap out of and the narrow slit too it slim to climb through.

Den-sister? Jaydra's mind touched mine. *Saffron in need?*

I let out a breath, relieved that Jaydra had not listened to me and had not left me. *I'm being fed breakfast. And I must stay to try and find Bower before we can escape.*

Good. All three leave this place together. Jaydra agreed with a firm determination to try and sniff out where Bower was being kept.

"Ma'am?" The girl wet her lips and stared at me.

With a glance at her, I asked, "Is there a river? A waterfall I can use to wash?" I looked the girl over. She was as thin as a stick. "You can eat some of my food while I do wash."

The girl shook her head and kept staring at me. I decided there were no waterfalls nearby. I pointed to the tray, took up a hot roll that I ate, and then used the water she had bought to wash as best I could under the white gown I wore. The girl's cheeks reddened. She turned away to pull another dress from the wooden cupboard.

I shook my head and crossed my arms. "I want my own breeches and jerkin, not that flouncy dress.

The girl's eyes widened. "But…"

"Aren't you supposed to do what I ask?" She nodded. "Well, fetch me my clothes." She ran out and came back with my skins, which had been brushed off. I dressed and the girl stood where she was, not moving a muscle.

I waved at the rolls. "Try one. And I don't look that bad, do I?" I pulled my hair back and tied it with a leather thong from my pouch. The girl hadn't brought back my knife, but everything else seemed in place.

Even though I didn't want to admit it, I felt better with food inside me and after a night's sleep. I started to plan.

Clearly the king recognizes I am a Maddox. He may even be trying to win me over to his side. I will demand the release of Bower—and then call on Jaydra to help us escape! It was a simple enough plan, and one that I hoped wouldn't require me to wear dresses… *They better not have hurt him…* I thought about Bower, looking at all of the food laid out before me and instantly felt sick. There was really no way that I could eat a thing while he was wherever he was, starving? Being beaten?

"Go on, girl." I said to her. "Break your fast. You look as if you need all the food you can lay hand to and it'll only go to waste otherwise."

The girl opened and closed her mouth, and shook her head. "I can't, ma'am. The king ordered me to bring the food to you. It's for you."

I was stunned at this strange behavior. Growing up with dragons had left me practical as far as the fundamentals of life were concerned. If you were hungry and you weren't stealing a den-mate's food, you ate. If you were tired and you weren't in danger, you slept. If you were thirsty, you drank. The idea of this girl not eating when she was clearly near starving and there was plenty of food for both of us, struck me as insane. "No one is going to mind. And no one is going to tell. Eat!"

"No, the king is great and terrible," She screwed her eyes shut and pinched herself on the arm.

"What are you doing?" I asked.

"No one disobeys the king, ma'am. If he said this food was for you, it is for you alone."

I scowled. This king sounded very unlike any den-mother. "If this is my food, I can do with it as I wish. And I want you to eat some of it. Fair enough?"

"I don't know." The girl stared at the floor.

"It's my food, so I can give some away. Besides, doesn't the king have someone else taste his food? I've heard stories that kings need to do that to avoid poison. So, you've got to help me out." I took two of the rolls, started to eat one and gave her the other. Gingerly, the girl took a bite. I nodded and smiled. She smiled back and we finished the rolls together and started into a plate of ham.

When we finished, the girl smoothed her gown. "After you are ready, I am to take you to King Enric." She frowned at my breeches and boots. "I was to offer you a selection of dresses."

"You did, but remember what I said about the food? Same goes for the dresses. If they are mine, it is my choice for what I do with them."

The girl nodded. "Yes, ma'am. As you wish. Please follow me." She led me to a stone stairwell that seemed to spiral down almost forever.

At every landing, tall, barred windows looked out onto the city and onto green gardens just below us. The view seemed to show every part of the city, every street and house. I could see the patchwork of stone, slate and thatch roofs, and colorful banners for the fair going up and what seemed like crowds of people in the streets. It almost looked like the view from the back of a dragon.

The palace itself seemed to have rich orchards and gardens close by, surrounded by tall walls. Beyond that stretched the wilds of the mountain and a rocky ridge. It would be easier to escape up onto the mountain—once we found Bower. Jaydra would be able to swoop down, pick us up and we would be far away from here before the Iron Guard could even react. Walking down the stairs I thought back to having seen that one metal guard, still twitching and moving as if it was alive, even though I could see nothing inside of it. Magic had split it in half—but was that the only way to destroy such a metal soldier?

We came to the bottom landing and the girl stepped back. A long corridor with a stone floor and paintings and statues on each side stretched out in front of me.

The girl waved me forward so I stepped into the long room and found myself looking down on yet another and even bigger room.

I stood in what seemed to be just part of an incredibly large space. A wooden railing stood between me and the lower floor, and steps led down on either side. Underneath me, I could see more doors and staircases. The room below was lit by a window in the ceiling made of colored glass and lights—dozens of candles—hung from the ceiling along with crystals. I'd never seen anything like it.

Looking around, I saw the paintings were all of my family—or of House Maddox. Every one of them had hair like mine. A few had the black-cloud birthmark in a spot where it showed. And every one of them seemed to be fighting something or someone—they were either riding horses into battle, or leaping across the decks of a ship, and even the women seemed to have swords in their hands or at their sides. They all stared out of the paintings with what looked like grim determination.

"Lady Saffron."

I looked around for where the voice had come from and saw the king dismiss a man in purple robes. The king strolled up the stairs to my side.

"King," I said with a nod.

"Please call me Enric. We are just about cousins, are we not? Or perhaps something even closer. I trust you slept well, Lady Saffron?" He lips curved up, but it did not seem much of a smile to me.

Why are you trying to be nice to me now?

None of this felt right. I stared at him. "I was unconscious very deeply, thank you."

The king's lips curved even more. "That is why I sent up a substantial breakfast. Using our magic always makes one hungry. You will need your strength if you are to ever gain control of it."

My mouth fell open. *My magic?* I stared at him, all thoughts driven out of my head. But of course he knew. I had tried to blast him into a wall and had only succeeded in doing that exact thing to myself.

"What do you know of magic?" I demanded.

He wagged a finger at me. "There is *so* much for you to learn!"

I started to demand that he teach me, but stopped myself and bit my lower lip. How dare he talk to me as if I had just hatched from an egg? I was den-sister to dragons! I crossed my arms. "I don't think I need you to teach me anything," I muttered.

The king waved at the paintings in the long room. "Look around you, Saffron! Look at all that House Maddox has achieved. You have no idea yet what a noble and ancient bloodline you carry."

I found myself looking at the paintings—I had to know my family. Even if I did not like them.

Enric strolled over to a portrait. "Hacan Maddox—my father who was king before me—who defeated the Red Pirate Army. This was Yulic Maddox, my aunt, who routed out the Witch of Haselbad from her rocky fortress. And my cousin, Mado Maddox, pacifier of the southern hot lands. And here is Hacon Maddox, liberator of Torvald. Great generals, heroes, explorers, and wise scholars. But the truth of our success lies in the fact that throughout our line the magic has coursed strong. We could never have achieved half of what we did were it not for the power within our veins, given to us by the might of the storms."

"Storms can give such things?" I said, frowning deeply.

He shook his head. "Do you think the House Maddox begins with Torvald? It was only in the last century that we came to this fertile land. Ah, yes, child there is so much you have yet to learn. So much of who you are and where we come from, and what gifts have been given to you."

Follow the truth in the blood. Wasn't that what Zenema had advised me?

To control my magic, I had to understand my family—I had to discover myself.

Did Enric know this?

"What if I don't want to know about my magic?" I said. I shifted on my feet, feeling oddly treacherous to myself.

Enric laughed. He raised his arms out to his sides, his green robes spreading out like elegant wings. His body lifted into the air and he floated into the middle of the vast room below us.

Even though I had grown up around dragons and magic, it was still unnerving to see another person use such power. And control it utterly.

"I can fly, as can you, Saffron. The power is strong in me, as it is strong in you." He hovered back to where I stood and landed lightly on his feet. "We are the last of our line, and the Maddox blood runs true in us. With that blood runs power, coursing through our veins." He put out his hand.

I shook my head.

Enric frowned and then sighed. He murmured words I couldn't quite hear, but the air swelled with his magic. It smelled of pines and spice. I was suddenly lifted into the air. My heart pounded and my breath caught in my chest.

I had never known anyone who could not just use magic for themselves but use it on others.

Part of me knew that I, too, would be able to fly like this if I could just control the power.

"Saffron, Saffron." The king whirled me around him. "You have no idea what you are capable of. You have no idea what our family has achieved. What greatness we can go onto claim."

With a wave of his hand, the floor changed into a perfect miniature of the city of Torvald. I watched in awe as Enric manipulated the image to become a map of the Middle Kingdom and then the world. I could see the coasts, the wilds, the mountains, and even the glittering blue of the Great Western Ocean and the Western Isles.

He changed the view so I could see the lands to the east, dry and dusty, a land that seemed plagued by storms.

"The House Maddox has traveled far to find our fate— and has ridden even farther," the king murmured, showing the vast lands of the east, with an inland sea I had never seen anything like.

"We have explored places of legend to these people. We have been where their very myths were created. And we have brought power with us, living inside of our blood."

With a clap of his hands, the images below changed into snow-clad mountains that seemed to exist at the edge of the world. It was as if we were dragons, flying to the very ends of the earth, scorched by the sun's rays and chilled by the moon's rising.

The view changed to a deep gorge and then to a grove where one tree, impossibly tall, stood at the very center, it's leaves blue and silver on one side and golden on the other. Fruits like stars hung in its branches.

This cannot be real.

I gasped. We flew closer and Enric reached out a hand, plucked one of the shining star-fruit. He held it out to me.

Stunned, I took it. In my hand, the star-fruit turned into a strange, luminous yellow-green fruit. When I bit into it, it tasted like coconut and mango, fresh, succulent and sweet.

"I can teach you how to use that magic within you, Saffron," Enric said, his voice low and soft.

He clapped his hands again. The taste of the fruit faded and the star-fruit disappeared from my hand. We stood again on the floor, but the huge room seemed dull now compared with what I had seen.

I shook myself and tried to remember this man had thrown Bower into the dungeon. He wasn't my friend—but he was my blood.

And didn't I need to learn to control my magic?

Zenema said I must follow my blood.

In my own way, I was actually more dangerous right now than Enric. He could target his magic—I could not. And someday my magic might just explode from within. I could become too angry, too furious over something, and then I might harm whoever was with me.

I wouldn't have to stay here forever. I wouldn't have to even agree to like him. And it would give me time enough to find Bower.

The king stepped closer to me. "Saffron, there is a prophecy that has been written about us. It babbles on about old and young uniting, and rebuilding the glory of Torvald. The rebels thought they could keep these words from me—they knew if I discovered their prophecy I might use it to build even more power. Now I can see the whole truth and not just part of it—this prophecy talks about us,

Saffron. You and me. Old and young—for I am older than you by a little bit, aren't I?" He smiled and took my hand.

I tugged my hand away. "What else does it say?"

"Oh, something about dragon's breath, which must mean smoke and fire…and from that comes the return of the True King. Don't you see what that part means? Torvald must burn. I've worked hard to bring in every bit of scum and every rebel to the city. I've planned this for months now. I've held out the promise of a fair—that's all it took. Food and frivolity and they flock to this…this wretched place. But the Iron Guard will seal it up. We'll watch it burn. We'll build fresh. When we stretch out our hands—our united powers—we shall rule the entire world!"

"No…wait…you want to destroy your city? Your palace?"

Enric shrugged. "My what? This is my prison. I cannot walk the streets without death threats thrown at me. These Salamanders, as they call themselves, wish to steal my throne. But I've outsmarted them. They'll be the ones trapped within Torvald's walls. My Iron Guards will shut the gates and keep everyone trapped like rats. They'll have their fair and their drink and food and then the dragon's breath will consume them and I shall rise as the True King."

"Breath? You mean fire? You cannot intend to burn everyone—to kill everyone. And we cannot…are we not cousins, or are you not my uncle?" She shook her head. "This is no plan at all."

"It is. It will be the prophecy come true!" Enric's eyes flashed. "It must come true, and it will just as I envisioned it."

Throat closed tight with loathing, I wondered what this man wouldn't do for power.

"We are the products of destiny, you and I, Saffron! We are not bound by any laws but those we make. We are the last two of our line, and we must preserve the power of the Maddox's for all time!"

The man was mad. But how else—and *who* else, would ever teach me how to use this gift inside of me? If he was telling me the truth, then he was the only one left alive who could!

Bower. The name blossomed in my mind.

"What about my friend? Bower of House Daris?"

The king blinked, as if for a moment he could not even remember the name. "Ah, yes. The young pup who kidnapped you? He is a traitor to the crown and a traitor to Torvald." The king shrugged. "However, if you like him, he will come to no harm. But I cannot have him endangering your life again!"

I pressed my lips tight. If I could have a promise that Bower would be safe, it would buy a little time. But I could not leave until we also found a way to stop the king from destroying Bower's city. I could not leave all these people to die.

I looked at the king, who was watching my face intensely. "I want to learn how to control my magic." I kept my tone flat and my voice even. I didn't want to betray that I had no intention of helping him with any part of the rest of his plan.

This time his smile warmed his eyes. "Excellent, my dear. You have come home at last, to your real family."

*　　*　　*

CHAPTER 16

IN A DARK PLACE

I was thankful I was not dead, but that was about the best I could do. I had been tossed into a small cell with only straw on the floor and a slop bucket. Rats squealed in the darkness, and water dripped constantly. Shivering, I curled up in a corner. The chains had been taken off my feet and wrists, but I couldn't remember how long ago I'd been tossed in here. I slept and woke, and sometimes a pan of gruel would be pushed into my cell through a slot near the floor of the iron door. Had days passed or just mere hours?

Given how my body still ached, I was going to judge not that long in this dark, cold cell. It was hard to tell what bit hurt the most—my sides where the guards had punched me, my back, my wrists, or my hands where I'd tried punching a guard.

Well, this is certainly an adventure, but not one I'd wanted. At least now I expected no better treatment than this at the hands of my king.

What happened to justice? What happened to a fair trial?

My head spun slightly from thirst and hunger—they never fed me much and only had pushed in a cup of water once. The only light entering the room was a grayish tinge that could be from dawn or late afternoon. It lit the cell high up, near the ceiling. A single vent, about the width of a hand and only a finger's width high was all I had. Even if I could climb, I wouldn't have been able to look outside.

Every now and then I heard the stamp of metal boots—the Iron Guard. It seemed to me they were unusually active. Or maybe it was just that I was used to them standing about.

I wasn't even sure if where I was—were the palace dungeons inside the palace? Were they underneath it? Up on the abandoned Mount Hammal? I strained to hear something that might help me know where I was, but could only hear a vague rushing of wind or water. Was I near a cliff? A river?

What made everything worse was also the not knowing.

After the guards started to drag me away, I had heard an almighty crash from inside the courthouse. A bag had been thrown over my head and I'd been thrown back into that prison wagon. When I woke in the dungeon, being dragged to my cell, I had no idea where Saffron might be or what had happened to her.

I had tried shouting her name, but no one answered. Not even a guard or a fellow prisoner   telling me to shut up. I wrapped my arms around my knees. I had been left with my fears.

Had the king taken pity on Saffron? Had he decided he wanted to keep one of his relatives close?

I kept thinking about what the king might have done to Saffron. The best I could hope for is that he'd exiled her. Or perhaps she had been able to escape using her dragon tricks, and she and Jaydra would never have to come back.

That thought brought me a smile and a sliver of hope. It also left me thinking about what would happen to me.

I doubted I would like whatever the king had planned for me, but I wanted to meet my fate with my head held high. And certain that Saffron was safe.

I had time enough to think about my father, and remember kinder years when he would read to me the prohibited stories after all of the servants had gone to bed.

He must have wanted me to know all the stories had to be kept alive. He read to me the stories of House Flamma—of the great Dragon Riders Agathea and Sebastian. I wasn't sure why those had always been his favorite legends, but I was at least glad now that we had shared some time.

I began to remember the long weeks where he would disappear on what he always said were trips to trade for goods. Odd merchants would come to our door, often late at night.

Was that the reason why that old man had helped me escape the city—had he known me for Nev's son? Was that the reason why Jakson had spoken the dissident's slogan to me, telling me to remember, 'The flame exists within'?

"What a fool I've been," I said, saying the words just to hear a voice—any voice.

It made sense now. My father had to have at least been in touch with the Salamanders. He, in his day, had been waiting for a prophecy to be realized that had never come true. He faced his own death, but he had made certain I would know the prophecy and know that House Maddox must fall one day.

A mixture of shame, pride and gratitude welled within me. I forgot my anger at him for leaving me when I had been so very young and in need of him. Even though I had been terrible at riding horses, and fencing and strategy, he had taught me the truth of the past. He had allowed me to read and to learn.

He knew that one day I might face hard choices just as he had. But I, too, had trusted the wrong friends.

I had trusted Vic when I shouldn't have. I had allowed Saffron to talk me into returning to Torvald when I knew better. And right now…well, right now King Enric was planning something and I didn't know what it was, but it could not bode well for Torvald.

But what could I do?

I'd fallen into a trap. I was as doomed as my father had been.

Had he been held here? Had he faced this dark place and knew his life would be over soon.

I thought about all the things I might have done if my life had taken a different turn. If House Daris had never fallen on bad times. I could have started building new opportunities for the poorest to work and helped to rebuild the city. If House Daris had been rich, we might have funded new farms and grain mills. We could have sacrificed some of the family profits from trade to help the city, which in turn would have brought even more trade to the city.

Remembering my time hiding in Monger's Lane, I knew the entire city was teetering on the edge of collapse. It wouldn't be long before the streets ran with fire and blood if the king kept up this level of oppression. Why was he holding a month-long fair to make everyone feel better for a time?

Closing my eyes, I knew I had made a mistake with Vic. I had expected the best of him. Was I now thinking that of the king?

If I were Enric, what would I do if I faced a capital ready to fall apart? What would I do if I faced people ready to be done with my rule?

Thinking back to how the king had swept Master Julian from the chamber, I realized the king would do the same to anything else that he viewed as standing in his path to power.

Cold swept into me, chilling me to my heart.

This fair—it was as much a trap as Vic had set for me in House Daris.

The king was luring people into the city—what he had planned for them I did not know. But suddenly I knew I had to escape. I had to warn the city. I had to stop a looming disaster—or Torvald would be no more.

Staring into the darkness, the harsh reality of the dungeon cell hit me hard. I might never escape. I might die with my city.

Longing settled deep inside me—oh, what would I trade to be on the road with Saffron and Jaydra and no bigger a problem than where would we sleep?

But that life was done. Somehow I had to warn Torvald that its king meant them as much harm as he meant me.

*   *   *

The king's gardens were nothing like the islands where I had grown up, but it was still agreeable to get out in the fresh air. I needed to think and plan—and find Bower. So far, I hadn't been able to do any of those things. Caitlyn, the girl who had first brought me breakfast, seemed to be my personal maid. I also had to wonder if she was perhaps a spy for the king.

It was my second day in the palace and the first time I had been allowed outside. Anywhere I went, Caitlyn followed like a skinny shadow. She had at least brought with her a covered basket of fresh rolls and tiny bottles of ginger and lemon beer. I'd already discovered the palace was huge—it would take far too long to search everywhere for Bower. My tower room had a staircase that led to the Rose Hall, the place where the king had shown me some of what the Maddox magic could do. I had thought at first that the Rose Hall had to take up most of the palace, it was so grand. Walking around today, I had realized that my tower and the gigantic Rose Hall were only one part of a structure that had to be ten times larger.

And I was still waiting to learn something about magic—and still wanting to leave as soon as I could. But I was worried.

Everywhere in the palace I saw images of just how much the people had been taught to fear and hate dragons. Paintings showed knights slaying dragons. The servants all used sayings that cast dragons as dangerous.

"Evil winds blow cold from a dragon's maw," Caitlyn had told me last night. I'd told her that a dragon's breath was hot, and that had gotten us into an argument over how no one's supposed to know anything about dragons.

Looking up at the dark ruins on the ridgeline near the palace, I asked her now, "Is that the volcano? The one that was said to be a home for dragons? I could see how it would make a good den, those high rocky walls, and lots of heat from below."

"My lady!" Caitlyn was staring at me, her eyes huge.

"What is it?" I asked. I turned to walk down yet another gravel path. All of the paths seemed to be graveled. Why did they do that when they had a perfectly good lawn to walk on instead?

"Dragons, ma'am. You're never supposed to talk about them like you know anything about 'em. It's against the king's wishes and the king is great and terrible!" Her voice had gone high and the words tumbled out almost too fast to follow.

"You mentioned dragons last night in that ridiculous saying of yours—cold winds from a dragon's mouth."

"That's different. We're allowed to say things like that. Just not things like—"

"Like how dragons live, or that they might have families, or that they might actually not be nothing but claws and fangs?" Her mouth opened and closed. I almost laughed, but it wasn't funny. Shaking my head, I told her, "Don't fret, Caitlyn. I won't tell anyone we had this conversation if you don't. I just think it odd that folks go on blaming everything on the ghosts of dragons. Why not blame this garden for not having trees to shelter us from the prevailing wind? Why not learn about dragons?"

"But King Enric is great and terrible, and he says—"

"What do you think? That's what matters."

She shook her head and shifted her basket to the other arm.

I would probably never get anywhere with Caitlyn. She was too deeply entrenched in the king's service and unable to believe he might be mistaken in any way. Was everyone like that? If so it was going to be even more difficult to find Bower.

Looking around, I decided the king's gardens weren't really gardens. Not in the sense I understood. A garden was meant to provide food and herbs. I'd seen dozens of gardens on my travels, and they'd been all sorts of sizes, but they'd always had more than grass and gravel in them.

We turned a corner and strode into yet another garden.

This one at least had tall hedges with flowers on them. They made a line next to a fountain that bubbled up clear water. Other trees or bushes had been chopped into different shapes like a triangle or a cube. It all seemed a little too tame to me.

I was used to thick vines with lush flowers, tall grasses that waved in the wind, scattering their seeds at random, and a hundred different types of trees. For a moment, I wanted nothing more than to be back on the islands, wandering one of paths made by the villagers, or a broad path made by dragons, or climbing up into a tress to pick melons.

Looking around, I wanted nothing more than to run over and climb a wall—but I noticed that no vines had been planted near the tall walls that surrounded the palace. No trees were planted anywhere near the walls—there would be no escape unless I could fly away.

And I can't do that unless Enric teaches me how.

I gave a snort of disgust. A cough behind us answered. I turned and King Enric stepped out from a gap in the hedge, flanked by two Iron Guards. I hadn't heard them approach, but considering the magic I had seen yesterday, I shouldn't be surprised that the king knew how to manipulate sounds as well as sights.

"Lady Saffron." Enric inclined his head, waved away his guards and sent Caitlyn away with a glance. She gave a curtsy and turned to flee, her feet crunching on the gravel path.

I glanced sideways at Enric and gave a start.

For the briefest of moments, I glimpsed deep, sunken eyes, yellowed skin with each vein and tendon clearly visible. I blinked and looked at the king and the image vanished. King Enric stood before me, dazzling in golden robes that fanned out at the sleeves and covered him to his ankles. Jewels that I had learned were called diamonds glittered on golden chains hung around his neck.

Was something wrong with me that I'd seen anything else other than the king?

"My lady?" The king stepped closer and frowned. "Are you well? You look as if you have been out in the sun too long? You must have a care for your wellbeing."

"King Enric," I stammered and brushed a hand over my forehead to wipe away the sweat that had gathered. I tried a curtsey—Caitlyn had tried to teach me one this morning.

"Please, no need for that. We are family after all… and, I hope we can be friends as well."

Suddenly, I wanted more than anything to be his friend. He smiled and I started to smile back, but…

Bower.

"Bower," I said. I took a step away from Enric. "You said he would be safe. But where is he? I haven't seen him, and you said he was going to be taken to the dungeons, and I need to know if he is safe before..." I let the words trail off.

Before what?

I didn't have an answer to that question.

A shadow seemed to darken the king's eyes. He winced slightly as if he'd been stuck with a thorn. "I had hoped I wouldn't have to break this news to you at once. Not after your terrible ordeal in traveling here, and your magic backfiring and your confusion and all."

"What confusion? Did something happen? What is wrong with Bower? Is he safe?" My heart began to thud against my chest.

"Bower of House Daris has gone…no, no, not dead. You need not look so stricken. I sent my guards to offer him a pardon. Such a shame. I had rather hoped he would stay and, perhaps, eventually come to take his place again and regain my favor."

"Why did he go? Where? It doesn't make any sense to me." I bit down on the words that Bower would not abandon me. I had not known him long, but I knew that about him.

The king gestured for me to walk with him. "I think that I might have made things worse. You see, I fear that the reason he didn't bring you straight to me when you first came to the city was that he was actually afraid I would be angry with him. Just think, Saffron, if Bower had announced he had found my last living relative. How could I have been angry at his petty criminal activities? You see, I knew of his reading habits. But I let it slide. They were, after all, just a few books. It all seemed so harmless."

I found myself nodding even though I didn't want to.

The king shook his head and let out a long breath. "However, I fear the young man has too much hate in him to ever want to understand me. I gave him the choice to join you, but he wouldn't take it. He said that he would rather die—so very dramatic, these young people. And, of course, by what he said, he has not known you long enough to claim a deep friendship, now has he?" The king raised his eyebrows, and I shook my head. "What could I do? The young man forced my hand. His other choice was to leave the city."

"He left Torvald?" I said my throat tight. Torvald was his home. This could not be right.

The king nodded and gave another sigh. "Just as he did once before. He left. Ran off yet again rather than just talk to me, his king!" Enric pinched the bridge of his nose as if it was all too frustrating and silly to bear thinking about.

He did leave before... And he told me when I first met him that he would never be able to take me back here, but I forced him.

I stared down at the grass and kicked at it with my boot.

Maybe everything the king had just said was true—and Bower had never intended to stay here at all.

But he left me.

 The thought rang in my mind. Bower left me, just as my father and mother had left me. I was left to fend for myself.

Anger coiled in my belly, hot and clawing at me. For a moment, I wanted to release my magic at Bower. I had thought him my friend, but he made his hatred of King Enric more important. Now I had no one to help me— except Enric.

"I am sorry, Saffron. Perhaps in time he will see the error of his ways. Maybe then he will come back to us. Especially when he sees what you have become under my tutelage."

I looked up, excitement stirring inside me, blotting out the anger. "When do we start? You said you would teach me to control my magic."

"Patience, child. I will teach you to use the power within our blood. The Maddox power." Enric grinned. "Together we will rule the world as it was always meant to be. We will remake Torvald. The prophecy will come true. And you will be my dragon queen." Reaching out a hand, Enric stroked a finger down my cheek.

I tried not to shudder. His touch chilled me. I turned away from him and it happened again—I saw the face of an old man, his nose huge with age, his teeth yellowed and long, his sunken eyes glittering in a winkled and lined face. A few pale hairs stood up on his bald and age-spotted head. His neck seemed lined and thick.

Pulling back, I faced him. But now he once again had dark hair and an unlined face. I blinked. What had I seen? Had it been the real Enric leaking out, or simply an illusion he had cast out for a moment as a test, part of him starting to teach me magic?

"My lady?" Enric frowned. "Have I gone too far, too fast? You are not accustomed to any attention, I know."

The truth slammed into me. This was not a test to start teaching me anything. No, he had been using his magic on me, to fool me into thinking he was young and handsome when he was in fact far older than me.

Heart hammering, I knew I could not let him know that I had seen past his illusion. I needed to use him the way he was trying to use me. He was trying to make me forget

Bower—trying to make me lean only on him. So, I would act as if I had nothing better to do than to learn about magic.

Turning away, I shook my head. "I need time to think. Time to adjust to all the changes. It will be easier when I know more magic…and know more about my blood."

And know where Bower really is.

"Of course, my lady, of course." Enric's voice changed and he said, his tone suddenly imperious, "It has turned cold out here. There is a chill from the mountain." He clapped his hands and two Iron Guards stepped from behind the hedges to his side. "Please see the lady back to her tower."

I opened my mouth to complain, but closed it again. Enric needed to think I was under his spell—he needed to think I could be made to agree to anything. I smiled and rubbed my arms, even though the sun still felt warm to me. "It is chill. I will go back."

His eyes narrowed but his mouth curved up. "Please do not take too long with your decision, my lady."

I turned away, but I had heard the threat under his words.

It was quite possible that my time was now as short as the little time that Torvald had left to it—and I still had not discovered where Bower was being kept.

*   *   *

CHAPTER 17

FROM THE HORSE'S MOUTH

Bower?

The dream was one I'd had before and I curled up tighter. I didn't want to wake up just yet. I was dreaming of having fallen asleep in my study, stretched out in my most comfortable chair, a warm fire crackling, the room smelling of leather and pages. Only a moment more here— that was all I wanted. I needed to forget for a short time every terrible thing that had happened or would be happening soon.

Bower!

The voice poked at me, like a thought in my head that wasn't mine, as insistent as a nagging conscience. Someone had invaded the sanctuary of my study. When I looked, however, I only saw pristine shelves with books intact and in perfect order. Did Cook want me? Or father? Was he alive still?

Foolish Bower, wake and look up.

The voice echoed in my mind, forcing me out of my chair. A wind whipped through the study, carrying off the books, snuffing the fire and leaving me cold and shivering.

All gone—my books are all gone.

Not gone—here. Look and wake.

What? What is that up there?

I glanced up and saw a small gap near the ceiling of the study. The books had fallen off the shelves, leaving a tiny strip of tired light that leaked in. I wanted to stay in my chair, not go back into the cold. I wanted to be comfortable again. Gripping the chair arms, I tried to hold onto the dream. I was not going to climb the wall of bookshelves to reach a gap that a voice in my head kept telling me had appeared.

This time a hot, snorting, growling breath tickled the back of my neck.

I woke to the sound of roaring wind—only it wasn't a wind, but a hot, fiery breath that shook my dream, scattering it like the torn pages of my books.

Blinking, my eyes hurting from the flare of light, I tried to shout out a caution to have a care. I couldn't get a word out past the roaring and growling. More and more of the gray, water spilled into the cell. I covered my head with my arms and wondered if I would die now.

The smoke in my cell began to lift, but it had set me to coughing and spluttering. I pried opened my eyes and squinted up at the light that was falling from the small grate far above and directly into my eyes. I was cold and stiff, but it seemed to me that fire had awakened me.

Was that even possible?

The light wobbled above me. A shadow moved and came back. Someone or something was up there. I heard digging noises and then something pounded on an iron grate.

Was that a horse?

A sensation almost like a headache buzzed behind my ears—a pressure more than a pain. It faded almost at once. Oddly, it seemed to be coming not from within me. It wasn't due to the battering I'd had, but seemed to be coming from the horse that was moving about near the grate.

"Jaydra?" I asked. What else could it be, other than a dragon disguised as a horse. I almost laughed at that absurd idea.

The digging paused. After more shuffling and a stream of soil that trickled down into my cell, the eye of a large horse appeared. An unusual eye, flecked with an almost luminescent gold and silver.

"Jaydra, it is you!"

Once again the buzzing pressure behind my eyes intensified. It was almost as if…

No, that can't be.

Was Jaydra trying to communicate with me—was that her mind just about knocking on me? I didn't quite understand it, but Saffron had insisted she could talk to the dragon. I knew the two of them had a special bond. I had certainly caught Saffron speaking aloud to what seemed like no one, but could Jaydra establish a link with me?

I almost grinned.

I was talking to a dragon, who was trying to answer me.

"Jaydra, I don't know how you found me, but thank you!" Shifting around, I staggered over to the other side of my cell so I might better see her. "Saffron isn't here. I think the king took her to the palace! Maybe I'm at the palace—I don't know. I do know this…as a horse, you might be able to get into the stables. I've been to the palace before and I know the stables are behind the main buildings, to the northern side. You should be able to find it by the smell of the horses and the hay. Even with your size, you should be able to get in. Find Saffron. Get her away from the king, please!"

The now familiar buzzing sensation scraped against the back of my eyes. I shrugged—I couldn't understand her. However, Jaydra gave a snort, banged once more on the grate and then her shadow and eye disappeared.

I almost wanted to laugh, but my side ached too much for that.

"Now all I have to do is to figure a plan to get out of here!" I told myself.

At least Saffron would be able to escape—Jaydra would help her. They might be able to do something to prevent the king from going through with any plan to destroy Torvald. And even though I was still imprisoned, a flash of hope had ignited inside me. There was at least someone— something—on the outside that was waiting for me to free myself.

It was a small consolation, but it was a start.

*   *   *

I ducked. The captain's quarter staff whistled over my head. He missed me, but it had been close indeed. He was one of the king's guards, so I didn't feel bad for trying to hit him as hard as I could. But he wasn't making it easy for me to do so.

Grinning, he tried to circle me. I wasn't going to let him best me.

I had asked the king again today when I would start to learn magic. He had sent word he was too busy with his plans for Torvald. That had set my blood running cold. Was time running out? I decided I could not wait. I had forced Caitlyn to take me down to the guard room, and had demanded some exercise. Enough insults tossed around, and the captain of the guard had accepted my challenge.

I just wished it was Enric I could smack with a staff.

The captain was both larger and taller than me. But I was faster. While he knew more, I had a few tricks I had yet to try with him. So far he had knocked me to the ground twice, and smacked my thigh with enough force as to leave me limping for a few steps. I rather thought he had no love for women, or maybe he just didn't think that I would make a worthy queen.

We'll see how weak he thinks I am!

Stepping back to our original positions on the flattened circle of grass, I took a fresh grip on the ash staff. The captain turned his staff over once—I knew now that meant he intended to feint. Well, what he didn't know was that I could be as fierce as a dragon. If there was one thing I learned from hard play with Jaydra it was that an attack must be quick and meant to draw blood.

I let the captain make the first move. As I'd expected, he jabbed in a feint. He wanted me to lunge at him and overreach myself so he could smack me on the back.

I ducked and spun and waited for his real attack to come.

Another jab came at me. I easily sidestepped that one. A flicker of annoyance tightened his mouth and flashed in his eyes. He did not like that I was refusing to try to parry his blows. This time he jabbed straight forward just as I was stepping forward, hoping to crack me a painful thump in my chest. Not a killing or a finishing strike, but hard enough to hurt.

But I saw the move coming and parried the blow.

The captain used my parry to reverse his strike, spinning his staff around quickly in the other direction, straight for my head.

I pushed one foot out to the side, crouched down and swung my staff upward to catch him in his ribcage. The blow knocked him out of the circle.

He hit the ground with a loud thud and a grunt.

I realized I fought best when I stopped thinking, when I let my dragon self through.

Saffron!

I staggered back. The captain was pushing himself up and dusting himself off.

Jaydra? Is that you? The thoughts I sent her were washed with worry for her—it seemed a very long time since I had last heard from her. Glancing around, I couldn't see her, but I knew she was in horse form. She needed me, and suddenly I was done with this captain.

"You got lucky," the captain said. I detected a slight wheeze as he stepped into the ring again and leveled his staff.

Bower needs Saffron right now. The horse-dragon's mind was strangely clear in my own, and I wondered if all of this hiding out in a city near so many other human minds and voices was making her more human as well.

"Again?" The captain gave me a dark look that told me I would not be so lucky this time, nor would I come away undamaged.

Eyes narrowed, I moved before he was ready, dropping to the ground and using the staff more like a dragon's tail, whipping it around to knock his feet out from under him. Rolling onto my feet, I slammed the staff into his head, knocking him senseless.

I stood and brushed the grass from my clothes. "That will teach you not to overestimate yourself or underestimate any opponent." I told him.

He gave a moan. I nudged a toe into his side.

Jaydra thought to me, *Too like gulls of the island.* I knew what she meant. The seagulls that lived in the Western Iles hunted in swarms. Together they were strong. One on its own, however, was loud and obnoxious and easily taken down.

I think that you are right, Jaydra. I greeted her more formally, letting her feel how glad I was at being able to talk to her again. *Where are you?*

Outside. Near a place with many horses and humans. The horses keep looking at me as though I might eat them. Jaydra snuffed a laugh.

And might you? I asked, sensing a flicker of her old humor.

Only if they keep trying to feed me grass. Jaydra talked to Bower. Bower is in a cave-box below.

Taking the staff with me, I set off to find Jaydra.

As big as she was, it wasn't hard to spot her. The other horses did seem nervous around her, dancing away.

A box? What do you mean?

I realized I had actually believed King Enric when he had told me that Bower had left the city. It was not just because I had known how much Bower despised the king, but Enric's magic had been more powerful than I had expected. I would have to be more careful and aware around the man.

A stone box. Below this place, Jaydra repeated.

It was difficult for her to correctly shape the thoughts around such human concepts as palace or prison. To her all buildings looked essentially the same—some came in bigger sizes, some smaller, some smelled more than others and some were fun to tear apart. They all came across as a sort of den to her mind.

Does it have bars? Metal on the windows or doors? Is it small? Dark or light? I tried to ask, feeling Jaydra try to understand my answer.

No… Yes. Small hole with metal. Just big enough to smell Bower. He was cold and dreaming—Jaydra had to wake Bower.

It sounded as if Bower really had been thrown into the king's dungeon! *We have to get him out. Thank you, Jaydra. You've done more than I've been able to manage so far.*

Saffron wanted family. King is no family. Enric magic smells bad. Jaydra's thoughts seemed matter of fact, as if she could have saved us all the bother of this trouble many days and weeks ago if I had just listened to her. That might have been true—but I knew that some things you had to learn for yourself. That wasn't always fun, but the lessons took better.

Wait just a little longer in the horse ground. I will come find you after tonight. I have to get Bower out of his cave-box and then we have to talk about what to do about the king.

A pleased wave of fierce satisfaction came to me from Jaydra, but it fell away.

I glanced around. I didn't care about the captain any longer—I needed a plan to get Bower out of his dungeon. It was good to have Jaydra close by—I had a feeling we might need to get away quickly. But we couldn't leave until we were certain the city was also safe. That might take even more work.

Glancing down at my hand, I thought about my magic. However, I didn't dare try it again. Last time I'd used it, it had sent me flying. *If only the king had taught me a few things.* Well, I couldn't worry about that now. If we got out of this, perhaps I could simply vow never to use magic again—but I feared that would be a vow I would all too quickly break. I'd wanted more than anything—even more than finding out the truth about my family—to learn how to control my powers. Now that seemed impossible.

The King had lied to me. He had used his magic to try and blind me. And now I wondered if he ever really intended to teach me anything—maybe he just wanted my powers. Or wanted to use me as a pawn in yet another plan he had to gain power. That didn't matter.

Bower was alive and I knew where he was at last.

Glancing around at the training equipment, I let a small smile curve my lips. I was going to need some supplies and tools if I was going to break Bower out of the king's own dungeon.

*   *   *

CHAPTER 18

MAGIC

Den-sister?

Jaydra's voice cut through my dream like a bird through the sky.

I'd gone to bed early, telling Caitlyn I was tired from a day of sparring. I didn't tell her I'd knocked the captain senseless. I'd also noticed that he and his guards were avoiding me, which was all the better for my plan.

I'd been in a light doze—I was too tense to sleep. The moonlight came into my tower room in a thin strip. I hadn't undressed, so I simply threw back the covers and lit the lantern on my table. My boots were soft and would make hardly any sound on the stone.

The palace sleeps, Jaydra thought to me. I knew she could hear everything—every breath, every dream. She would be able to alert me of any danger.

Guards, I thought to her.

Cold and lazy. In dens or standing near fires. Not warm like Jaydra.

I sent her my thanks and felt under the pillows for two long-handled knives that I had pilfered from the training today, as well as some padded greaves. It wasn't a lot, but it would have to do for now.

I couldn't ask Jaydra how long until dawn. Time in the form of hours wasn't something dragons ever understood—they knew now and all of the past, but they tended to confuse dreams and the future. But Jaydra would smell the morning dew—she would sense the warmth of the sunrise. I asked her to let me know when dawn was close. We had to be gone by then.

The door of my tower room was always locked, but I had fed Caitlyn most of my dinner and slipped a bit of cloth into the lock so that when she had locked it, the key had not actually locked anything. I'd held the door shut so she would try the door and think she had locked it. I felt bad about fooling her, and hoped nothing too bad would befall her. But if we managed an escape, the king would be after us—not poor Caitlyn.

Slipping onto the stairs, I propped my staff against the wall, held up the lantern and pulled the door shut behind me. I had the knives tucked into my belt at my back. My heart was pounding. Taking up my staff again, I ran down the stone stairwell and out to the Rose Hall.

Anyone there, Jaydra? I asked as I paused at the ground floor.

Closing my eyes, I lifted my head and allowed Jaydra to sense as much as she could through my senses. As a dragon, she could smell a fish deep under the waves—she found my ability to smell and hear clumsy and limiting. But she sent me word that the hall was clear.

I hurried across the marbled floor and to the door that let out into a small courtyard. I put out the lantern. From here, I would have to stay to shadows and moonlight.

Across the way from the Rose Hall stood the Imperial Lodge, a shorter building made of stone. I ran across the courtyard. I didn't want to stumble across any half-sleeping guards, so it was better to keep to open spaces. Jaydra approved of this idea.

Easy to be quiet and unseen…marble noisy.

I'd never been inside the Imperial Lodge. Caitlyn had told me the king held most of his meetings there, but no one slept in the lodge or lived there. She had said it was one of the oldest buildings in the palace, and that it had a lot of rooms underground—to me that meant it must have access to the dungeons. Jaydra had sent me an image of where she'd found Bower—she'd also sent me an image of the trees and plants around his very narrow window. I'd taken a walk around and I knew where he was—the trick now would to find the right route to reach him.

Saffron…halt!

Jaydra sent me an image of a guard, walking toward me, making his rounds. I froze. I had reached a shuttered window. I flatten myself against the stone and held my breath. If I was discovered out here, I might be able to get away with a story of wanting a walk or not being able to sleep. A guard might let me go. However, once I got into the dungeons, I would have to do away with any guard who found me. The king might want me for his own reason to be his queen. But he might not want me after I had shown I could see through his magic. And any excuses I could make would not extend to Bower or Jaydra.

I waited and heard the plodding walk of a palace guard. He carried an oil lantern in one hand. A broad-brimmed helmet shaded his eyes. I knew he hadn't spotted me, for he yawned and kept on walking, almost looking half-asleep. He strolled across the courtyard, lantern held high.

He was going to pass right by me—he would see me for a certainty unless he was almost completely blind. My hands itched to use the trick to hide myself. But if it went wrong, it would rouse the entire palace.

Saffron? Jaydra's mind brushed against mine in warning. I had no time to ask her what was going on where she was. I took a deep breath and thrust the staff out, tripping the guard.

He started to fall. He seemed too surprised to shout. I flipped the staff and landed a blow across the back of his neck.

He hit the ground with a thud and lay still. His lantern hit the stone wall and shattered. I held my breath and waited. No one called out to ask what had happened. No one raised an alarm. But the sound might have been loud enough to attract another guard.

Grabbing the man by his ankles, I dragged him into the lodge. I went back for his helmet, which had fallen off, and kicked the lantern under the bushes near the window. Inside the lodge I found a cupboard large enough to hold the guard. I rolled him inside and started to toss his helmet in after him. But I realized it could be put to better use.

I pulled off his cloak and threw it over my shoulders. Metal gleamed from his belt in the moonlight. Reaching down, I found he wore a set of keys, as did many of the guards. They had to be ready to open doors in case of fire.

Taking his keys and his helmet, I left him locked away. He would not wake until long after dawn.

Not long now, Jaydra—what was wrong? I threw my mind toward her and hurried to the nearest door. Jaydra did not reply. I could not even sense any emotion from her. She had fallen oddly silent, as if she had fallen asleep or had to hide herself.

Jaydra? I asked again. *Den-sister?*

Still no response. Worry spiked within my breast. For a moment, I wanted to abandon Bower and race over to the stables. However, if Jaydra was hiding, my thundering over there might put her into more danger.

Jaydra would also tell me to save Bower, as she was a dragon and could look after herself. I set to opening the door again. It swung open and I found myself in an elaborate hall with myriad of arched doorways leading into even more rooms.

The Imperial Lodge had an elegance about it that the Rose Hall lacked. To me, it seemed that Rose Hall had been built to show King Enric's power and glorify House Maddox. But this building lacked all the paintings of brave deeds. Instead, the decorations were of buildings or bridges, and even a few landscapes of Torvald. I wondered if this place showed what Torvald had once been like.

I passed every grand door—I was searching for the smallest, most unobtrusive door, and one that looked sturdy enough to withstand an axe. I found it at the far end of the main room. Iron bands crossed the door. The posts and frame looked sunk into the stone of the floor. I was certain this door would lead to the dungeons—it looked like a prison door.

I went through almost the entire set of keys until I found a heavy, iron one that fit the lock. I winced, expecting the lock to squeak and growl with rust. Disturbingly, the lock turned easily and the door swung open on silent, well-oiled hinges.

This door must be used often, I thought with a sense of despair. How many others were down here, besides Bower? I could not save them all. A wave of fetid, damp-smelling air rose up from the darkness. I stepped into a narrow, stone corridor and pulled the door closed almost completely behind me. Without any light, and with my heart beating fast, I had to stop and wait for my eyes to adjust to the darkness.

It was not the pure pitch black of the deep caverns and tunnels I knew from my childhood of scrabbling over dragon hides in dens so deep that it was easier to close my eyes to see. Light filtered down from torches set at long distances apart. Instead of blackness, a soft light revealed a set of stairs that led downwards. I hurried down the steps to the bottom, keeping one hand raised with fingertips just gently stroking the wall in case I came across a doorway. In my other hand, I held the staff at the ready. The scrape of rat claws and the drip of water grew louder.

I reached a long corridor with doors that stood open and empty cells. At the end of it, I glanced left and right. To the left I could see a little more light, but to the left seemed utter blackness.

Jaydra said a grate opened onto the outside—and that must mean moonlight!

I turned to the left and strode down the stone hall, my stolen cloak flapping around my ankles. I found more empty cells.

But no other prisoners.

These dungeons had to be well used, given the ease with which the door opened and the rank smells that left me wrinkling my nose. But now they stood empty. Did that mean a lot of prisoners had just recently been released, or had they been...?

No, I didn't want to think about the alternative answer. I strode toward what looked to be the very last cell.

This door was locked, but I found the key more easily. Opening the door, I peered inside.

The cell looked to have enough room for three people to lie down. In one top corner, I glimpsed the small grate. The moon gave me enough light to see someone was trying to stand.

"Bower!" I gasped the word. Anger sparked inside me for how he'd been left—dirty, bruised by what I could see of the dark shadows on his skin, and his face marked with cuts that looked as if they might fester. My hands twitched with the desire to let out my powers—to blast this place. I could feel the anger changing into magic, starting to pour out of me. The room brightened, and I knew I was the cause of that. But I could not stop it—could not control the power. It was going to burst out of me.

And then Bower said, "Saffron, what are you doing?"

*　　*　　*

Saffron was glowing—there was no other word for it. Light seemed to pour from her skin as if she honestly was on fire. She blazed in the darkness like a beacon. My mind seemed to be working sluggishly, but I remembered she had said she couldn't really control what she did. Struggling to my feet, I put my back to the wall.

"Saffron, what are you doing?"

The glow started to fade from her skin. She gulped down a shaking breath and stretched out a hand, sketching what seemed to be letters in the air—ancient ruins. I recognized the likes of them from the oldest scrolls I had ever seen.

The glow flowed to her fingertips and condensed into a blinding ball of whiteness. She flicked a finger and the ball launched itself at the wall. I ducked, and it hit just over my head, sending a cascade of bits of stone and leaving the wall glowing red hot. Moving away from the heat and destruction, I stared at the crater she had made—it wasn't enough to get us out of here for the stones still stood, but I worried now that the structure might be compromised and this place could fall down on top of us.

"Bower," Saffron said again. This time she sounded more like herself—her voice earlier had had both a tight anger in the word and an echo of something I found unsettling. It was as if for a moment she had become something larger. In fact, it was a lot like when Jaydra had changed form into a dragon—Saffron had seemed not to take the shape of a dragon, but I sensed a power from her that might have destroyed not just this cell, but the entire dungeon and us as well if she had loosed it.

I began to wonder if she might be more of a danger even than King Enric.

Was this what happened to someone who lived with dragons? Had the king been right in saying dragons changed what a person was and made them something dangerous?

Saffron stepped closer and smiled, looking like herself again, no longer glowing from within, but the stones cast an uncanny light over her face, and I could again see the resemblance between her and the king in the sharp cut of their faces and the bone structure. I shivered. "I'm here to rescue you. We have to get going. Can you walk?"

I nodded. "I'm just—tired. And hungry. If you see something to eat, grab it, will you?" Pushing off the wall, I managed to walk over to her. My legs shook. I needed water more than I needed food, but it seemed a very long time since I'd had much of either of those things. I wanted to touch her to make certain she was real and that this wasn't another dream, but I didn't dare. Not after what she'd just done to the wall. I wasn't certain what had set her off. "I thought I would never see you again."

Saffron flashed a smile, but her eyes seemed very bright. She gave a sniff. "Of course it's me. I am not Vic. I would never leave a friend in danger."

"But we can't leave. King Enric has a terrible plan."

She nodded. "He told me. There is some prophecy about dragon breath, which the king thinks is fire and smoke, and some kind of true king coming out of that, so he thinks this means if he burns Torvald to the ground he will both kill all those who oppose him and become this true king. He wanted me to stand with him, so I had to let him think I was considering it. I mean, he is family." She pulled a sour face, and then her mouth set into a line of grim determination. "He's been telling a lot of lies and blood-family doesn't seem all I thought it would be. But I don't think he's lying about his grand plan."

I nodded. "No, I think to secure more power, the king would lay waste to all of the Middle Kingdom."

She pushed a staff at me. "Here, you look as if you could use this. "Ready?"

Leaning on the staff, I waved for her to go first. She turned, but paused and turned back. "Oh, you may need this." Pulling out a long knife from behind her back, she twirled it and handed it to me hilt first.

Staring at it, I shook my head. "No, you better keep that for now. The shape I'm in, I'm likely to cut myself."

She gave a snort but moved ahead, knife held out in front of her.

My eyes burned from the smoke in the cell, I glanced back at the wall that Saffron had blasted. How had she done that? How had power poured from her fingertips? How had she known to sketch the runes in the air? Had the king taught her this—or did she just know?

It suddenly occurred to me that she really was of House Maddox—she had the same blood as the king. The thought unsettled me. But for now, we had to escape this place.

No guards came to check on us—which I thought a touch odd. Saffron led the way down a long corridor with cell doors that stood open. The place seemed oddly empty, as if the king had taken everyone from the place. Was this more of his plan? Had he put all of his enemies back into Torvald, released them under the pretext of doing something noble for the fair celebration to mark a turning point in his reign? If so, I knew he must be doing that to make sure they died along with the rest of Torvald.

I knew if the king closed the gates, there would be no escape from the walled city. The king could burn it and everyone would die. Once there might have been dragons and those nobles in the city who were Dragon Riders and could have flown from danger—that time was no more. We had to stop the king.

Through my fog of pain and hunger, I followed Saffron, leaning on the staff she had given me. The steps proved more difficult for me, and then we eased through a door and into a room that I recognized as being part of the Imperial Lodge. I'd been hidden below a place I had come to before, long ago, when my father had still been welcome at court and I had been a boy.

"I know where we are," I told her.

Saffron glanced at me and waved for me to take the lead. "What's the best way to the stables? Jaydra is waiting for us there and hiding."

I frowned. "Saffron, we can't leave Torvald to a horrible fate."

"I know. But first we have to get to some place safe. Then we can figure out what we can do."

It was my turn to nod, and then I walked ahead of her, trying to be quiet with the staff and not thump it hard against the floor.

We stepped out into the dawn. A silver light traced the eastern sky, sharpening the ridgeline above the palace. The thin, watery light streaked clouds into colors of red and orange.

I pulled in a sweet breath of clean air, but the acrid scent of smoke tickled my nose. And something else as well—something sour and old, like flowers that had wilted in a vase and were rotting or like meat gone off and now infested with maggots.

Turning to tell Saffron we could use the path to the right to get to the stables, I saw she had frozen still. For a moment, I thought she was glowing again, but it was just the dawn starting to bring color and shape back to the world. Saffron's eyes seemed to pale and her gaze went distant and she uttered but one word.

"Magic."

*   *   *

CHAPTER 19

WHERE YOU BELONG

The world smelled of magic. Or rather of Enric's magic. I knew the scent of it now, I knew he had to be using all his powers. But to do what?

Smoke hung in the air and I feared we were too late to stop the king—he was starting to burn Torvald. But I heard no alarms from the city, no cries, and no shouts. The palace, too, seemed oddly silent. Not even a morning bird had begun to sing.

I looked to Bower and found him staring at me, his mouth twisted up on one side and down on the other as if he wasn't happy about something. Fear flashed in his eyes for a moment to be replaced by what I hoped might be a touch of warm gratitude. I wondered for an awful moment what he really thought of the power that had slipped out of my hand in the cell—I hadn't been able to control it.

Anger had stirred the power—as it always did. I'd hated to see Bower looking so poorly. My hand seemed to move on its own, sketching a symbol that seemed to be something I knew in my blood—Maddox blood. Maddox magic. Only Bower calling my name had pulled me back into myself and kept me from releasing a power that could have killed us both.

I was still a danger to those around me—still unable to control my powers.

How will Bower look at me when he realizes I have the same magic as Enric?

Bower must hate the king—I did as well. But all too soon, Bower might start to fear and then hate me. I didn't want that to happen. I would have to control my anger better so I did not allow my powers to take hold.

Dragging in a breath, I told Bower, "That stink. It's King Enric's magic. You do know he's not a young man— he's old. Ancient. He uses illusion to make everyone think him handsome."

Bower straightened. "I knew it! I knew there was something that was not right with him. I've seen a shimmer a few times—like I do with Jaydra at times."

Suddenly, I was the one worried about Bower. He shouldn't have ever seen the shimmer of illusion around Jaydra—or the king. I remembered Jaydra had said there was something special about him. Now I started to wonder just what made him different from anyone I had ever met. Did he have power and not know it? But why had I sensed nothing from him? Why did my power surge in ways I couldn't handle, but Bower's abilities seemed content to be quiet and soft?

It wasn't fair.

It was also nothing I could do anything about. But I could find Jaydra.

Casting my mind out, I tried to sense where she might be hiding. I found her at last, crouched in a small, dark room that smelled of straw and hay, her muscles coiled as if ready to spring into the air. She still had the form of a horse, but her tail whipped and lashed far more like a dragon's tail.

I touched minds with her. *Jaydra, what is it? I lost touch with you before.*

Many metal soldiers. I smell magic. Something is happening. Jaydra known now to be a dragon! I wasn't able to share all of her senses in the same way she could use mine. I could feel the tension in her body, I could also smell the magic in the air both through her and my own nose. But I could not really see through her eyes. I could, however, hear the clank of metal boots.

"Saffron?" Bower asked and touched a finger to my arm. His face looked as if he had been on the losing end of a fight. He licked chapped lips.

I gave a nod. "It's Jaydra. She says the Iron Guard seem to be on the move. They seem to know she's a dragon."

"How—" He cut off the word, and then spat out, "The king. You said he has magic and he's using it."

Tugging on Bower's sleeve, I told him, "Something is happening. We need to get to a place where we can see what's going on."

Bower pointed up to a gray, stone tower. "There's always that or the roof."

The tower he'd waved at looked a lot like the one where I'd been kept, except this tower seemed to have a flat top at the peak, not a sloping roof. I glanced at Bower. "Sure you can make it up the stairs?"

He shrugged. "Do we have a choice? Besides, I might find some food or water on the way."

Leading the way and leaning heavily on the staff, Bower led me to a narrow staircase that curved up the outside of the tower. It had no railing and so I stayed close to the stone tower wall. I kept glancing behind us, wondering why I was not seeing any guards.

The long flight of stairs left us both panting hard.

On the tower's flat roof, we could see the mountain behind the palace and the ruins on the crest of the ridgeline of hills and down into the city. Smoke curled up from the city, and at first I took it to be fires started for morning meals or perhaps set out for the fair and some kind of entertainment. Bower limped to where a low wall stood between us and a very long fall.

Below us the Imperial Lodge seemed to be only slate gray roof. The palace gardens seemed extensive, the green of grass and hedges wandering around buildings. We stood even higher than my tower room had been. I felt almost as if this was a place for dragons to perch. Even the vast Rose Hall seemed small from this height.

Stretching out a hand, Bower pointed to the city. "Look—it's begun. Fires."

Frowning, I stared down at the city. "But…no one has set an alarm. No one is trying to—"

"Escape?"

I whirled. The king stood with his back to the sunrise, his figure silhouetted in the morning light. He hovered before us, suspended in mid-air, using his magic to fly that he had shown me before.

Power pulsed around him, glowed from his skin as if he was made of nothing but fire and light. He was so much better at magic than me! He could swat me like a fly! But instead, when he spoke he did so with a slow, measured charm.

He shook his head and sorrow leaked into his voice. "Saffron, Saffron, Saffron…after everything I thought to give you—this is how you betray me?"

Anger erupted in a burst, scalding my stomach and throat. I forgot my earlier vow to keep it contained—I tried. But it flared like a fire given fresh fuel. "How I betrayed you? You lied to me." I threw my arm wide, gesturing to the city. "And now you betray your people— you want Torvald to be ashes.

Enric shook his head. "The prophecy must come true. If I do not make it happen, it will take place on its own, without my guidance. Old and young must unite to rule the land from above. Upon the dragon's breath will come the return of the True King. What you see now will be the rebirth of the glory of Torvald." Enric's voice had begun to rise, the way a wind could start to howl before a storm. A breeze seemed to start from around him, rising fast into a whirling wind that whipped at me. He floated closer, his robes gleaming in the sunlight, jewels winking from his fingers—his face pale and perfect and his black hair not moving an inch despite the wind. "Are you not borne to me on the dragon's breath, out of the far west? Are you not young. And I am so very old."

He smiled. The shimmer Bower had described rose up around him. The image of the young man faded. For a moment, young and old both seemed to be part of his face—he was both handsome and an old man.

Bower gasped, and I shuddered.

Enric spread wide his arms. No longer did his robes stretch over bulging muscles. Instead, his form seemed thin and bent, as if magic had sapped the strength and flesh from him. His black hair faded into baldness, leaving only strands of white hair over age-spotted skin. His skin faded into pale whiteness, lined with deep grooves around a mouth that pulled down at the corners. His eyes still glittered deep in sunken sockets.

How old must he be? Eighty? Ninety? Over a hundred? Or was this the cost of magic? I didn't know if the magic preserved his life, extended it, or had the magic aged him into this almost corpse-like being?

His magic swirled around him now—I could *see* it as well as smell it. Waves of ugly purple, black and red held him aloft, left him floating just outside the tower's low wall as if he stood on a cloud of magic. He *did* look majestic—but it was a terrible majesty to inspire only fear and loathing.

Enric lifted a hand. Waves of magic wrapped around me like a dragon's tail. Invisible, icy fingers seemed to wrap around my throat.

"You thought I would let you go? With the power you have in your blood?" He drifted closer. I struggled against the iron-like clamp on my throat. From the corner of my eye I could see Bower had also been caught and was being held. "You will help me fulfill the prophecy. You will...or you will see your friends, your Bower and your Jaydra die. So, watch now as the prophecy comes to life!"

Struggling against his magic, I thought I saw the shimmer around Enric that Bower had described. Had he reached the limits of his power? I knew with my own magic that it came with a cost—that it could drain me. Or was he so powerful he could use magic as if it was a thousand bright jewels to be scattered at will?

There was but one way to find out. I pushed against the invisible hold wrapped around me—I struggled and grunted.

Enric smiled and shook his head. He waved his hand and suddenly I stood next to Bower, staring down at the city. Licks of orange flames rose from rooftops. Black smoke curled into the air. And still no shouts or cries or alarms sounded. I knew then that Enric must have set magic over the city, perhaps to hold everyone still as I was being held.

"The prophecy beings," Enric shouted. "I will be back for you after Torvald burns and we will build a new, greater capital for our world."

With a clap like thunder, Enric vanished.

He had to have extended himself too far—I was sure of it. I could feel it in the magic that held me—it was weakening, easing. It would fade soon. But soon might not be soon enough.

"Saffron, we must do something." Bower choked out the words. I glanced at him, saw his face had gone pale. Enric's magic hold around him was killing him—but seeing Torvald burn would even be worse for him. "Saffron, I saw what you did in the cell. You're a Maddox—just like the king."

"We're nothing alike," I snarled.

Saffron? Jaydra sent me her worry—she would be by my side in an instant if I asked. But I could not bring her to me.

Anger bubbled inside me, molten hot. I could not let it out. But it bled up to my skin, it sizzled in my veins. The king was not going to kill me. No, he would keep me alive and imprisoned. He would keep me by his side and use me—and my powers. He would work to bend my will to his—and what if he succeeded?

Could he draw the magic from me—or make me willingly use it to bring him more power?

Next to me, Bower spoke again, his voice tired and strained. "You have to do something, Saffron. Use your powers like you did in my cell. But this time let them go."

I shook my head and kept seeing the old man who was my family as he floated before us. "What if I become him?"

Bower gave what sounded a mad laugh. "You'll probably kill us both, but if you save Torvald it'll be worth it." I glanced at him and he gave me a crooked smile. "Let it out, Saffron. You won't kill me or Jaydra—I know that. Just blast the walls of Torvald and wake everyone up. You can do it."

For an instant, Bower's faith wrapped around me, warm and somehow comforting. The power within me changed as well, shifted from blazing heat to a fire that felt…felt like a friend's kind hug. His confidence became mine. What had that old magician said to me—make a friend of magic. Could I?

And then I thought of Enric, gloating and staring at me with eyes too much like my own. Fear blazed up to mix with my anger. I bit down on it, tried to shove it back. But Jaydra gave a cry.

She burst from the stables in full dragon glory, and I knew she was about to tangle with the Iron Guard. She was in danger—as was Bower's city.

I let loose my anger and my fear—and every ounce of power.

Magic like a green and gold fireball burst from my hands shattering the cold around me. I reached out, eyes closing and head falling back, but still I could see. And the world pulsed red.

*   *   *

Watching power and magic burst from Saffron was like watching a terrible summer storm erupt into something deadly. I wasn't sure we actually would survive this—but I wanted Saffron to think we might. The air around us crackled. Bolts of lightning sparked from Saffron's skin. She held up her hands and began to sketch the ruins again.

I shivered, but I could not look away.

I was watching her call magic to life!

Her power seemed to be called from the air, from the clouds now scudding in and forming over the tower as if they'd been awakened by Saffron's power. Colors swirled around us— beautiful greens and golds that leaked from Saffron's skin and turned to snap at me.

I had no idea of her powers, and this seemed nothing like the king's ability to float or hold us still or make himself seem young. The king's magic seemed to have more in common with nightmares that crept in while you slept. Saffron's power looked like that of a volcano exploding as I had seen in drawings in books.

And she has no control over it.

The thought shook my bones and rattled in my chest. The Saffron I knew had vanished—next to me stood a glowing power that was about to be unleashed. Saffron might not just knock holes in the walls around Torvald and wake everyone—she might blast the palace, the city and everything within miles into dust.

I had to help her, so I called out over the whirl of wind now tugging at Saffron, "You can do this. Aim for the walls of Torvald—send it out. Use it, my friend."

Something shifted within Saffron. She rose into the air, unsteady at first, rocking and stopping, and then she settled into a steady hover above the tower. I held my breath.

She opened her eyes. Her face shone with the green and gold colors of her powers. She spoke a word in a language I'd never heard and at the same time I heard Jaydra roar.

Light and power spilled from Saffron's hand. It shot out not as a blast as it had within my cell, but as bolts that blasted into the city walls. The tower shook and rumbled. It tipped and I staggered, free now from the king's dark, holding magic, but still the city burned. The lightning spread from Saffron's hands, spilling upwards into the clouds. The air crackled and thunder boomed, shaking the world even more.

Suddenly, the city seemed to wake with screams and bells ringing alarms. People poured from houses, some streaming toward the gaps in the city walls, fleeing. "You did it," I called out to Saffron. "It's done."

But still the magic poured from Saffron. The clouds overhead rumbled and rain let loose, pouring down on us and on the city. It burst out almost like a waterfall and now I feared we were replacing fire with flood. Glancing at Saffron I knew she'd lost control—the power wasn't being controlled, it was pouring out of her. Her skin was no longer glowing, but had taken on a greenish cast. Would this kill her?

Taking a deep breath, I ran and jumped, grabbing her legs and dragging her from the air.

For an instant, her power seemed to resist and I hung in the air. I closed my eyes, certain now Saffron would blast us all to bits. So I did what I'd done in my cell and called out her name.

She fell to the stone tower platform with me. I landed on bruises and let out a grunt. Saffron lay still and unmoving. Sitting up, I glanced down at the city.

Holes had been blasted in the walls—the Iron Guard still stood by the gates, but people were fleeing through the rubble of the walls. The king could mend them eventually, but for now it would be a long time before anyone thought of Torvald as a safe haven. The rain had changed from a solid sheet of water to a steady patter—it would help put out the fires. Torvald would not burn. Not today.

Turning, I glanced at Saffron. She lay still, her face pale. Lines that looked like streaks of green lightning skittered over her skin and sank back into her. I was almost afraid to touch her.

But the palace had woken as well.

I could hear bugles calling out—an alarm perhaps. The king still had his Iron Guard, which he could send after us. We could not stay.

Looking up into the sky, I thought the word and then called out, "Jaydra!" She had seemed to know when I was talking to her when she'd found me in my cell—I hoped she would hear me now.

I heard another roar and a crash from where I knew the royal stables to stand. Jaydra lifted into the air, her scales gleaming sea-blue bright in the sun, her wings spread and roaring. Horses neighed and shouts of alarm spread through the palace. Jaydra swept down on the tower, picking up Saffron in one claw and me in the other. It was not the way I preferred to fly, I decided. But it would do.

Torvald vanished behind us and Jaydra, her wings sweeping the air strong and steady, flew into the west with us.

*　　*　　*

EPILOGUE
UPON THE DRAGON'S BREATH

"Magic," I repeated, watching Bower's expression. I didn't know which of us looked the worse, Bower with his bruises now yellow and purple and his cuts half healed or me. My hands still shook, I could stand only for a minute or two, and even just walking down to the golden sands of the shore had left me out of breath. Bower had gotten his much-needed food and water—or so Jaydra had told me—and I had slept for three days and three nights. Or so Jaydra had told me.

The memory of what had happened on the tower blurred in my mind—I could recall giving myself to my anger, my hatred of Enric, to the fear weaving through me. I'd mixed them into something that was all churning emotion and had set them loose. Next thing I knew, Bower was calling my name and then I hit something hard and woke to find myself in Jaydra's claws and flying over the sky. That had been a relief.

Bower lifted a hand and wagged it. "I think I saw that." His mouth twisted into a wry and somewhat pained smile. "And felt that. But you didn't end the world."

"Not for lack of trying," I mumbled. Reaching over, I touched the ugly bruise that was just starting to go down. Bower flinched and I pulled my hand back.

I sat on both hands, tucking them under me and digging my fingers into the cool sand where they could do no harm. "I'm sorry."

"For what? Saving Torvald?"

"For not being able to heal you. Like I said—it's a curse. Magic." I spat out the word.

Bower let out a breath and turned to watch the low ocean waves shush in against the sand. It was low tide and the sun was just starting to think about setting. "The king's a curse. He will probably search for us—well, for you. From the way he spoke, he does not want to let your power out of his grasp."

I wrinkled my nose and knew I had to tell him the truth. We were friends—we'd saved each other. Swallowing hard, I dug my fingers deeper into the sand. "Do you hate me now you know who I really am? Now you know what is inside of me. Maddox magic."

Bower glanced at me, his eyebrows lifted high. "You can't control who your family is. I know about that. You can only pick good friends and maybe that's a better family."

Pulling out a hand, I stared at it. It looked like my hand again, but I could feel the power under my skin, hot and ready for my anger to call it out. "Enric—I have his magic."

"Trust me, you don't." Bower sat back, stretching his legs out in front of him and propping himself up on his elbows. He'd changed into the clothes we wore in the Western Isles—soft skins sewn together and we'd both left off our boots. The air brushed my skin with salt and ocean spray and a hint of flowers from the islands. A fish jumped in the ocean, scattering white spray. Bower tipped his head to one side and said, "I saw it, Saffron. I saw the magic as I imagine Jaydra might. Yours was beautiful green and gold. The king's was—"

"Ugly purple, black and red." I finished, nodding. "Like your bruises. How is it you can see magic?"

Jaydra told Saffron Bower has something special.
Jaydra landed on the sand behind us and folded her wings tight. She smacked her lips and gave a belch that smelled of smoke and fish.

I glanced at Bower again. "You don't mind me having magic?"

Bower shrugged. "It'd be nice if you could control it just a little more. But the king's power left me wondering if too much control is a bad thing. Maybe he strangled his magic into submission and that twisted it?" He shrugged, winced and put a hand to his ribs. "So long as you keep it a healthy green and gold, what do I have to mind? That's like saying I mind that you have frizzy hair.

I put a hand up to my tied back hair. The ocean air had left it with even more curls. "But I'll never have a normal life. I can't—the anger. It can come out anytime." I wrinkled my nose. "I certainly don't have anything like a normal family."

Bower sat up and held out his hands in front of him. "Well, don't get angry about it."

Laughter bubbled up inside me. It cooled my anger and I let out a giggle. "Well if you insist. You know, all I wanted was to find out who I was. Instead, I find my family comes from a long line of crazed, evil sorcerers."

"Not all of them," Bower said. "Your parents would not have left if they didn't want to get away from what was being done. And what is normal? My father was gone most of the time when I was growing up. I hardly knew my mother. I'm just as much an orphan as you."

A shadow passed overhead and I looked up to see Zenema's vast shape. She circled once and glided down to land next to Jaydra, who gave a welcoming chirp. For the four days we had been here, Zenema had been gone, visiting a den on one of the other islands. I stood, happy to see my den-mother again. Well, more like relieved. I wanted to pour out my story to her, to ask her what should I do now—I had followed my blood but it had not led anywhere that I wanted.

However, instead of welcoming me back under her wing, Zenema swept her head down in a low, respectful bow and said in low, clear words that anyone could hear, "Hail Bower, King of Torvald."

Bower's mouth fell open.

So did mine. I recovered first and stuttered, "Zenema? You can speak the human tongue? And what do you mean King of Torvald? Did Enric die or something?"

Zenema snuffed out what sounded like a dragon laugh to me, and Jaydra curled her tail around her, looking like she had settled in for one of the den-mother's ancient tales.

Zenema spoke again in a voice like warm honey sizzling on hot coals. Somehow Zenema sounded like she had always sounded in my thoughts—full of dignity, wisdom with a hint of amused fire. "Welcome home, den-daughter, and welcome to my island, True King."

Bower started to shake his head. "No, you have that wrong. I'm Bower of House Daris."

"Zenema?" I asked. Zenema had never been wrong. Oh, she had said I should follow my blood, and I had—she had not been wrong that I would learn about myself. I just had not cared much for what I had learned.

Bower's mouth pulled down, and then he said, his tone stubborn and final, "My father was Nev of House Daris. My mother—"

"Came from House Flamma," Zenema said.

Bower sucked in a breath. "No," he said, the word firm and final.

I kept staring at him. Bower—a king? How was that possible? He didn't know anything about fighting or survival. He had shown the worst instincts I'd ever seen, trusting that false friend of his.

Can you not feel he is dragon-friend? Zenema sent her thoughts to me, a shimmer of excitement quivering inside her.

She turned to Bower and spoke aloud again. "Dragons sense the true master of Dragon Mountain—that is you, Bower of House Flamma-Torvald. Your father might be of House Daris, but your mother brings you the blood of kings. We are bonded, Bower, dragon-friend. There is a connection there that cannot be denied, for you are the last True King, the last of the House Flamma-Torvald."

Zenema bowed again. Jaydra inclined her head as well. She had been telling me she had felt something about Bower. Now I knew why he could see magic, and he had been able to call to Jaydra to carry us away from the palace tower.

I knelt in the sand and bowed my head. "You are the True King of prophecy. You have come from the dragon's breath to take back your throne."

Bower tugged on my tunic, trying to get me to stand. "Stop that. Stop saying that. I'm Bower of House Daris."

Lifting her head, Zenema towered over us. "You dare name Zenema of the Western Isles a liar?"

Bower's face blanched and then reddened. "Would I even make a good king? What if I end up choosing poor advisers—people like Vic? My father taught me well, but mostly he'd taught me to question myself, and I have to wonder if the people really prefer Enric?

"The king who would tax them to death but also would give them a fair to celebrate his rule—and then try to kill them all?" I crossed my arms over my chest. "I can see why the people might love such a king. Love him to leave!"

Zenema touched a claw to my shoulder and turned to Bower. "Your mother came from House Flamma-Torvald. Her mother, as a child, had been hidden by the Dragon Riders. I know for I am a dragon who once lived within Dragon Mountain."

Both Bower and I sucked in breaths. Zenema snuffled out an amused breath. "Yes, and that is why my Jaydra finds her human—finds you, Saffron, to be her rider. But, you, Bower-child, you have as much to learn of yourself as does Saffron-child. Learn you will together now."

"A king without a crown, a horse or even so much as a city," Bower muttered.

I thumped his shoulder. "Then we shall have to take back your crown, Bower of House Daris. Or should I say King Bower of House Flamma-Torvald. As a child of House Maddox, it is my blood-duty to make things right between our houses. We shall take back your kingdom." I grinned. Bower's mouth twitched. Leaning closer, feeling the rightness of my words and Jaydra's pleased expectation of battles to come, I told him, "And for your steed, you will ride on the back of a dragon!"

END OF 'DRAGONS OF WILD'
Book 1 of the Upon Dragon's Breath Trilogy

Keep reading below for an exclusive extract from my bestselling novel, **Dragon Trials**.

Thank you for purchasing 'Dragons of Wild'

(Upon Dragon's Breath Trilogy Book One)

If you would like to hear more about what I am up to, or continue to follow the stories set in this world with these characters—then please sign up for my mailing list at

http://www.subscribepage.com/b7o3i0

You can also find me on me on

Facebook: www.facebook.com/AvaRichardsonBooks/

Homepage: www.AvaRichardsonBooks.com

SNEAK PEEK

Have you read the #1 BESTSELLING dragon riding epic 'Dragon Trials'?

Blurb

High-born Agathea Flamma intends to bring honor to her family by following in her brothers' footsteps and taking her rightful place as a Dragon Rider. With her only other option being marriage, Thea will not accept failure. She's not thrilled at her awkward, scruffy partner, Seb, but their dragon has chosen, and now the unlikely duo must learn to work as a team.

Seventeen-year-old Sebastian has long been ashamed of his drunken father and poor upbringing, but then he's chosen to train as a Dragon Rider at the prestigious Dragon Academy. Thrust into a world where he doesn't fit in, Seb finds a connection with his dragon that is even more powerful than he imagined. Soon, he's doing all he can to succeed and not embarrass his new partner, Thea.

When Seb hears rumors that an old danger is re-emerging, he and Thea begin to investigate. Armed only with their determination and the dragon they both ride, Thea and Seb may be the only defence against the Darkening that threatens to sweep over the land. Together, they will have to learn to work together to save their kingdom…or die trying.

Dragon Trials - Return of the Darkening Trilogy Book 1 is available at AvaRichardsonBooks.com/

DRAGON TRIALS

(RETURN OF THE DARKENING TRILOGY BOOK 1)

Exclusive Excerpt

I heard the Dragon Horns blowing on the morning of the Choosing, just like everyone else. However, unlike everyone else I was already up and awake, well into my fourth or fifth hour of the day.

That's what it is like as a blacksmith's boy. There's always ingots to be hauled in, bellows to be primed, wood to be chopped and the foundries to be cleaned. My dad is the blacksmith for Mongers Lane, and I have to be up before the crack of dawn to make sure the forge is ready when he starts work.

Which probably won't be until midday if he was out at the inn again last night. A twinge of embarrassment and shame warmed my face. My father liked his flagon of ale at the end of a working day. He also seemed to like it in the evening and halfway through the night as well.

Stop that, Sebastian, I chided myself. *It's not right to think ill of your father no matter how much he drinks!* I didn't mind the work. It felt good to be up early and to get everything ready for the other apprentices and junior smiths. I even made time to chop some wood for Old Widow Hu a few doors down. I always tried to do what I could for her because the poor woman was nearly blind, needing all the help she could get.

But the dragons—I loved to see the dragons. All of my short seventeen years I had been dreaming of them— the freedom they knew of flying through the air, above the world and all its troubles, the power of every muscle, the strength of every wiry sinew. They are such beautiful creatures. They offered the steady loyalty, strength and wisdom of a horse, but with the playfulness, speed, and sometimes the temperament, of a cat.

Sometimes we work on the rider's tack, which was such an honor, but sadly that didn't happen often enough to please me. The Dragon Riders of Torvald usually got their kit remade and polished at one of the bigger, throne-endorsed smithies. But every now and again, a few small buckles or harness-clips filtered down our way to be seen to.

I would hold them in my hand, imagining which part of a rider's kit they corresponded to, taking care to re-tool the fine designs etched into their surface, polishing and polishing until they gleamed as good as new. It was one of the few paid jobs that my father let me do by myself, knowing I would put the extra work in just because I loved dragons.

I'd seen a flash of one last year. A brilliant scintillating flash of blue and green that soared over Mongers Lane. It moved as fast as a hawk. For a moment, I swore I had looked up past the towering, crowded houses of the street down here and had seen it looking down at me with eyes like the golden green of a summer lake or the first flush of spring leaves. No one believed me of course. They said I was imagining it. That dragons only had eyes and noses for their riders, but it had happened. I knew it had. I'll never forget it.

This morning, I was working extra hard trying to clear my duties for the day, hoping I might get to finish early enough to see the last few choices of the day. Everyone would talk about the choices for the next five years. How this blue dragon or that white wyrm approached their rider. Did they go on foot? Did they snatch them from their windows?

I moved the final barrow of split logs, seeing a whole collection of end-pieces, scrappy tops and tree-hearts left. It would be too much work to break them down and feed them into the kilns. Besides, they would give an uneven burn, so I loaded them onto a wheelbarrow and decided to take them to Old Widow Hu. She would be pleased for the free firewood, and Father couldn't do anything with them anyway.

Mongers Lane was a tight little community, more than just a lane really, but not much bigger than one. The poorest district in the city, with people living in makeshift houses next to each other, cheek by jowl, my ma said. I knew it wasn't much, but I liked living here. The people were honest.

Old Widow Hu had a hovel poorer than most, a collection of mud and brick walls and wooden beams almost leaning against the stronger houses next door. As I neared her home, in the background I could hear the cheers and gasps as the dragons must have swooped overhead. I knocked on her oddly-fitting wooden door and waited as a breeze blew down the alley behind me.

It took a little while for Old Widow Hu to answer her door, but I didn't mind. When she did, she peered past me and blinked, then looked at my barrel. "Oh, thank you Sebastian, but you've already done me such a kindness," she was saying in a cracked and croaking voice.

"These are free, ma'am. I'd like to think someone might take care of my step-mam if ever she got older and had no one around." I heaved the wood onto the pile by the side of her door. I was forced to jump back immediately as a few of the tiles fell off her roof above us.

"Oh, dear goodness!" Old Widow Hu was looking up at me.

She must not be able see me, I thought. "It's okay, Mrs. Hu. It's just me, Sebastian."

"N-no, Seb..." her voice quavered. "I think there's someone to see you." She hurriedly stepped back into her hovel.

Oh no. It must be Father. He must be annoyed at me for something.

I turned and came face to face with the long, sinuous, muscular neck and the strong snout of a red dragon. It had golden-green eyes, eyes the color of the sun glinting off polished gold or seen through the leaves of a beech forest at midday. She was beautiful.

How do I know it's a she? I thought, but I knew. I just knew.

She didn't look like a dragon to me. She looked—she just looked like herself. Not a thing, not a lizard or a beast. I could feel something stirring in my breast, my heart thumping and a lump in my throat as I raised a hand up to her.

She put her snout on the edge of my fingers, letting me touch the sensitive mouth that I knew surrounded her teeth and then huffed a warm breath of pine smoke and coal-dust over me, fluffing my thatch of hair.

You're playing with me, aren't you? I smiled, blowing air back onto her snout.

With a sudden sneeze, the dragon shook its head and made a chirruping noise, oddly musical, like a bird.

"Seb! Seb! What are you doing?" a voice shouted, alarmed and fearful—my dad, his drunken gait exaggerated by the alarm and anger in his voice.

The dragon then did something I had been hoping for all my life, but never expecting. It seized me with its front feet, black talons the length of my whole forearm curling gently against me and not even hurting a tiny bit, and launched itself into the air.

"You've got the wrong boy!" I heard my father yell, along with the Old Widow Hu's reply, "no, I think that it's got just the right one!"

Dragon Trials - Return of the Darkening Trilogy Book 1 is available at AvaRichardsonBooks.com/

Made in the USA
Lexington, KY
12 March 2017